BAD PRINCE CHARLIE

John Moore

ACE BOOKS, NEW YORK

THE BERKLEY PUBLISHING GROUP
Published by the Penguin Group
Penguin Group (USA) Inc.
375 Hudson Street, New York, New York 10014, USA
Penguin Group (Canada), 90 Eglinton Avenue East, Suite 700, Toronto, Ontario M4P 2Y3, Canada
(a division of Pearson Penguin Canada Inc.)
Penguin Books Ltd., 80 Strand, London WC2R 0RL, England
Penguin Group Ireland, 25 St. Stephen's Green, Dublin 2, Ireland (a division of Penguin Books Ltd.)
Penguin Group (Australia), 250 Camberwell Road, Camberwell, Victoria 3124, Australia
(a division of Pearson Australia Group Pty. Ltd.)
Penguin Books India Pvt. Ltd., 11 Community Centre, Panchsheel Park, New Delhi—110 017, India
Penguin Group (NZ), Cnr. Airborne and Rosedale Roads, Albany, Auckland 1310, New Zealand
(a division of Pearson New Zealand Ltd.)
Penguin Books (South Africa) (Pty.) Ltd., 24 Sturdee Avenue, Rosebank, Johannesburg 2196,
South Africa

Penguin Books Ltd., Registered Offices: 80 Strand, London WC2R 0RL, England

This is a work of fiction. Names, characters, places, and incidents either are the product of the author's imagination or are used fictitiously, and any resemblance to actual persons, living or dead, business establishments, events, or locales is entirely coincidental. The publisher does not have any control over and does not assume any responsibility for author or third-party websites or their content.

BAD PRINCE CHARLIE

An Ace Book / published by arrangement with the author

PRINTING HISTORY
Ace edition / May 2006

Copyright © 2006 by John Moore.
Cover art by Walter Velez.
Cover design by Annette Fiore.
Interior text design by Stacy Irwin.

ISBN: 0-441-01396-1

ACE
Ace Books are published by The Berkley Publishing Group,
a division of Penguin Group (USA) Inc.,
375 Hudson Street, New York, New York 10014.
ACE and the "A" design are trademarks belonging to Penguin Group (USA) Inc.

PRINTED IN THE UNITED STATES OF AMERICA

10   9   8   7   6   5   4   3   2   1

To Mom and Dad

It was a dark night—not a stormy night, not at all—but very dark, and that was good for ghosts. To be more explicit, it was a good night for *seeing* ghosts. Ghostly ectoplasm has a faint luminescence about it, so the darker the night, the easier it is to see a ghost. In theory, you should be able to see them during the daytime if you are in a totally dark room, but for some reason this never happens. Nonetheless, a deep, dark, non-stormy night is quite an advantage if you want to find ghosts, and even better if you want to see and avoid them. How the ghosts feel about this is not known.

The castle itself was rather new as castles go, having been completed only a generation earlier, but it had a traditional design, with square walls and towers. Most of the other castles being built at that time had round towers, which gave their archers overlapping fields of fire, and round walls, which were less susceptible to collapse from tunneling. Damask Castle was built on a mountain of rock, though. No one was going to tunnel under its walls. And square rooms are so much easier to live in. The furniture fits better.

There was no drawbridge. There was no moat. Neither Damask Castle, nor the city that surrounded it, nor the cultivated plains that lay beneath the mountain fortress, had water to spare.

None of this mattered to the guards patrolling the parapets of Damask Castle. The castle was parapet intensive. There was no good reason for this. The architect just liked parapets. At the time the castle was built, parapets were the hot thing in castle architecture. They ran all along the outer walls, the inner walls, the ramparts, the rooflines, the towers, and the citadel. They took a lot of patrolling.

"You have to wait until it gets really dark," one of the guards told Oratorio. "That's when he really stands out. Otherwise you'll walk right past him. Even a bit of moonlight will wash him out." The guard's teeth chattered a little, but that could have been the cold. The wind was bitter, and the temperature dropped quickly in the dark reaches of the night.

Oratorio looked up. On the horizon a few stars could be seen, but thick clouds overhead made the sky impenetrable. And the moon would not rise for several hours.

"It's the king," said the other guard.

"The ghost of the king," corrected the first.

"Don't be nitpicky, Turic. He knows what I mean."

"Rod, how did you know it was the king?" asked Oratorio.

"It looked like the king."

"You saw its face, then?"

The two guards looked at each other. "No, not really," said Turic. "But it had the image of the king."

"What image was that, exactly?"

"It was carrying a bottle of cheap rotgut."

"Ah," said Oratorio. That did rather point to the king. Oratorio was a knight, however, and he felt he had to show some logic and leadership to the two guards. "We don't want to jump to conclusions, though. The king died just this week, a ghost appears, naturally the tendency is to assume . . ."

"It was a bottle of Old Duodenum," said Rod. "We could see the label."

"That's his favorite brand, all right," Oratorio conceded.

"Aye, and it was like no other spirit I've seen. The look of it, a horrible putrid yellow. And a rank smell."

"The ghost?"

"The liquid in the bottle."

"Yeah, that's Old Duodenum. Some batches are like that. The quality control isn't really great. Well, boys." He clapped a hand on each of their shoulders. "As the ranking guard on duty tonight, it is up to me to confront this apparition. If the king—may he rest in peace—has sent back his shade, I can only surmise that he has something important to say to us."

"Good thinking," said Rod.

"I concur," said Turic. "You're just the man for the job, Oratorio. Although, of course, we'll be right behind you. And indeed, it probably is the king and not some demon from Hell that has taken on the appearance of the king in order to trap you."

"Say what?" said Oratorio.

"'Tis not at all unlikely," said Rod. "It takes a brave man to confront an apparition of this sort. Remember that haunting at Lockhaven Manor? The drowned little boy, and his appearance, and the sad weeping from the boathouse? Aye, but of those who ventured inside, the poor lad to comfort, came out none of them again, but their gruesome remains were collected at daybreak and buried in very small caskets."

"'The poor lad to comfort'?" repeated Oratorio. "'Came out again none'? Why are you talking backward?"

"Ghost stories sound better in archaic language."

"He's right," said Turic. "Not about talking backward, but about apparitions. Tricky devilish things, and not above taking on the appearance of a loved one to lure the unwary. We all know it happens—sailors who are lured overboard by the appearance of a ghostly maiden, or mothers who follow their spectral child into the graveyard, and in the morning their drained or decapitated bodies are found, the features twisted into expressions of utmost horror, mute testimony to the terrible . . ."

"Yes, yes, all right!" said Oratorio. "You don't have to go on about it."

"There!" said Rod.

It was faint, but they all saw the dim white glow, rippling like moonlight reflected on a puddle. It was at the far end of the parapet, moving at the speed of a sedate walk, and it passed behind a wall only moments after they first saw it.

"Same as last night," said Turic. "It's taking the outside stairs up the south tower. Are you going after it?"

"Of course," said Oratorio. "I said I would confront the apparition, didn't I?"

"You're not moving."

"Well, I didn't say I would do so right this very minute. A good soldier does a reconnaissance first. He collects information. He studies the situation. I should probably come back for a few more nights before I make my move, to see if I can pick up a pattern of behavior."

"He's over there," said Turic. "That's his pattern of behavior."

"He's going up the tower again."

"All right then." Oratorio raised his lantern, so he could see along the parapet, and quietly made his way to the bottom of the tower stairs. As with the other towers, the stairs were wide enough for only one man and rose along the outside wall in a clockwise direction, which gave the defender above more room to swing his sword, while limiting the movement of the attacker from below. The candlelight gleamed on the dark stone. The steps rose above his head and disappeared into the black night. "We don't want to go charging up these steps in darkness," he whispered. "We're liable to miss one and plummet to our deaths. That may be exactly what it is luring us to do. But using the lantern will reduce our night vision, and we won't be able to see it. So this is the plan.

"I'll go first, leading the way with the lantern. You two will follow close behind, but my body will shadow most of the light from your eyes. So you should still be able to see it when we reach the top. If it's there, draw your swords and try to corner it. Ready?"

He glanced back over his shoulder, frowned, then marched back to the blockhouse. "You said you'd be right behind me!"

"Well, right behind you is a rather nebulous term," said Turic.

"Right," said Rod. "I mean, who's to say just how far behind is right behind? I think it's entirely possible that a fellow could be right behind another fellow and still be a pretty fair distance off."

"Exactly."

"Shut up!" said Oratorio. "Get out your swords. We're going to charge up those stairs. I'll lead the way. You're going to be behind me, right behind me, which means if I get atop that tower and you're not there with me, you're going to be joining that demon in Hell. Is that clear?"

He raised his lantern so he could see them nod. He nodded curtly back, turned away, and held his lantern close to his chest. When he judged they had regained some of their night vision, he said, "Let's go!" and took off briskly down the parapet. At the stairs he hesitated only long enough to make sure he heard the clump of their boots behind him, then trotted up as quickly as he dared in the dim light. For the final corner he quickened his pace, and leaped onto the roof with his sword thrust out in front of him. Nothing attacked. He stepped quickly to the side, out of the way of the two men following, who also reached the roof with swords at forward guard. Oratorio shut his lantern, and all three men looked around for the ghost.

It was easy to spot. There was a dim white glow in the middle of the roof, flat against the stone. Moving closer, the men could make out the faint figure of a man, lying on its side, clutching a bottle. Its hair and beard were matted with sweat, and a thin line of ectoplasmic drool ran down one side of its jaw. Its eyes were closed. They fell silent, listening carefully. Above the background of chill wind they could hear, rising and falling, the unmistakable sound of a drunken snore.

"Oh yeah," said Turic in disgust. "No doubt about it. That's the king, all right."

In a distant place, in a distant time, twenty kingdoms (give or take a few) were spread out in a broad band between the mountains and the sea. They were fairytale kingdoms, lands of enchantment, where the laws of nature could be bent to the rules of magic. This did not matter a good deal to the inhabitants. Magic in the Twenty Kingdoms was not unlike open-heart surgery today. It required skilled practitioners with decades of training, the results were often unsatisfactory, and it was financially out of reach for most of the population. Even those who could afford it used it reluctantly and as a last choice.

But when it worked the way it was supposed to, the results could be spectacular.

However, on this day there was nothing magical on the road from Noile to Damask. It was overshadowed by mountains and overhung by leafy branches, that still dripped steadily from the morning's cold rain. The mountain pass was cold even this late in the spring; the peaks to either side were still snowcapped. Puffs of steam came from the mouth of the horse pulling a dogcart through the forest, and from the mouths of the two young women driving it. The one who held the reins was red-haired, green-eyed, and singularly beautiful, although with a slightly petulant look to her full lips. Her hands were covered by lambskin gloves, and a dark fur coat protected her excellent figure. Her companion, no less enchanting with fair hair and blue eyes, kept her hands sheltered inside a good wool cloak. They were cheerful, for they had the exuberance and confidence of youth, but they were also wary, for they were coming to a narrow bridge that was known to be a favorite spot for robbers.

And, indeed, they were not disappointed. Before they got to the bridge they heard the rushing of the Matka River, and then they heard voices filtering through the trees, and then, turning a bend in the road, they saw the bridge ahead of them, and a coach and four. It was stopped in front of the bridge, the first two horses with their feet already on the planks. Four men, swords drawn, surrounded the coach. Their leader seemed to be in deep discussion with someone inside the carriage.

The red-haired girl stopped the dogcart and murmured, "Gentleman Dick Terrapin, the notorious highwayman."

Her companion widened her eyes. "Is he really a gentleman?" she whispered back.

"I wouldn't count on it, Rosalind. Men give each other the strangest nicknames. 'Big Jim Smith' is usually a small man, and anyone called 'LittleJon' is invariably a giant. If he has a name like 'Howie the Hairy,' you know for certain—"

"That he's bald," finished Rosalind. "Shall we go back?"

"I don't intend to do so. They've already seen us, and we can't outrun their horses. Let's see what 'toll' they will extract from us to cross that bridge."

Dick Terrapin had been plying his trade as a road agent for nearly six years, which was a remarkably long time to be playing a dangerous game. His origins were unknown, but somewhere along in life he had picked up a gentleman's education, and he did not mind putting it on display. He did indeed share some of the characteristics of the nobility, in that he was greedy, rapacious, and preferred to take money without working for it. He nonetheless had a certain code of honor, and that was never to leave his victims completely penniless. The occupant of the coach had already resigned himself to handing over his moneybag.

But he was a first-time visitor to Damask, and had to rely on Dick to tell him how much he was losing.

"Give it to me once more," he said to Terrapin. "A fourthing is one fourth of a penny. That makes sense. And then you have pence, tuppence, thruppence, and . . . four pence."

"No," said Terrapin. "Four pence is called a groat."

"A groat."

"Right. And nobody calls it thruppence. It's called a thrupenny bit."

"And then twelve pence is . . ."

"A shellac. And there's twenty shellac to the ponce."

"That doesn't make sense. Why not twelve, or twenty-four? It would be more consistent."

"That's just the way they do it. There's also the gimme, which is one ponce and one shellac."

"So the gimme is twenty-one shellac?"

"Correct."

"Not twenty-four?" The passenger still didn't want to give up his idea of monetary symmetry.

"No. Now a shellac is also called a barb. So if someone asks you for 'barb and tenner,' you would pay him . . ."

"One shellac and ten pence," finished the passenger.

"No, one shellac and six pence."

"Stop," said the passenger. "That's enough! You're making my brain hurt. Take the money. Just leave me enough for a meal and a room in Damask tonight."

"Should run you about three barb," Terrapin said, handing him back some coins. "Don't let them charge more than five. Some of those innkeepers are absolute thieves."

"You ought to know," said the passenger sourly, slamming the door. The driver flipped the reins, and the coach crossed the bridge and soon disappeared into thick forest.

The band of rogues turned their attention immediately to the dogcart. Two men blocked the entrance to the bridge, a third took a position on the left side of the cart, while Terrapin himself removed his hat and bowed low to the red-haired girl. "Do I have the honor of speaking to Lady Catherine Durace?"

"I'm sure the honor is mine, sir," said Catherine. "But I'm afraid your face is not familiar to me. Have we met?"

"We have not had that pleasure," said Terrapin. "My name is Terrapin."

"Mercy!" said Catherine. Her hand flew to her breast, as though to quiet a palpitating heart, but putting it closer to a dagger concealed in her cleavage. "Not Gentleman Dick Terrapin, the notorious highwayman and bandit leader!"

Almost imperceptibly, Terrapin puffed out his chest a bit. Rosalind looked around at his three accomplices. Each man reacted instinctively to the glance of a pretty girl, straightening his collar and sucking in his stomach. Rosalind gave them a benign smile. Beneath her cloak, she gripped the shaft of an oak cudgel.

"You do me a disservice, Miss," Terrapin told Catherine. "We are but humble toll collectors, whose task is to see that travelers get across the bridge safely. You may be assured that once our modest fee is paid, you may travel all the way to Damask without fear of robbery."

"Alas," sighed Catherine. "Our family's fortune has greatly diminished over the years. I fear that I will be unable to pay your toll, however modest it may be."

In his years of highway robbery, Gentleman Dick had heard every sad tale a traveler could conjure up. "We take barter, my lovely. If you would be so kind as to hand over your jewelry."

"They ain't wearing jewels, Boss," said one of his minions. "Not even a ring between them."

Terrapin's smile slipped. "Search the luggage."

Two of his men were doing this already. "Nothing, Dick. Just clothes, and nothing fancy at that."

"We are on our way to the king's funeral," explained Catherine. "Finery would be inappropriate."

"Experienced travelers," said Terrapin. "You left your valuables at home. Very wise."

"I have been on a few trips, yes."

Terrapin's smile was back, but this time it did not make him look friendly. "Fortunately, a woman always has something of value."

Rosalind gave a tiny gasp. Dick's men suddenly seemed larger and coarser, and uncomfortably close. Her hand tightened on the wooden club. Catherine seemed unconcerned. "Please don't bandy words with me, sir." Somehow the dagger had gotten into her hand. "I would not lightly surrender such payment."

Terrapin held up a hand. "Now, ladies, surely we can avoid such unpleasantness. He put the hand on the edge of the cart and leaned inward. "I propose a little contest. Are either of you familiar with the tale of Oedipus and the Sphinx?"

Catherine sighed. "Alas, no. My parents did not approve of advanced education for girls. Instead, I was tutored in more traditional womanly arts, such as needlepoint and baking muffins." Despite the danger they were in, Rosalind had to hide a smile.

"The Sphinx," said Terrapin, "guarded a crossroad in ancient Greece. It was an animal with the head of a woman and the body of a lion."

"Of a female lion?"

"The myth does not specify the gender of the lion, but one presumes it was also female. The ancient Greeks were a little kinky but they weren't *that* strange. In some versions it also has the wings of an eagle."

"What kind of eagle?"

"*Aquila heliaca*, the imperial eagle," said Dick. "A migratory species, but native to the plains of northern and coastal Greece. Now quit stalling, young lady."

"Sorry. Carry on."

"The Sphinx posed Oedipus with a riddle. If he answered correctly, he could pass unmolested. Now, ladies, I will present you with the same question. If you answer correctly, you may continue your journey. If you cannot answer, you must surrender your charms without a fight."

"Are you quite certain you wouldn't rather have a muffin?"

"The offer is tempting, but no. The riddle of the Sphinx is this: What animal goes about on four legs in the morning, two legs in the day, and three legs in the evening? You can see the Sphinx already ruled out minerals and vegetables, so that narrows down the scope considerably."

"Indeed it does," said Catherine brightly. "Why, the answer is obvious. It's Bad Prince Charlie."

It was one of the few times in his life that Dick Terrapin was at a loss for words. He looked at Catherine and cocked an eyebrow, waiting for her to elaborate on her answer. When she merely continued to smile at him, he said, " 'Bad Prince Charlie'? I'm afraid that's incorrect, my lady. But why would you answer 'Bad Prince Charlie'?"

"Because I see him coming right now. He travels on four legs when he rides his horse up to you, preparing to skewer you like a holiday goose. He walks on two legs when he dismounts to run his blade through your kidneys. And he stands on three legs when he pulls out his sword and leans on it while watching the blood spurt from your painfully writhing body."

Terrapin looked down the road. A black horse was trotting toward him. The rider was a young man wearing cavalry boots and spurs, dark breeches, and a black leather riding coat. He was hatless, so the wind ruffled his thick black hair. From this distance it was impossible to see his expression, yet to Dick it seemed that a thundercloud was approaching—indeed, that dark clouds followed the young man where ever he went.

"On second thought, I've consulted with our panel of judges and they've decided to accept your answer," he said hastily. "What do we have for the lucky winners, Jerry?"

His men were already piling boxes into the dogcart. "A set of designer cardboard luggage, a luxury three-day, two-night all-expense paid cruise aboard the *Noile Trident*—meals, lodging, transfers, tips, port fees, and reservation fees not included—and a pair of beautiful ladies' gold-tone pendants with genuine certified diamond chips. Taxes are the responsibility of the winner."

"Then we're off," said Terrapin. "Nice meeting you, my lady. We must do this again sometime." He turned around to find himself staring a black horse in the face. "Um."

The rider was leaning to one side, evaluating the occupants of the dogcart. He had deeply set black eyes that didn't seem to look at you so much as glower. "Is there a problem here?"

"No," said Terrapin.

"I wasn't asking you."

"I think we're fine, Charlie," said Catherine. She had adopted a familiar tone, but her voice held no warmth. "We were just about to continue on to Damask. Am I correct to assume you are going the same way?"

The young man nodded. "What news of Noile? Has the plague reached there?"

Catherine's face clouded. "Alas, yes. I rather hoped the mountains would protect us, but the first case struck some months ago, and the numbers grow each week."

"I have been away at the university and have not had news of home, but I fear it will be the same."

"Is it the situation in Bitburgen?"

"Even worse. These things seem to follow a pattern, starting in the major population centers, then spreading along the trade routes, and eventually reaching even into the small towns. We can only hope that it runs its course quickly."

"At this point it shows no sign of diminishing."

"The plague?" said Terrapin. "Excuse my interruption, but when you speak of the plague, are you talking about . . . surely you don't mean . . ."

"Yes," said Charlie. "Coffee shops."

The thief made a noise of disgust. "*Coffee shops*. They seemed to come out of nowhere, and now Noile is infested with them. And the prices. Ten pence for a tall macchiato! It's ridiculous. It's . . ."

"Highway robbery, Dick?" Charlie swung a leg over his horse and dropped lightly to the ground.

"I wasn't going to say that," said Terrapin, taking a step back and putting his hand on his sword.

Charlie glared at him, then turned back to the girls. "I won't keep you any longer. Thank you for the news. Perhaps we will meet again in Damask." He slapped their horse on the flanks and it started off. Catherine looked affronted at this sudden dismissal. Rosalind, for reasons she couldn't explain, found herself wishing the horse would move away faster. Bad Prince Charlie made her nervous.

When the dogcart was over the bridge, Charlie returned his attention to the bandit leader. "Dick, you accosted me when I left to begin my studies. Do you recall what I said to you then?"

Terrapin attempted a display of bravado. "You don't scare me now, *Charlie*. I know you're not a legitimate prince. And you're not in Damask, either. You have no authority here. I'll do as I please. You may be good with a sword, but you can't take on my whole gang."

"What gang?" said Charlie.

Terrapin turned to look around. His men had melted into the bushes the moment Charlie had dismounted. When he turned back to face Charlie, the prince had his sword out of its scabbard. Terrapin gave an involuntary little jump.

"This road," said Charlie, "is the only road connecting Damask to the port of Noile, which is open year round.

Therefore it is important to our trade. I want it kept free of bandits and road agents. Do I make myself clear?"

"Yes," said Terrapin.

"Good." Charlie sheathed his sword and mounted his horse. "Being as this is a joyous occasion in Damask, I will let you off easy today. Next time I see you . . . but there isn't going to be a next time, is there, Dick?"

"No," said Terrapin. "Joyous occasion? What are you talking about? Everyone who passes on this road is going to a funeral. The king is dead."

Charlie flipped the reins. The horse started off, shoes clip-clomping on the wooden bridge. "That's the joyous occasion I'm talking about."

⚜ ⚜ ⚜

Early in the history of Damask, a man named Joseph Durk staked a claim to one of the few springs that ran reliably all year and built a brewery. Durk knew his craft. He brewed a pretty good lager, using high-quality hops and a cold fermentation process. Joe Durk didn't worry much about selling the beer. He just brewed the kind of beer that he liked to drink. Other people drank it without complaint, and everyone agreed that Durk's was a good beer. If you were in Damask, you drank Durk's.

His son, Thomas Durk, inherited his father's brewery. Thomas also opened a brew-pub. He sold his own beer, as well as laying in a few barrels of imported beers to keep up interest in the place. Most of the customers drank Durk's. But for Thomas, it wasn't enough to know that people drank his beer. He asked himself an important question: Why don't people drink *more* beer?

He pondered the matter for several years while he observed the customers in the pub. He funded research. He commissioned studies. And he came to the surprising conclusion that people didn't drink beer because they didn't like the *taste* of beer.

Oh sure, they drank it. They drank it because it was something cool on a hot day and wet on a dry day, and the bubbles felt good on the tongue. They drank beer because it went well with particular foods, and it carried with it a certain aura of conviviality and good times. They drank it because their friends drank it. They drank it because it gave them a little buzz. But they didn't really *like* the taste.

Another brewer might have shrugged off this knowledge, but Thomas Durk knew an opportunity when he saw it. If the patrons didn't like the taste of beer, he'd give them beer with less taste. The obvious thing to do was to water down the beer. To his delight, sales went up. He was not only selling more beer, he was making more profit on the beer he sold.

There was a limit, however, to the amount of water he could add to the beer. Too much and it actually tasted watered-down, didn't look right, and of course, didn't give the same buzz. Durk experimented with his brewing process. He replaced some of the hops with sprouted grains— barley, wheat, and maize. Flavor decreased. Sales went up each time. But when he finally settled on rice, he knew he had a winner. His beer was beautiful to look at, modestly alcoholic, and virtually tasteless. Soon Durk's Beer was the number one beer in the Damask.

And *that* was a source of unending irritation to his grandson, Tommy Durk. Tommy was a beer aficionado. The family did not let Tommy manage the brewery yet. Someday, he knew, he would have control of the brewery and then they'd start making real beer again, beer a man could be proud off. In the meantime, he had charge of the brew-pub.

He did a pretty good job with it. He stocked a variety of microbrews from all over the Twenty Kingdoms—top-notch stuff, if you liked beer. The food was also good (for pub food), while the barmaids were pretty and buxom (no complaints there) and wore kirtles. In the evening there was a fiddler to keep things lively. In the summer the windows were opened to let in the breeze and a couple of small boys were hired to swat flies. In the winter the windows were shut, the fire was lit, and the air grew thick with the smell of pickles, cheese, smoked sausage—and beer. It was pretty big, as taverns go, but it was full this past week, with so many people coming into the city for the funeral, some even coming over the mountains from Noile. Tommy worked alongside the barmaids and tried in vain to educate the customers.

"Steve," he asked a regular. "Why don't you try this? It's an Alacian light amber. It's a mild lager, maybe a bit darker and maltier than your usual, but low on the hoppy side, with a hint of juniper."

"Pint of Durk's," said Steve.

One advantage of owning a tavern was that you overheard things. Once he had listened to the conversation of a pair of bricklayers. They were building a brick house for a wealthy merchant. But they were planning to cheat him and use inferior mortar between the bricks. That night Tommy went to the merchant's home, delivered his information at the tradesman's entrance, and suggested it was worth a tip. The servant who answered the door listened to his news in stony silence, then shut the door in Tommy's face. Tommy figured he had learned a lesson, put it down to experience, and went back to the tavern.

Except a few days later a man, not the wealthy merchant, arrived at the tavern with a handful of coins for Tommy. And instructions on how to earn more tips.

He was thinking about that now as he wiped down a table for a customer. "Got something special just in, Mr. Carter," he said. "You owe it to yourself to try this. It's a wonderful red ale from Deserae. The caramel malt gives it sweetness, but the hops dominate. Deep gold color, high alcohol content, and a slightly fruity background make this . . ."

"Let me have a schooner of Durk's," said Carter.

"Coming right up."

One day the man came back and told Tommy that he wasn't allowed to sell his news to anyone else. But to make up for the lost income, he would be paid a small retainer. Tommy agreed immediately, since he had never thought to try selling his news to anyone else. He knew, of course, that he was not the only one gathering news. He was a small part of a network, and it might be a very large network, and there was no telling who else was in it or where the information was going. But there was nothing to be gained by thinking about it. He kept his ears open and husbanded his coins.

The barmaid was gesturing urgently to him. Tommy looked where she was pointing. Catherine Durace and a companion were seating themselves in the dining room. (Tommy ran a respectable tavern—ladies were not permitted in the bar.) He hurried to put on a clean apron and fill two glasses with his finest new import.

"So good to have you with us again, Lady Catherine." He set the glasses on the table. "Compliments of the house, allow me to present you with this Bellringer Abbey Special Dark. It comes from an abbey in Illyria, where monks have been brewing it for nine hundred years."

Catherine put her hand on the glass. "And it's still cold!"

"Amazing what those monks can do. But if you like a good brew, milady, if you're a woman of judgment and discerning intelligence, if you're looking for something new to please your palate, then you can't go wrong with this Illyrian double dark premium lager."

Lady Catherine looked up at him with her deep green eyes. "Why, that sounds delicious, Tommy—it's Tommy, isn't it?"

"Yes," said Tommy, feeling ridiculously pleased that she remembered his name.

"But what I'd really like now is a nice glass of Durk's."

Tommy's smile slipped the tiniest bit. "Certainly, mi-lady."

"And I'd like a glass of Durk's Light," said Rosalind.

"Coming right up," said Tommy, sighing inwardly. He delivered two new glasses, brought the dark beer back to the bar and sipped one glass. He was gratified when a new customer walked up to the bar and said, "What's that you're drinking?"

"Bellringer Abbey Special Dark. Try one. Compliments of the house." Tommy passed the man the second glass and looked him over. He wasn't wearing insignia, but the cut of his tunic and his overcoat told Tommy he was a military man.

"Well, thank you much. Say, this is pretty good."

"You think so? You must not be from around here."

"From Noile. Folks here told me that Durk's was the best beer in the country, but I dunno. Tastes watery."

"Staying long?"

"I'm starting back home tomorrow. But I expect to be back before summer's end. And don't worry. I'll be with men who will drink anything."

Tommy thought about this. There were a lot of people from a lot of countries in Damask now, so it wasn't unusual to find a Noile soldier. But this one expected to be back with more soldiers? That might be worth a tip.

⚜ ⚜ ⚜

Charlie stood at a window of the north tower, looking over the foothills, and across the plains of Damask. There were still trees on the hills below, light green with young leaves, and on the plowed land of the plains, the dark brown of the earth was striped with rows of deep green shoots. Wild-flowers grew on the banks of streams that trickled down from the hills. A light spring rain was falling, coating everything in view with a wet sheen. The view that lay beneath Charlie's stern gaze, the thatched houses with their neat little gardens, the baby goats sheltering under the trees, the cultivated fields, carried all the promise of spring, the promise of fertility and growth and rebirth.

Charlie knew it was a trap.

From time immemorial the Gray Mountains of Noile, so called because of the smoky mist that collected in their hollows, had been considered impassable. It wasn't that they were particularly high, but they were crisscrossed with near vertical rifts and ravines, and so covered with dense thickets of thorn trees, that they turned back the most intrepid traveler. It was only a hundred years ago that a band of political exiles from Noile, and their ragtag army of followers, carved a passage through the mountains. There they found the richly forested hills of Damask, and the smooth green plains beyond, and they made their big mistake. They stayed.

He turned his attention back to the interior of the room. It was set up for a large meeting, with a long table, sixteen chairs, and decanter of water. Tapestries hung on the walls, one of them depicting a map of the Twenty Kingdoms. At one end of the room was a pedestal with a bust of Charlie's great-great-grandfather, one of the founders of Damask. At the other end was a stand with a blank flip chart. Today, a glass of water had been set out at only three of the chairs. A bowl of grapes sat on the end of the table. Charlie's uncles were by the door, giving orders to their courtiers and various hangers-on, then shooing them outside. When they were through, the two men locked the door and wearily sat down. When they looked like they were settled, Charlie took a seat also.

"I want to thank you for joining us, Charlie," said his uncle Gregory. "It is good of you to give us some time."

"We know you're anxious to get back to school," said his uncle Packard.

Charlie shrugged. He was not, in fact, particularly anxious to get back to the university. Nor was he particularly anxious to stay in Damask. And he wasn't particularly fond of his uncles, who reminded him of a pair of elderly jackals. They were old and skinny and crafty, with lined faces and feral smiles, and they seem always to be on the lookout for carrion. Charlie reached for a grape.

"The king," said one of them, watching Charlie carefully, "left no heir."

Charlie gave a short laugh. "For God's sake, Uncle Packy. You don't have worry about my feelings. You know by now that I'm not sensitive about it."

The two older men relaxed. "Okay then, Charlie. You can see the situation. It's up to us to pick out a successor to the throne."

"What? It's not going to be one of you two?"

"There are issues, Charlie," said his uncle Gregory. "Noile again. Young Fortescue has got that country pretty well stabilized now, and once again they're looking to take Damask back."

"Great!" said Charlie. "It's about damn time. Let them have it."

His uncles exchanged glances. "Why do you say that, Charlie?"

"Oh, come on." Charlie kicked back his chair and went around the table to the other window. The one that faced east, toward the mountains. "Look at them. I studied up on this during my last semester. They call mountains like those a rain shield. All the clouds bump up against them and dump their rain, and the rivers run through Noile to the sea. We get the little moisture that works its way through the valleys, and a couple of rebellious streams that decided to buck the crowd and flow west. It takes a minimum of thirty inches or rain per year to support farmland, they taught me, and we get twenty-seven."

"An average of twenty-seven." Charlie turned around to see his uncle Packard was now standing at the other window. There was bitterness in the old man's voice. "Sometimes you get more. You get a good year and the crops are lush, and then the next year is even better. The third year comes and you start thinking your luck has changed and maybe you can make something of your estate after all. And then come years of drought, and you're worse off than ever."

"Our ancestors thought it was a paradise, damn them," said Gregory. "I'm sure it looked like that, with the grass and trees." He snorted. "Six inches of soil over bedrock. It must have taken hundreds of years for those oaks and magnolias to grow. Once they logged them out, that was the end of it."

"Now they're grazing goats on the land," Packard added. "That will finish it off in a few more generations."

"So we're agreed," said Charlie, as they all returned to the table. "Let Fortescue have it."

There was a long, meaningful silence, except the meaning of it was not clear to Charlie. He looked at his uncles and they looked back at him. Finally he said, "Okay, out with it. You asked me here for a reason, so let's hear it."

"Fortescue doesn't want it." said Packard. "All right, I know I just said he wants it, but he doesn't think it's worth fighting for."

"A sensible man," said Charlie. "It isn't."

"But they'll fight for it anyway," said Gregory. "The nobility will want to hold on to their lands and titles to the very end, and the people will stay loyal to their monarch. It's all that patriotic indoctrination we get in the schools. Very hard to let go of, even after you're an adult."

"And Fortescue can't just invade on a whim. He needs a reason. Otherwise it will damage Noile's relations with the other kingdoms."

"Yep, you got a problem all right," said Charlie. He sat again, tilted his chair back, and yawned. "Excuse me."

"Unless the king is overthrown," said Packard. "Unless there's a revolution. Lot of civil unrest and all that."

"Right," said Gregory. "Then everyone will be happy when Fortescue comes in and restores order."

"What?" Charlie brought his chair forward with a *clack*. He frowned at his two uncles until the puzzle pieced itself together in his head. Then he laughed, long and hard. "I get it. I get it! You've sold out! Fortescue is paying you to turn the country over to him."

"I resent that accusation," Gregory started. "We . . ."

"All right, yes!" snapped Packard. "We sold out. Does that bother you, Charlie? You already said Damask would be better off under Noile rule. And you never cared much for the place anyway."

"I still don't. And don't get me wrong. I have no problem with it. Hell, I admire you two for it. I'm glad somebody will finally get something out of this wretched little country."

Packard relaxed. "Okay then. We need a bad king. Someone to raise taxes, abuse his power, anger the nobility, oppress the commoners, and give both classes someone to rise up against. Then Fortescue moves in on the pretext of restoring order, arrests the king, sends him off to a comfortable exile, places his puppet on the throne, and pays us off."

"Sounds like a plan. Not that I care all that much, but mild curiosity compels me to ask: Just what poor schlub do you plan to put on the throne? Cousin Richard? Abusive and oppressive doesn't really sound like his forte. And who is that kid Aunt Lydia dotes on? James? Jason? I think he'd have a little problem inciting an uprising. The worst thing I can imagine him doing is forgetting to feed his goldfish."

"It's not an easy decision to make," said Gregory. "So many members of our family are well qualified and deserve to rule. To be crowned King of Damask is an honor that . . ."

"We were hoping you would do it," said Packard.

Charlie stared at him.

Compared to most other young adults, Charlie had been around a bit. He had traveled all over Damask and Noile, and had paid visits to the courts of all the surrounding kingdoms. He had caroused in their cities and read in their libraries. He had even been to sea for a short while. He had studied at Bitburgen which, like any famous university, was well skilled in the art of convincing its students that they learned more than they did. All this had left him with the impression that he was knowledgeable about the world at large, and that no one in Damask could say or do anything that would surprise him.

But now he had to admit he was taken aback. He looked from one uncle to the next, did it again, and finally said, "Why me?"

"It will be a tough job, Charlie. We won't deny that. The new king will have to make a lot of tremendously unpopular decisions. All hands will be turned against him."

"All kings have their detractors. And what does it matter? Unless I'm totally misreading the situation, you're going to be running things behind the throne anyway."

"The problem is that we still have to live here afterward, Charlie," said Gregory. "So does the rest of the family. So do all the nobility. We can't lose the country and then stick around. Even if we have to relocate back to Noile, it will be no different. We've all got relatives and connections and investments there, too."

"We need someone who can pack up and leave afterward, Charlie. You never liked it here. We know you didn't plan to come back. Fortescue will depose you, there will be a bit of a show trial, and then you'll be exiled on pain of death. You'll be back in Bitburgen in time for the fall semester. I'll bet you could even get work-study credit."

"You'd have to fill out the forms," said Charlie absently. "Though I really can't see myself . . ."

"We'll cut you in on the take, of course. And it will be generous. Packy and I have our faults in some ways, but we're not greedy. You know we'll give you a fair share."

"That's not an issue. My mother left me a generous legacy."

"Everyone can use a little more."

"So can Richard or Jason, I imagine."

"It will never work with Richard. The man is too damn friendly. You know what I mean, Charlie. Those big blue eyes, and that big smile, and that infectious laugh. Everyone likes him. The man practically oozes charisma. The people are not going to rebel against him. And even if they did, it would break his heart."

"And then there is Jason. It's not really that he's fat. He's just sort of . . ."

"Pudgy," said Charlie.

" 'Cuddly' is the word," said Packard. "I've actually heard girls say he was cuddly. Like a stuffed toy, they said. Not all fat people are jolly. I've known plenty of fat kings who were mean bast—um—mean to the core. But you can't be cuddly and evil."

"And you think I'm evil?"

"No!" Packard and Gregory said, almost in unison. "Not at all, Charlie."

"But you look the part," continued Gregory. "You've got the image. You're *Bad Prince Charlie*."

"Oh, come now. You know how I got that name."

"Most people won't remember. You look tough, you've got an attitude, you always dress in black. . . ."

"What? I don't always dress in black."

"You don't?" Gregory was surprised.

"You're dressed in black now," said Packard.

"I've just come from a funeral. We were all dressed in black. *You're* dressed in black."

"Yes, but you *look* like the kind of guy who always dresses in black. That's my point. You've got an image. You've got a reputation. You intimidate people. Those brooding dark eyes, that scarred face . . ."

"My face isn't scarred!"

"Yes, it is. There. On your chin."

"That's a shaving cut. It will be gone in a few days."

"Well, you look like the kind of guy who ought to have a scarred face."

"I'll mention that to my barber. I'm sure he'll be pleased."

"Also." Gregory started to speak again, but stopped to give Packard a hesitant look. Packard nodded. "Once again, I hope I'm not rubbing a raw nerve or anything. Please forgive me if I do, Charlie. But there's also the issue of your being illegitimate."

"No raw nerve," said Charlie lightly. "I'm okay with it now."

"Well, you used to be quite sensitive about it. I remember at your eleventh birthday party you blacked young Cantinflow's eye with a pork chop."

"With a pork chop?" said Packard

"It was one of those double-thick pork chops they serve at Almondine's."

"Oh yes. Those are great. A pity the cooks here at the castle never learned to do them that way. Either they come out raw in the middle or overcooked and dried out."

There followed a minor digression on the subject of grilled pork, with or without Almondine's signature apple chutney*, before Gregory returned to the subject.

"It's just that some people will always support the king, no matter how much of a rotter he is. As I said before, all that stuff we teach them in schools about upholding the law and being good citizens. But when the heir is illegitimate, it makes it easier to depose him."

"Of course, plenty of kings have been illegitimate," put in Packard. "It's generally not a problem unless someone

---

*This looks like a good place for a footnote. Terry Pratchett and Susanna Clarke use lots of footnotes and they write bestsellers, so maybe I should also throw in a few.

makes an issue of it. We probably won't have to make an issue of it. It would just be another card to play if we needed it."

"I don't know if you know this, Charlie, but after this is all over, we could have you declared legitimate by the Council of Lords. Really, Packy and I thought it should have been done years ago, but the king wouldn't have it."

Charlie waved his hand. "I keep telling you, don't worry about it."

"Well, the offer is open if you want to take us up on it. I expect someday you'll have kids of your own, and it might be important to them."

"I'm afraid they'll just have to suffer the ignominy." Charlie placed one booted foot against a table leg and slid back his chair. He stood and leaned forward with his hands on the table. "My dear uncles, you have my admiration. Selling out your country for a mess of pottage, double-crossing your highborn friends, betraying the trust of the people—it's the kind of underhanded scheme that makes me proud to be a part of your family, however tenuously. For I can't think of any country that more needs to be sold out, or any group of nobles that more deserve to be double-crossed than those of Damask. Congratulations."

He clapped his hands a few times in applause, then turned his back on the old men and started for the door. "Nonetheless, you can count me out of the game. I may well be bad as you think I am, but underhanded scheming is not my idiom. Now, if you'll excuse me, I'm planning to fail a lot of courses this semester and I have a lot of books that I need to ignore."

"I understand, Charlie," said Gregory. "Thank you for hearing us out. We'll get someone else. I hope we can count on your discretion."

"Of course."

"I expect Catherine will be disappointed," said Packard. "I'm sure she was rather hoping it would be you."

Charlie stopped with his hand on the doorknob. "Catherine?"

"Lady Catherine Durace."

"Lady Catherine Durace?" Charlie paused, as if in thought. "About twenty years of age, as tall as my chin, impeccably dressed, a melodious voice, slender legs, a narrow waist, a thick mane of hair as red as a summer sunset, delicate lashes, soft pink lips formed into a perfect pout, flawless light skin with just a hint of freckles across her nose, and green eyes that flash like emeralds in firelight when she's angry, and sparkle like wavelets on a morning beach when she smiles? That Catherine Durace?"

"Ah, you know her then?"

Charlie took his hand off the doorknob. "I . . . think I may have heard of her." He retraced his steps back to the conference table, pulled out his chair again, and spun it around. He looked at it thoughtfully, as though trying to decide if he should sit down again. And then he did sit down. "Tell me more."

❧ ❧ ❧

Of course there had been a state dinner after the funeral, a somber affair, as befitted the occasion, with toasts and speeches and cold meats. Men fiddled with the buttons of their black coats and soberly reflected on their own mortality. Women hid their faces behind black veils, dabbed their eyes with black handkerchiefs, and speculated about the cost of one another's dresses. All agreed that the late monarch, despite a teensy little bit of fondness for the bottle, was one of the finest dead men to ever rule Damask. Catherine and Rosalind played the roles that were expected of women—looking pale and wan, and eating very little. Now they were making up for the lost opportunity, with a late supper in the dining room of the castle. They were seated at one end of a long table, still wearing their mourning clothes, but with the veils pushed back over their heads. The only other occupants were two solicitors at the other end of the table, talking in low voices on some technical point of law. A trio of logs burned steadily in the fireplace. Candles provided a small pool of light around the two girls.

Catherine reached for a loaf of brown bread and tore a piece off the end. "It went very well, I thought. I do so like it when it rains at a funeral. Not thundering rain, you understand, but a dreary little drizzle adds so much to the atmosphere. It makes the whole affair seem so much more—well—funereal."

"Oh, I agree," said Rosalind. "When the world seems gray and bleak, you can tell yourself that life is filled with misery and despair, and the departed did well to quit it when he did. Whereas, on a bright and sunny day you feel the loss of an early death so much more. Did my dress pull across the back?"

"No, it looked fine."

"I thought it might be too tight. I'm not sure I trust my new seamstress. The men looked very good, don't you think? Especially Bad Prince Charlie. That was so wild, the way he stood up to those bandits in the forest. Don't you think so?" Rosalind looked at her friend carefully. "Do you find him attractive?"

Catherine picked up a pat of butter with her knife. "I suppose."

"He was looking at you."

"Oh, look, here's Oratorio. He must be getting off his shift." Catherine waved her bread. "Oratorio, come sit here with us."

Oratorio, in uniform, holding his helmet under his arm, bowed low from across the room. He paused a moment to warm himself at the fireplace, then took the seat next to Rosalind. "Good evening, ladies. Ah, three more months of this, and I'll have completed my service to the crown. In the meantime, how pleasant to have your company at the end of a long watch. Have you eaten yet?"

"We were just starting."

"I wonder if I could get an omelet," said Rosalind.

"No," said Catherine. "Not in Damask."

"Unless you want dried eggs," said Oratorio. "And you don't."

"Oh yes, I'd forgotten that you don't have eggs in Damask. Some sort of curse, right?"

"Not a curse," said Catherine. "More like a spell that went awry."

"And in truth, we can have eggs. You can have duck eggs or goose eggs, if you want them badly enough. It's the chickens that don't survive here."

"All due to a sorcerer named Thessalonius," said Catherine. "He eventually turned out to be pretty good. In fact, he is now the Royal Sorcerer for Damask. But this was many years ago, when he was just starting out."

"He killed all the chickens?"

"He drove them out of the country. He was actually trying to drive the snakes out the country. He heard about someone else doing it in some other land, and he thought it was a good idea. But he made a mistake somehow, and instead of driving out the snakes, he drove out the chickens."

"Well, it was a good idea," said Rosalind. "I don't like snakes. Ick."

"Eventually he did figure out how to drive away the snakes," put in Oratorio. "Then he had to let them back in again."

"Goodness, why?"

"Rats," said Catherine. "Snakes eat rats and mice, so the vermin were infesting the granaries. Ground squirrels, too, eating the crops when they were still young shoots. It turns out we needed snakes. So a properly humbled sorcerer, sadder but wiser, had to reverse his big spell and let them in. No doubt there's a lesson there for us all."

Rosalind thought this over. "If he could reverse the spell that drove out the snakes, why couldn't he reverse the spell that drove out the chickens?"

"A quick thinker," said Oratorio. "I like this girl." Rosalind gave an involuntary little wiggle. "Because," he continued, "Thessalonius didn't know what his mistake was when he drove out the chickens, so he didn't know how to reverse it."

"Thus no omelets," finished Catherine. "No soufflés. No egg salad. No popovers."

"No cakes," said Oratorio. "No custards. And worst of all, no eggnog." He attempted to put on a tragic expression. "During the winter holidays, we have to drink our brandy straight up."

Rosalind patted his hand. "That must be terribly difficult for you."

"It is indeed. But we're tough in the guard. We can deal with hardship. Plus, every autumn we have the chicken festival, where cartloads of cold fried chicken and hard-boiled eggs are brought over the mountains. Everyone picnics in the parks."

"But still, no eggs, or cakes, or custards, or chopped liver, or chicken soup. I'd think people would be pretty mad. Why did the king keep him on?"

"He didn't just keep him on, he promoted him. No one knows why, but Thessalonius and the king were pretty close. And then, when the king died, Thessalonius disappeared."

"Really?" said Catherine. "I didn't know that."

"No one has seen him in weeks. Packard and Gregory gave us orders to keep an eye out for him."

"He might just be in mourning somewhere. What about Bad Prince Charlie? Why do they call him Bad Prince Charlie? Is there a story behind that?"

"*Yes*," said Catherine severely. "I gave him that name. He treated me in the most ungallant manner. He betrayed my trust."

Rosalind looked at her, wide-eyed. Catherine wore a grave expression, and she twisted her napkin in a fretful manner. The blond girl looked at Oratorio, who was leaning forward, listening, and back to Catherine. This was new to him. She said, "Don't hesitate, girl. Tell us about it."

"He invited me to dinner. You must remember, this was when I was young and innocent."

"And you're not young and innocent now?" asked Oratorio.

"Alas, no." Catherine sighed. "Years of sorrow have left their mark upon my careworn cheek."

"He asked you out to dinner . . ." prompted Rosalind.

"Yes. He sent a carriage for me. It was quite a nice restaurant. We were dining out on the terrace, late in the evening. He poured chilled wine into my glass. It was a warm summer night and I was a bit heated. I drank it down quickly, perhaps too quickly."

"Oh dear." Rosalind knew where this was leading. She glanced sideways at Oratorio to see how he was taking it. The young soldier looked stern.

"There were so many distractions. The moon shining on the terrace, the warm breeze bringing the scent of roses, a trio of musicians playing romantic airs. There were multiple courses to the meal, and several different wines. He kept filling my glass before it was empty. It was so hard to keep track of how much I drank. But I thought I could trust him."

Oratorio and Rosalind nodded gravely.

"My head began to swim. The candles seemed but a blur of light. The waiters cleared away the dishes and brought out the dessert tray. As if from nowhere, a snifter of brandy appeared in front of me. I told him I didn't want it. I'm sure I told him. But he urged it upon me. That final, after-dinner drink pushed me over the edge. I could no longer think clearly. And it was then, when my defenses were down, my protective instincts stripped away, that Charlie took cruel advantage of my weakness."

Oratorio's lips were set in a grim, tight line. Rosalind seemed struck with horror at what she was about to hear. "Oh, Catherine!" She leaned across the table, her voice dropping nearly to a whisper. "Surely he didn't . . . no . . . not Prince Charlie . . . not what I'm thinking!"

"I fear it's true."

"You mean—*he ate your dessert!*"

"Yes!" The red-haired girl gave a heartfelt sigh. "And it was chocolate, too!"

Oratorio stood up. "Cute, ladies. Very clever. I admit I was taken in. Now, if you'll excuse me, I must be off."

The girls laughed. "Now don't be mad at us, Oratorio. We were just having some fun." Rosalind patted his chair. "Sit with us, Oratorio. Our food is just arriving."

"Oh, I'm not angry, Rosalind. I'll be back a little later, if you're still here. But now I have a duty to perform. I must deliver a message to our Bad Prince."

⚜ ⚜ ⚜

Charlie walked through the hallways in something of a daze. He had spent a long evening with his uncles, mapping out a strategy. Now his brain was reeling from information overload.

He would not actually be crowned the king of Damask. Instead he'd rule as prince regent. He had talked it over with his uncles and all had agreed that was the best plan. "It's so much harder to depose a crowned king than a regent," explained Packard. "There's a mental barrier that people just don't want to cross, no matter how bad you are. So we'll stall for time while you whip the country into shape. We'll tell them we're planning a big coronation ceremony."

"We'll do it at the chicken festival," said Gregory. "When the carts come over from Noile, it will provide a cover for Fortescue to move his people in."

Charlie was more interested in Catherine.

"She's a good choice," said Gregory. "The House of

Durace have always been contenders for the throne. Well, you know what a new king does when he takes a disputed throne. His first move is to arrest all the other potential rivals. If they're adults he executes them, and if they're children he locks them up in a tower."

"Hold it," said Charlie. "I am *not* going to arrest some child and lock him in the tower."

"No, of course not. But Catherine's a good choice. She is a candidate for the throne, both here and Noile. In a distant way, perhaps, but she's still a believable choice."

"Of course, if you do want to grab a kid," said Packard, "I wouldn't object to that little pestilence Allen Durace. What with practicing with his drum set outside my window . . ." Both Charlie and Gregory glared at him. "It was just a suggestion," he finished.

"Catherine is tremendously popular," continued Gregory. "And very well connected. She has friends everywhere. So, of course, people will be very upset when we spread rumors that she is being cruelly mistreated at your hands."

"Especially when they hear that you're—ah—forcing your attentions on her. To take her virtue will make you seem particularly fiendish."

"I want to be quite clear on this. You're going to tell people that I'll be—um—*ravishing* Catherine Durace?"

"Well, we have to choose our terms carefully. If a man is really good-looking, it might be called ravishment. If he's one of the nobility, it's considered seduction. If he's a commoner, it's just rape. But any way we go, her supporters will read between the lines and be outraged."

Charlie ran a finger around the inside of his collar. "But Catherine has agreed to this? That I can—um—take advantage of her charms? You are quite, quite sure?"

"We've explained everything to her. She promised her total cooperation. Like you, she knows that in the end, this will be best for the people of Damask."

Charlie stopped at the corridor leading to his bedchamber. He leaned against the wall. *The people,* he thought. *Can't forget about them. I've got a lot of responsibility now.* Still, it was difficult to stay focused on his duties, because it was hard to get Catherine out of his mind. A mental picture of her laid back on satin sheets, her hair spread across a pillow, kept intruding on his thoughts. *What I need is a good night's sleep. Things will sort themselves out by morning.* He looked down the hallway, but decided to seek out the king's bedchamber instead. "Might as well get right into the role."

The king actually had a suite, with a reception area, an office, a bedchamber, a dressing room, and a sitting room. Courtiers and official visitors went through the reception area into the office, which connected to the bedchamber. Castle staff and private visitors went through the sitting room into the dressing room, which also connected to the bedchamber. A pair of windows looked over a courtyard, another pair looked over a cliff-top view of Damask. Charlie went into the sitting room and immediately said, *"Gagh."* He crossed the room and threw open a window, then opened a second window. Aloud he said, "The whole place stinks of tobacco and cheap wine. Why didn't the servants air it out?"

"I don't smell anything myself," said a man behind him.

He was of late middle age, dressed in loose and badly fitting mourning clothes, his hair inclining to gray, his body inclining to fat, and his face prematurely lined in that way that results from decades of excess tobacco and booze. In fact, he was smoking a pipe and nursing a bottle of fortified wine as he spoke. He was sitting in an armchair with one leg crossed over the other.

"I don't doubt it," said Charlie. "Pollocks, that's you I'm smelling, dammit." He crossed the room, took the pipe and bottle from the older man, and flung them out the window. There was a distant tinkle as the bottle crashed on the cliffs. "What are you doing here?"

The man looked regretfully out the window, then turned his attention to Charlie. Somewhat stiffly he rose to his feet and bowed. "It was my duty and pleasure to serve as the king's Faithful Family Retainer during his reign, and now I offer my services to you, my liege."

"You're calling yourself a Faithful Family Retainer? I thought you were more like his drinking buddy. Which, I grant you, meant putting in a lot of long hours."

"I admired your father for that. It is easy to make good decisions when you're sober. It takes a real statesman to rule when you're plonked."

"I see. Pollocks, I'm trying to remember. You've served my family since I was child. You were my father's closest associate and boon companion. You knew my mother well. And in all those years as my father's advisor, did he ever, even once, actually take any of your advice?"

"I am pleased to tell you that no matter how badly impaired the king's judgment became, he always retained enough sense to ignore my advice completely."

"Good for him. Well, thanks for the offer of service, but, in truth, I've made plenty of bad decisions all on my own, and I'm sure I can continue to do so without your help. Now, if you'll excuse me, it's been a long day and I'm going to turn in."

"Good idea, Sire. It's a long, steep ride, and we'll want to get an early start."

"What? Long steep ride to where?"

Pollocks pretended surprise. "Why, to the Temple of Matka, of course. It's a tradition. Upon taking power, the ruler of Damask visits the High Priestess of Matka, and learns what fate she foresees for the country."

"It's not a tradition. The country hasn't even been around for a hundred years. That's not long enough to call something a tradition."

"Someone has to start traditions," said Pollocks, one of the few people in the kingdom who had no problem contradicting a king to his face. "Your father paid his respects to the High Priestess and so did his father. The people here worship her. They will have more confidence in your rule if you visit and learn the future of Damask."

"Pollocks, you would be surprised at what I know about the future of Damask. I expect to be very busy in the days to come. I will have better things to do than listen to some crone spout a lot of gibberish."

"It's not gibberish. She's made some amazing predictions. Thessalonius consulted her."

"Yeah, where is Thessalonius anyway?"

"I haven't seen him." This statement was immediately followed by a knock on the door. Charlie went to open it but found that Pollocks had smoothly passed him and opened the door for him. Charlie half expected to see Thessalonius. Instead, he found himself face to face with a slim young man in a guard's uniform. "Sir Oratorio of the Royal Guard," announced Pollocks.

"Great," said Charlie. "I've been prince regent for three hours and already here's a young nobleman looking for favors. Sorry, not tonight. I'm tired. Come back tomorrow." He firmly removed Pollocks's hand from the knob and pushed the door closed.

"Prince Charlie, I'm Oratorio. Don't you recognize me? We were students at Bitburgen together."

Charlie opened the door again and studied the guard's face. "No, I don't. You're saying we were classmates?"

"Um, no, Sire. We didn't share any classes but we saw each other a few times. Um, freshman orientation? The homecoming dance?"

"Sorry, no.

"Rush night? The big pep rally?"

Charlie shook his head. "Doesn't ring a bell. Come back tomorrow during regular office hours. Good night." He shut the door firmly and turned into the room. "Pollocks, why are you still here? I don't need . . . Wait a minute." He did an about face and opened the door again. The guardsman was leaving with a dejected air. "Come back. Let me think. Oratorio. Fraternity type, right? You got drunk at the homecoming dance, tried to drive a four-in-hand into the ballroom, and got it jammed in the front doors?"

Oratorio reddened. "Your Highness, I wasn't the only one who . . ."

"Didn't you get arrested for dressing in women's clothing and trying to sneak into the girl's dormitory disguised as a housemother?"

"That's not exactly what . . . I can explain . . . you see . . ."

"Yeah, okay, I remember you now. What is it you want?"

Oratorio came to attention. "Prince Charlie, I must tell you that I saw your father."

"We all saw him. Lovely funeral. Good embalming job, if you appreciate that sort of thing. Very natural looking."

"No, Sire. I mean tonight. On the ramparts. I saw his ghost."

"Of course. You saw his ghost. On the ramparts. Yes, I see." Charlie looked at Pollocks and rolled his eyes. Pollocks gave an imperceptible nod back.

"It's definitely him, Sire. And it's not the first time he has appeared. Other men have seen him also."

"Well, we can't have that, can we? Talk to my secretary in the morning and we'll see about getting in an exorcist. It's the door down the hall. Don't come to this one."

"No! Your Highness, the ghost wants to speak with you. He has something to tell you."

"Then wait here." Charlie went into the bedchamber, where he found a small writing desk. He opened a drawer, removed a pot of ink, a quill, and square of foolscap, then dipped the quill in the ink. Returning to the sitting room, he handed the quill and paper to Oratorio.

Oratorio took them. "Um, what is this, Sire?"

"Pen and paper. If you see another ghost, take a message. I'm going to bed."

"I think the ghost expects you to speak to it yourself. He seemed very agitated. I'm sure it's important."

"Oratorio, I didn't care much to converse with my father when he was alive. I certainly don't intend to do it now that he's dead. Now I'm tired. If I don't get a good night's sleep, I get irritable and short-tempered."

"I guess you don't sleep much," Oratorio muttered. He knew Charlie mostly by reputation, and the prince was reputed to be short-tempered and irritable most of the time. He stood there for a long minute, still foolishly holding the quill, while Charlie turned his back and walked to the open window. Pollocks opened the door again, and the two men, with backward looks at the prince regent, stepped out together. Before they could close the door, Charlie spoke again. "Wait. Come here, both of you."

Pollocks and Oratorio exchanged looks, then quickly joined the prince regent at the window. Charlie pointed to the courtyard below them. It adjoined the dining hall, and was meant for eating outside during pleasant weather. Now it was lit by a handful of torches. It had a few tables, a nice view of the mountains, and rows of pots along the walls, where one of the cooks was growing spices. Two young women, wrapped in long coats, were walking along the perimeter of the courtyard, examining the potted herbs and discussing their contents. Charlie pointed to one of them. "That's Catherine Durace, correct?"

Pollocks looked over his shoulder. "Lady Catherine Durace. Yes, Sire. Born and raised in Damask. She's been living with relatives in Noile until recently. She returned for the funeral. I haven't heard that she plans to leave anytime soon."

"And who is the other one?"

"Rosalind Amund," Oratorio answered. "Lady Catherine's lady-in-waiting. I believe her father is a justice on the Noile court."

"Hmm. Pollocks, do we still have those rooms in the south tower for detaining political prisoners?"

"Certainly, Sire."

"Nice rooms? Big? Comfortable?"

"Oh yes, Sire. They're all as nice as your own room, and of course, the suite at the top floor of the tower, which is meant for detaining our most influential prisoners, is quite luxurious."

"Is it ready for use? Clean linens, fresh towels? Ashtrays emptied? Has the minibar been restocked?"

"I'm afraid I couldn't say, Sire." Pollocks found the line of questioning disconcerting. "It hasn't been used in a quite a while."

"Well, check. Get the servants out of bed and give the place a dust-off. Put a basket of fruit on the table and mints on the pillow. You know what I mean. Oratorio!"

Oratorio instinctively came to attention. "Yes, Sire."

"Get a couple of guards in here. Make sure they look presentable. Clean uniforms, buttons buttoned, that sort of thing."

"Yes, Sire." For the second time, Oratorio and Pollocks found themselves going out the door together. Once again they exchanged quizzical looks. Then each shrugged and went down the hall in separate directions.

Charlie leaned his elbows on the windowsill and watched the scene below. Catherine had pushed back her hood, and her long hair shimmered gold and red in the flickering torchlight. Her face, rising from a dark fur collar, was softened by shadows. The pale oval seemed to float over the dark cloak. Charlie closed his eyes and listened to her voice, which seemed to hold a musical sweetness. He opened his eyes again and focused on her lips. They were, he decided, the most perfect lips of any woman alive. He wondered what it would be like to . . .

"The guards are here, Sire," said Oratorio, standing at his shoulder. Two burly men were standing behind him. Their beards were still damp, indicating that Oratorio had sent them to a washbasin before bringing them in.

Pollocks returned, with a pear in his hand. "The tower room is ready, Sire. Complete with mints, fruit basket, and little bottles of shampoo and conditioner."

"Good, good." Charlie suddenly straightened his shoulders and flung the window full open, so the frame made a loud crash against the wall. The two girls in the courtyard looked up. He pointed dramatically at Catherine. "Arrest that woman!"

❧ ❧ ❧

Lord Gagnot thought that Charlie was one of the most sensible young men he had met in a long time. The prince didn't insist on any sort of ceremony, but rose from the throne when Gagnot came in, escorted him to a table that was piled high with accounting books and invoices, and invited Gagnot to pour himself a drink. Gagnot told him a few stories of riding and hunting on his estate, and found himself warming to this young man who listened so attentively and made appreciative comments. Gagnot found it admirable that Charlie was respectful to his elders, even when he outranked them socially. His Lordship paused in his storytelling to pour himself another whiskey, and that was when Charlie casually mentioned that he had passed Gagnot's estate on his way into town, and what a lovely manor house he had.

"Yes, isn't it? We just remodeled the whole thing. Added a new wing, too."

"It's quite impressive."

"You must come to dinner so you can see the inside. I don't know much about decorating, myself, but my wife did an excellent job picking out the new carpets and draperies. The furniture's all heirloom, of course."

"I understand Lady Gagnot likes to give lavish parties."

"Oh yes. We both love to entertain. Wait until you see one of our parties. We'll be sending you an invitation to the autumn ball."

"Thank you. Of course," said Charlie, smiling gently, "it did seem a rather large place to be supported on an estate of that size."

"Hmm? Oh yes. Well, it does take a bit of careful money management. But we know how to spend our money wisely. Lady Gagnot knows how to stretch a shellac."

Charlie put his hand on one of the ledger books and casually slid it over. "The Council of Lords put you in charge of the public granaries, did they not?"

"Hmm? Oh yes. They asked me to take the job and I accepted. Just one of the many responsibilities I have taken on in the service of Damask."

Charlie flipped the ledger book open. He compared an entry in it with an invoice. "And yet it seems that the inventories don't match the amount of grain that was deposited for storage."

"Uh, probably some clerical error. I'll have it looked into."

"Perhaps you should look into the granaries themselves, as I did this morning. They should be nearly full. Instead they are nearly empty."

Gagnot put his glass aside and exhaled through puffed cheeks. "All right, Charlie, I can see where this is going. You want a cut of the action, right? Well, I'm sorry, Your Highness, but I just can't do it. I'm paying too many kickbacks to the Council of Lords as it is."

"You're betraying your public trust. You're stealing grain from the public warehouses, selling it to your cronies at rock-bottom prices, and taking a kickback for letting them make enormous profits."

"I'm not keeping the entire payoff." Gagnot was growing exasperated. "That's what I'm telling you. There are so many other nobles and government officials with their hands out that I'm just about losing money on the deal." This was merely a negotiating ploy. Gagnot was really making a huge profit. He sat back in his chair and rested his hands over his ample belly. "I can give you a small cut now, maybe a bit more after the price increase."

"What you're doing is illegal."

"It certainly is not, Your Highness. I'm authorized to dispose of surplus grain and set the price."

"As well as immoral and unethical. The way the year is going, we're going to need that grain to feed hungry people. And we'll need it soon, Lord Gagnot. People will be suffering."

"Suffering? I should say not, Prince Regent. They won't be suffering. They're commoners. They're used to being hungry."

"Oh yes," said Charlie. "Now that you've explained it, I see what you mean. As long as the nobility has plenty to eat, there isn't a problem. Excuse me, Lord Gagnot." He closed the ledger books, got up, and left the room, almost immediately encountering Oratorio in the hall. "Ah, Oratorio. Just the man I wanted to see."

"And I wanted to see you, Sire," said the young knight. He looked nervous. "It's about the ghost. He appeared again. I took a message this time."

"Not now, Oratorio. I don't have time for ghosts. I'm going to see the wizards. But first I have a task for you. Lord Gagnot is in that room. Find a couple of guards and arrest him."

Oratorio was starting to think that he could not see the prince regent without having to arrest someone. "Very good, Sire," he said moodily. "The tower again?"

"The Barsteel," said Charlie, referring to Damask's infamous prison. He continued on his way. Oratorio went off to collect another pair of guards. No sooner had Charlie rounded the corner than Packard and Gregory stepped out of the shadows. This did not seem odd to Oratorio. Packard and Gregory were men who spent a lot of time standing in shadows. He bowed to them and they, in turn, fell in step with him.

"Ah, Oratorio," Gregory said. "Going to arrest another one, eh? Our prince regent has been busy this morning."

"I'm afraid so. Lord Gagnot this time. To the Barsteel."

"The Barsteel? Is Charlie aware that it has been out of use for years? In fact, I believe the bottom level is being leased to a coffee shop."

"He's filling it up again, sir. There are still cells on the upper levels. And it wasn't totally out of use. The Marquis de Sadness is being held there."

Gregory knit his brows. "I can't place him, although the name sounds familiar. The Marquis de Sadness?"

"Oh, you know him," said Packard. "He wrote those kinky books. You know, the ones where he said he derived erotic pleasure from making women unhappy."

"Oh, right. Throwing his socks on the floor, leaving the toilet seat up, belching at the dinner table."

"Sometimes he waited until Friday afternoon to ask a woman on a date, totally upsetting her plans for the weekend."

"A very cruel man," confirmed Oratorio. "Well, he'll have some company now.

"Excuse us, Oratorio," said Packard. He put his hand on Gregory's shoulder and the two men fell back a few steps so they could talk quietly. "Did Gagnot give us *our* cut from those grain sales?"

"Oh yes. He's paid up with us."

"Excellent." Packard joined back up with Oratorio. "The Barsteel, eh? Well, I'm sure if the prince feels that way, there must be a good reason."

"It's not for me to say, sir."

"Oh, come now, Oratorio." Packard gave his shoulder a squeeze. "Your father and I are old friends. Gregory and I have known you since you were a baby. You can speak freely around us."

"Well . . . yes," Oratorio conceded. He remembered that he was talking to the two men who had put the prince in power. "Charlie is just starting his rule. It's really too early to judge. He seems to want to crack down on corruption, which I guess isn't a bad thing."

"And Lady Catherine?"

"I suppose he has some reason for arresting her, even though I can't think what it could be. People are pretty upset about that."

"When matters of state become as confusing as this," said Gregory, "I often ask myself what the old king would have done. But I suppose you know that better than any of us, eh, Oratorio?"

"Sir?"

"Well, the rumor is that you saw his ghost on the ramparts last night."

"It wasn't just me," said Oratorio defensively. "Lots of guys have seen it."

"They say it spoke to you."

"It gave me a message for Prince Charlie."

"What was the message?"

"It was a confidential message, sir. For Prince Charlie."

"Of course, of course. And what did our prince say when he received it?"

"I haven't had a chance to give it to him. He has been busy."

"We'll be having lunch with the prince today," said Packard. "It would be no trouble to deliver the message for you."

It was not an unreasonable offer, Oratorio considered. Either of the king's brothers could have taken the throne. There were any number of family members they could have chosen. So clearly they weren't trying to grab power for themselves. They had put Charlie into power, in fact.

Oratorio had grown up in an atmosphere of court intrigue, but for once there was no reason to suspect subterfuge. Nonetheless . . .

He stopped and faced the two elderly men. "I'm sorry," he said truthfully, "but it's just not the kind of message that can be passed along."

"It's up to you then," said Packard heartily, dropping his hand from the knight's shoulder. "We won't detain you any longer, Oratorio. Come and see us if you ever want to talk." He and Gregory slowed their pace and let Oratorio get out of earshot again.

"I don't like it," said Gregory. "We didn't figure on the king coming back as a ghost. Who knows what he has to say? I went up there myself at night trying to spot him. Didn't see a thing."

"Considering the circumstances, I really don't think either of us wants to meet him again."

"I don't want Charlie to meet him, either. He could undermine Charlie's trust in us."

"Maybe. He could also tell Charlie his secret. That would save us a lot of effort."

"We'll find it," said Gregory. "We have time. There are only so many places it can be."

The castle had a weather map. As a child Charlie had loved to look at it, and even now he thought it was the coolest thing in the wizards' tower. It lay on a large table, a three-dimensional model of Damask, Noile, and the surrounding areas, with tiny rivulets of water flowing through the streams and rivers, ice that formed and melted on the mountaintops according to the season, and clouds that floated above the surface, reflecting the precipitation patterns in real time.

What the wizards' tower lacked was wizards. Thessalonius was still missing, and Damask couldn't afford to keep even a small staff of experienced wizards. Charlie found himself meeting with a journeyman and two apprentices. The journeyman had been hired from a temp agency, a young man trying to build up some work experience. The two girls were bright enough, but were only here for the semester on a work-study program.

It was Jeremy, the journeyman, who had to give Charlie the bad news. "It doesn't look good, Your Highness."

"But the crops seem okay."

"For now, Sire. We're still getting some rain. We'll continue to get some. But already we're down nine inches for the year. The reservoirs are down to seventy percent level. If the pattern continues, the grain harvest will be poor. We'll get a harvest of sorts, but the tonnage will be seriously short."

"How about the orchards?"

Jeremy ran the projection again. Lines of small clouds formed at the shoreline and moved across the table, spraying tiny showers on mountains the size of bread boxes. Rivers, snaking down the mountains in little grooves, ran into Noile. A handful of tiny streams, each hardly more than a scratch, trickled into Damask. "The early summer stuff will be close to normal. But the late-maturing fruit will dry up on the vines and trees. Nothing will make it to autumn."

Charlie put his finger on the groove that represented the Organza River, letting the water flow around the tip. "It's just a projection, right? Have you got any confirming data?"

"Evi, show him the caterpillars."

Evelyn, the taller of the apprentices, brought over a pasteboard disk. It was covered with number, lines, and brightly colored gradations. A handful of striped caterpillars crawled around it. "There are various formulas for predicting the weather based on the number and thickness of the their stripes."

"I did that when I was a kid. That actually works?"

"Oh yes," said Evelyn. "I did a term paper on it. Let me find it. Tweezy, do you have it?" The younger girl, who had the appearance of a blond mop, stepped forward and showed the prince a bound report. It was written on pink notebook paper, and the i's were dotted with little hearts, but the writing was clear and concise. "The formulas don't agree about just how severe it's going to be, but they all predict a shortfall of rain."

"Jeremy, can you *make* it rain?"

The journeyman stepped back before he answered, to stand in front of a screen of light blue glass. Charlie noticed that whenever a wizard discussed the weather, he always stood in front of a blue screen and made odd sweeping motions with his hands. Charlie had never asked why. He assumed it was part of the magic of weather prediction. "No," said Jeremy firmly. "I can't. Not me, not Thessalonius, not anyone else. Weather systems are just too big. There's more energy in one thunderstorm than in all the magical spells ever devised put together. And don't believe all that talk about the flapping of a butterfly's wing in Angostura causing a thunderstorm in Illyria. The great wizard Ambergris thought he could work with that. He spent years doing calculation after calculation, filling up reams of paper with his charts, creating what he called a map of the solution, looking for something called an 'attractor.' Then, when he was finally satisfied with his work, he traveled to the foothills of Alacia and at a precise place and time set loose a single butterfly. And look what happened."

"What did happen?" asked Tweezy.

"Caterpillar infestation," answered Charlie. "Took them ten years to get it under control. You can bet the orchard growers weren't happy with him.

"You can't blame the caterpillars," said Evelyn. "They just did what they were supposed to do. Ambergris should have been careful not to use a pregnant butterfly."

Charlie was getting the idea that she rather liked caterpillars. "He could have used a male butterfly."

"Humph," Evelyn and Tweezy said together. They glared at him with expressions that clearly said, *Typical male attitude.*

"The point being," said Jeremy, trying to get back on topic, "that it's tough enough just trying to predict the weather, much less trying to control it."

"Okay then, how good are your predictions?"

"Not good at all. Oh, we do all right up to maybe three days in the future. But a savvy farmer can do nearly as well. Out past a week into the future, we can't do anything without Thessalonius."

"This is important, Jeremy. Farm production is critical this year. How good is Thessalonius?"

"Pretty good." Jeremy gestured at the table map. "Prediction is his specialty. He has spent half of his life on it. Which is not to say he is *very* accurate. But he has managed to develop *some* real power of prediction, and you know, that's extremely rare. Pretty much everyone else in the Twenty Kingdoms who claims to be a seer is a fraud. Of course, there's the High Priestess of Matka. She's supposed to be pretty good. But she's rather cryptic."

"Excuse me, Your Highness," said Evelyn. "But the Organza River is flooding again."

Charlie removed his hand from the model and shook the water off his cuff. "Did Thessalonius leave any notes? Are there any spells or guides that can help you improve your accuracy?"

"If he wrote anything down, it will be locked in his study. We can't get at it."

"I can. I'll bring up a couple of workmen to take the door off."

Jeremy shook his head. "I'm sorry, Sire. He not only locked it, he warded it with protective spells. We can't get past them."

The prince glared at all three of them. "Knock it off. I'm in no mood for nonsense. I've never met an apprentice yet who couldn't get into his master's cupboards, and I find it hard to believe that a sorcerer's apprentice is any different."

Jeremy's face grew stern. "I'm sorry, Your Highness. It's out of the question. The agency would fire me if they found out I'd removed a master sorcerer's protective ward. I'd never get another job if that happened. And it doesn't matter because I can't do it anyway."

"Nor us," said Evelyn. "We'd get kicked out of school for sure. But neither of us knows enough magic to undo a protective ward. Right, Tweezy?"

"Um," said the younger girl.

The other three stared at her in silence, until Evelyn said, "What? You mean to tell me you got into Thessalonius's study?"

Charlie couldn't see Tweezy's face. He could only hear the hesitant mumble that came from behind a mass of blond curls. "Um, maybe. Only once. I didn't touch anything. It was an accident!" she finished defiantly.

"You removed a protective ward by accident?"

"It could happen!"

"Right," said Charlie. He put a hand on the girl's shoulder and gently propelled her in the direction of the chief sorcerer's private rooms. "Have another go at it, Tweezy. If you get it open again, send word to me immediately."

"Yes, Your Highness."

It was evening by the time the prince returned to the throne room. On his first day of rule, the halls outside had been crowded with courtiers, solicitors, ministers, and consuls. After a few days of throwing corrupt officials into the slammer, the halls were now eerily empty. Those officials he did pass tended not to meet his eyes and walked away quickly. Oratorio, on the other hand, was waiting for him. Charlie stopped and gave him a questioning look.

"It's about the ghost," Oratorio started.

"I'm not interested, Oratorio."

"Well, I'm sorry, Your Highness, but it's scaring the hell out of the men. You really have to see it yourself to understand the effect it has, all floating and eerie and sepulchral. If you could just hear what it has to say, I think there's a good chance it would go away and then we could all get back to normal."

"Did it talk to you?"

"Yes, Sire. And I took down the message, as you requested."

"Then what is it?"

Oratorio took a twist of paper from his breast pocket, but the prince said, "Just tell it to me, Oratorio. I'm sure you remember it."

"Yes, Sire. Um." The knight paused to clear his throat.

"Come on, out with it."

"Very well, Sire. The ghost said, 'Tell that little bastard if he doesn't get his royal rump out on the ramparts tonight and hear me out, I'm going to give him a haunting he'll never forget.'"

"Huh. Well, I have to admit, that does sound like Dad."

"Yes, Sire. He seems to have caught the king's turn of phrase quite nicely."

"Too bad I've got other plans for tonight. If he appears, tell him he's penciled in for tomorrow."

Oratorio, looking unhappy, nodded. Charlie left the throne room and went back to his suite. Pollocks was there. Pollocks was always around, it seemed. He had brought a thick roll of diagrams into the small office. Now they were spread over the desk. Charlie joined him. "Are those the public works programs?"

"Yes, Sire. I brought everything I could find out of the files."

"Good. We'll need something to keep them employed when the crops fail."

"Here's one for a new opera house."

"No. I can tell right away that we can't afford it now. We'll be buying food with every penny in the treasury."

"Here's something about adding some new parks."

"Too easy. Won't employ enough people."

"We've got a few other civic improvements that don't amount to much. And then there's this." Pollocks showed him a mass of construction drawings. "I can't make out what this is all about."

Charlie studied them. "Sunken roads?"

"If you say so, Sire."

"That's gotta' be it. But why would we want a grid of roads going through mostly farmland? Look how extensive this is."

"I couldn't say, Sire."

Charlie studied them some more. "Cheap to build, though. Just scrape the dirt down to bedrock, which in our case is usually only eight inches below the surface, and bank the dirt along the side. No material cost, but labor intensive, which is what we need. The only equipment is shovels, and it will keep a lot of men busy. Okay, we'll do it."

"Do we need these roads, Sire?"

"We need a public works project and this is fully engineered and ready to go." Charlie rolled up the drawings and handed them to Pollocks. "Bring them to the Interior Minister and tell him to get ready. People will be coming in from their farms once their gardens start drying up."

"Yes, Sire."

"Tell him to keep track of the level in the city wells. Institute water rationing when they get to forty percent of normal."

"People won't like that, Sire."

"They don't have to like it." Charlie left the office and went into the dressing room. He opened a closet, looked inside with surprise, opened another closet, and looked in that one with puzzlement. He pulled a bell rope that summoned his valet. The man appeared quickly—he must have been already on his way—bearing a tray loaded with hot towels, a basin of water, a bowl of shaving soap, and a razor. Charlie pointed to the closet. "What happened to my clothes?"

"I put them away, Sire. On order from your uncles. They took the liberty of supplying you with a brand-new wardrobe."

"Everything is black!"

"Yes, Sire."

"Even the underwear is black."

"Yes, Sire, but it is silk underwear. Your uncles said that black clothing suited you. Would you like me to shave you now, Sire?"

"Yes, fine . . . no!" Charlie took the tray from his hands. "Ah, no. No, I'll shave myself. Thanks anyway." His valet bowed out. Charlie dressed with particular care, noting that, except for the monochromatic color scheme, his uncles had somehow found a tailor that was familiar with his size and taste. He carefully aligned the ruffles of his collar and laced up his breeches so the waistband lay flat against his trim stomach. Looking in the glass, he combed his hair several different ways before deciding on his usual left-side part. A few strokes with a towel brought a final luster to his already gleaming boots. He started to comb his hair again, but told himself he was only stalling, and put the comb away.

From another cabinet he took a silver wrapped box, opened it and inspected it. It held some of the finest chocolates that could be obtained in Damask. He replaced the lid, put the box under his arm, and picked up a dozen carefully wrapped roses. Deciding he was as ready as he was ever going to be, he made his way to the south tower.

Catherine was allowed to receive visitors—had been receiving a steady stream, in fact—but tonight, Charlie had instructed the guards to turn everyone else away. He hesitated before knocking, wondering if it would be more in character to simply barge in. He decided that even a bad prince could be polite. He knocked twice. Hearing no answer, he turned the handle and let himself in. He was not prepared for what he saw.

He was prepared to see Catherine, of course, and he did see her, although even that sight exceeded his highest expectation. She stood on the other side of the room, bathed in soft candlelight from a dozen strategically placed tapers. Her long red hair was artfully disarrayed, falling down to her shoulder and beyond, partially covering her face and concealing one eye. Her perfect figure was clad only in a long silk gown of sea-foam green. It had no sleeves or straps. It simply clung loosely to her breasts, seemingly without support, and rippled down to the shadows between her thighs, the translucent material hinting at the lush pleasure beneath its folds, without actually revealing anything. The gown was slit along one side, allowing Charlie's eyes to follow one slim, creamy thigh down to her high-heeled slipper. Her hands, splayed out against the opposite wall, boasted nails of deep red, and the same glossy red coated her rich, full lips. Lady Catherine Durace presented a sight that most men could only dream about. She was more beautiful—far more beautiful—than Charlie had ever dared hope, but he quickly upgraded his hopes to deal with that.

He was not, however, prepared to see a woman who seemed scared to death.

She was pressing herself against the far wall as though hoping to disappear into it. Her lower lip was trembling, and her uncovered eye was casting about as if searching for a means of escape. She was breathing stertorously, her breasts rising and falling in a way that kept drawing Charlie's attention even when he knew he should be looking at her face. They both stared at each other, silent, unmoving, until Charlie felt constrained to break the ice.

"So," he started cheerfully. "How do you like these rooms? Pretty nice, eh?"

Catherine brushed the hair off her face in one jerky, spasmodic movement. She fixed her eyes on him. She said nothing.

"I brought you some flowers." Charlie held them up. "And some chocolates." He gestured with the box.

Catherine continued to say nothing.

"They're really good chocolates," said Charlie.

No response.

"Well, I'll just put them on the table here." He laid the bouquet and the box on a table in front of him, between two candles. Catherine backed away as he approached, slithering along the wall.

"What do you want?" she whispered hoarsely.

"Um. I just dropped by to say hello and see how you were getting along. So the rooms are okay, huh? How about the food? Everything fine there? You don't have to answer, just nod your head. Maybe we could talk for a little while. We haven't seen that much of each other. This might be a good time to get reacquainted. How have you been? Your hair looks nice."

Catherine slid against the wall until she reached the side of the bed. It was a large, sleigh-style bed, with a great curve of varnished mahogany for the headboard and a smaller piece for the foot. The white silk sheets gleamed like a snowdrift under a winter moon. "Don't toy with me, Your Highness." She suddenly threw herself backward, sinking into the down mattress. Pillows bounced around and over her, hiding her from view until Charlie moved closer. She was lying spread-eagle, with her eyes screwed shut and her hands clenched into tight fists. "Go ahead," she whispered through clenched teeth. "Do what you came to do. Let's get this over with."

"Excuse me," said Charlie. He left the room, closing the door quietly behind him, nodded to the guard, and walked swiftly down the inside stairs until he was out of the south tower, where he then crossed over to the west wing of the castle. Both of his uncles had a suite on the floor below the king's rooms, across the hall from each other. Charlie took a long look at each door, taking deep breaths and counting to ten to control his temper. He gave up at seven.

"Get out here," he yelled, pounding on one door. He crossed the hall and hammered on the second one. "Get out here right now!"

The door behind him opened. Packard and Gregory came out of the same room, where they had been smoking and drinking port. "Charlie? What's wrong, my boy?"

Charlie pointed upward. "You told me she was in on the game!"

"You're speaking of Catherine?"

"Yes, Catherine! She thinks she's really a prisoner."

"No, no she doesn't. Charlie, she was fully briefed on the whole plan, right from the beginning. She knows everything you know. We went up to give her a progress report ourselves, just this morning."

"Well, there must be some miscommunication because I just went to see her and she's scared to death of me. She thinks I'm going to rape her."

"Ah." Gregory and Packard exchanged smiles. "Don't worry about it, Charlie. It's an act. It's all part of the plan to make you look bad."

"Why would she put on an act when there's no one in there but the two of us?"

"I expect she wants to stay in character," said Packard.

"Exactly," said Gregory. "Also, lots of girls have some sort of fantasy about being taken by a handsome and forceful young man. They want to be carried up the stairs two at a time, flung onto the bed, their bodices ripped. That sort of thing."

. "Don't tear the bodice for real," said Packard. "That will get her upset. Those things can be expensive. Loosen the stays and gently tug it open. Just have a tough expression when you do it."

"Are you telling me I'm supposed to *rape* Catherine as part of the plan?"

"Not rape, ravish. Ravish is the word they use."

"What's the difference?"

"Well, legally there's no difference. But in those novels they read, they always say that the hero ravished the girl."

Charlie put an arm up against the wall, then rested his head on the arm. "Rape or ravish, I'm not comfortable with taking a woman by force. This wasn't what I had in mind for us."

"Charlie, you're not doing either one," Packard said patiently. "It's a bit of performance art, to make the rest of Damask think you're mistreating her. She's just carrying it a little too far."

"You're a man of the world, Charlie," said Gregory. "You know what women are like."

"No," said Charlie. "Actually I don't."

"Oh, come now." Gregory winked at him. "You've been two years at the University of Bitburgen. We know they accept women now. We know what college students are like. We've all heard stories about the parties and the scandalous behavior of coeds. You're a good-looking young man of independent means. I'm sure you had your share of flings."

"Of course not," snapped Charlie. "I was an engineering major."

There was a long period of embarrassed silence. "I . . . I'm sorry, Charlie," said Gregory finally. "I shouldn't have said anything. I didn't know."

"Catherine won't know, either," said Packard buoyantly, clapping Charlie on the shoulder. "Off you go, my boy.

She's waiting for you and no doubt wondering what's taking you so long."

"Just follow your instincts," said Gregory. "And if she says anything about school, tell her you changed majors."

There were a lot of stairs between his uncles' quarters and Catherine's suite in the prison tower, but Charlie took them without much notice, lost in a mental haze. He navigated the turns on instinct, for his vision was turned inward, focused on a mental picture of Catherine, sprawled across the bed in her silk nightgown. Charlie knew there were many things in life that were more important than getting laid, but right now it was hard to imagine what they could be.

The reverie was broken by the guard. "I'm sorry, Your Highness. I tried to stop them, but there were too many of them. They just kept coming, from all over."

"Who?" said Charlie, but he found out as soon as he turned the corner. It appeared that every woman in the castle, from the noblest ladies to the newest chambermaids, was gathered in the hall leading to Catherine's rooms. They stood aside to let Charlie pass, but they gave him uniformly dark and dirty looks, contempt and revulsion plainly shown on every face, and Charlie could hear the whispers behind him as he passed. "Beast!" "Animal!" "How could he do that to her?" For the second time that evening, he knocked on Catherine's door.

This time she answered it. The picture she presented was quite different from what he had seen half an hour before. Her eyes were puffy from crying and her makeup was streaked with tears. The nightgown, he noticed, seemed to have been torn in a rather lewd way. He leaned forward. "Catherine? Are you okay?"

She shut the door in his face.

The whispering behind him grew louder. Charlie turned around. It stopped instantly, but he was washed by an almost physical wave of hostility, emanating from Catherine's supporters. As one woman, they folded their arms and glared at him.

"Oh for God's sake," muttered Charlie, and went out onto the ramparts.

The ghost drifted across the parapets. There was a chill wind blowing over the stonework, but the ghost didn't feel it. Since his death he had constantly felt cold anyway. He didn't like being dead. One day alive, breathing, drinking, surrounded by toadies, bootlickers, yes-men, and groveling sycophants, as a leader should be. Ruling a small kingdom, but one that had potential. Suddenly he was cold all the time, he felt like he couldn't breathe (he couldn't, of course, but it wasn't a pleasant feeling), and it was lonely up here on the walls. Twice he had managed to sink down inside the castle for a few minutes. There he had seen himself in a mirror, and it was a depressing sight. He hated himself in white. It made him look fat.

His only consolation was that he had fallen asleep on his final night with a bottle in his arms. At least he had that with him. He took a drink now, and blew on his hands to warm them. It didn't have the slightest effect.

A voice behind him said, "Whither thou, Ghost?"

The ghost jumped a foot in the air.

"Dammit, Charlie," he said irritably. "Don't sneak up on me like that."

"I wasn't sneaking. You're the one who's drifting around silent and translucent."

"Well, you're hard to see. What's with the black clothes? No, let me guess. You've decided to become a ninja, right?"

The prince looked down at his clothes and gave a small, resigned shrug. "Yes. Exactly right. Dad, it's cold, it's dark, it's night, I've had a long day, and I'm tired. Let's get this over with. You called me out here to tell me something, and I suspect it was not to comment on my sartorial habits. Come on, out with it."

"Don't rush me, Charlie. This is important." The ghost took a pull from its bottle. "You didn't happen to bring anything to drink, did you?"

"I stopped drinking when I left Damask. Alcohol makes me short-tempered and irritable."

"Oh, that's what does it, eh? Okay, I'm not going to repeat this, so listen up." The ghost put one hand on its hip and held the other one out in what was apparently supposed to be a dramatic gesture, although the bottle in its fist somewhat lessened the effect. It spoke:

> But soft, the gibbous moon and starry night
> Give witness to the secret I reveal
> For whence I journeyed to the Land of Nod
> And there did meet a most unnatural death
> There in my bed, while deep in slumbered bliss
> Foul poison entered in my trusting veins
> Thus curdled blood . . .

"What the hell are you going on about?" Charlie interrupted. "Are you trying to do iambic pentameter?"

"Quiet! I'm dead, I'm bringing you a message from beyond the grave. Of course it's in blank verse. There's a protocol to these things."

"Well, save it for the open-stage poetry slam at the Cuppa Java."

The king was momentarily thrown off topic. "What is it with those coffee shops?" he muttered. "They're everywhere. One and three for a mocha frappuccino? Where do people get the money to burn?"

"If we could return to the subject."

"Charlie, I did not die from natural causes."

Charlie gave him a *like-I-care* look.

"I was poisoned, Charlie."

"I'm not surprised. Alcohol poisoning is the first thing I'd suspect."

"Not alcohol poisoning!"

"You were bit by a snake?"

"Two snakes. Packard and Gregory. My own brothers. They poured poison—extract of hebenon—in my ear while I slept."

"No kidding? That really works?" Charlie patted his pockets, looking for a pencil stub. "Let me write this down. I may need to try it someday. Extract of hebenon?"

"Dammit, Charlie! Your uncles murdered me!"

"Good for them. They should have done it years ago. I'm sorry I didn't think of it myself."

The ghost glared at him. "Your sovereign and father was murdered. It's your duty to avenge my death. What are you going to do about it?"

"Give them a medal? No, too public. Perhaps just a thank-you note and a bottle of wine."

"Charlie . . ."

"Dad, I have to ask myself a question. In what way, exactly, is Damask worse off by your death? And you know, nothing is coming to mind."

"So you've turned against me, too," the ghost said bitterly. It looked despairingly over the ramparts.

"I've never been for you."

"Why? What have I done to deserve your opprobrium?"

"You must be joking. You want the whole list or just the top ten? Let's start with something you didn't do. Specifically, you didn't marry my mother."

The ghost did its best to look innocent and aggrieved. "Really, Charlie, is that what's bothering you? Come now, I'm hardly the first man in the kingdom to sire a child out of wedlock."

"You banished her from the castle. You threatened her with death if she ever came in your sight again."

"Yes, well, that was for her own protection. To stop rumors."

"Rumors! You denounced her in public! You called her a slut and a whore!"

"Foul lies! Honestly, Charlie, you know that a king always has opponents who will try to smear his reputation. You should know better than to believe stories like that. Where did you hear such nonsense?"

"From you. When you got drunk and started bragging to your cronies about your sexual conquests."

"Um, okay, but the point was that you were around to hear those stories. I recognized you as my son, didn't I? You *are* called Prince Charlie, aren't you?"

"You know damn well that's an unofficial title. You didn't recognize me as your son until everyone else in the kingdom was already calling me Prince Charlie, when it became obvious that we looked so much alike."

"Don't change the subject," said the ghost, changing the subject. "Did you come out here just to whine about your unhappy childhood? I tell you Packard and Gregory are not to be trusted. They're up to something. You've got to warn the new king."

"Warn the new king?"

"Right. Tell him to be on his guard. Whom did they pick, anyway? Was it Richard? Richard is the obvious choice."

"I thought so, too," said the prince. "But no. They offered it to someone else."

"Jason, I'll bet. I'm not surprised. I always thought he was pretty stupid. That's the kind of guy they want."

"You think so?"

"Oh yes. I know my brothers, and they'll pick some dumb chump they can easily manipulate. That's why you've got to act quickly. Get in to see whatever brainless idiot they've set up on the throne, and persuade him to come to the ramparts at night so I can tell him about . . ."

"It's me," said Charlie.

"It's always about you. As I was saying, get the fool up here where I can talk to him."

"You're talking to the fool now. It's me, Bad Prince Chump."

The ghost stared. "Ridiculous. Why you?"

"Thanks for the vote of confidence, Dad. Now let me ask you something. You said you were murdered while you were sleeping in bed, right?"

"Right.

"By someone pouring poison in your ear. While you were asleep, right?"

"Right."

"Okay, so if you were asleep, how could you know who poured the poison in your ear?"

The ghost sputtered. "I know because . . . because . . . I'm a ghost, dammit. Ghosts know these things."

"Totally convincing. Okay, Ghost, you've said your piece. You are released. No longer must your tortured soul haunt the environs of your sad demise. You may continue your interrupted journey to that ethereal plane to which we all ascend upon our dying breath. Et cetera, et cetera."

The ghost looked exasperated as only a ghost can. "All right. God only knows what Packy and Greg are up to, but I've got to trust you. Charlie, I've got something else important to tell you."

"I don't want to hear it. Ciao." The prince started to walk off.

"I mean it. This is important."

"I'm sure it is and that's why I don't want to hear it. I know how ghosts work. You're going to start telling me something, and just when you get to the critical details, you're going to fade away, or be interrupted, or yanked down into Hell, leaving me with an impenetrable mystery to solve. Well, forget it. I've got enough to do already."

"You have to find Thessalonius."

"I'm not listening."

"Quit fooling around. Get your hands away from your ears. Would I go through all the trouble of haunting these ramparts night after night just to tell you half a secret? Now start acting like a king . . ."

"Prince regent, actually."

"Like a prince regent and pay attention." The ghost once again assumed a dramatic pose. Charlie rolled his eyes but sat down on the wall and listened.

> *Destruction of the city is at hand*
> *If weapons magical are come to light*

"Not verse again," the Prince muttered.

> *Too strong the power that in this kingdom lies*
> *Sorcery that can wreak a havoc great*

"That last line doesn't scan."

"Shows what you know," said the ghost. "It's a trochee."

> *Thine uncles seek to make this weapon theirs*
> *And thereby to destroy Noile's strength*
> *Their army shall be rendered into mush*
> *Like boiled zucchini too long 'ere the pot*

"Enough!" snapped Charlie. "Get to the point. You're telling me that Thessalonius developed some sort of magical weapon?"

"Yes. One with immense destructive power. If ignited at the right place and time, it can destroy an entire army."

"And you think Uncle Packard and Uncle Gregory want to use it to invade Noile?"

"Exactly. I know them well, Charlie. Territorial expansion has long been an ambition of theirs. They suspected that Thessalonius had developed a Weapon of Magical Destruction for me, and they wanted it. They poisoned me when I refused to even consider their schemes."

Charlie shook his head. "Dad, you have it completely wrong. They don't want to take over Noile. They want Noile to take over us. They've already sold out to Fortescue. They put me on the throne to have someone that Fortescue could easily overthrow."

The ghost shrugged. "Fine, have it your way, Charlie. That only makes it worse. Fortescue is the last person who should get his hands on a WMD. You can't deny that *he* is warlike and ambitious. He'd use it without a second thought."

Charlie made a sound like an exasperated sheep. "Bah." He turned away and leaned over the wall. There were still a few lights in the city below, glowing in the windows of late-night taverns and restaurants. He watched them for a while, thinking that he wasn't prepared for this. He had expected to walk out tonight and meet a typical ghost with a typical secret—"The will is hidden behind the cupboard" or "The gold is buried beneath the old oak tree" or "The real heir was switched at birth with a swineherd's daughter." Now he was getting dumped on with another important responsibility.

He turned back to the ghost, who had emptied the last few drops out of the bottle and was licking the rim. "All right. I agree for the moment that Thessalonius made a WMD and is hiding it somewhere. Tell me where it is and I'll see that it is destroyed. Does that make you happy? And why did you even allow him to build such a device if you weren't intending to use it?"

"I can explain that," said the ghost. "We intended to—hark!" It cupped a hand to its ear.

"What?"

I hear the feathered herald of the dawn
The harbinger of early morning light

"The what?"

"I heard a cock crow."

"You did not!"

"Yes, I did. There it is again." The ghost began to fade away.

"We don't have cocks in Damask!"

"Um, it was a peacock then." The ghost was little more than a white shimmer.

"Peacocks don't count! Get back here!" Charlie screeched. He grabbed at the ghost, but his hands passed through empty air. Overbalancing, he ended up hanging over a parapet, looking at the courtyard below. A handful of guards were staring at him curiously. He straightened up and waved. "Just talking to myself a bit. Not a problem. Carry on." He backed away from the stone wall and stood for long minutes, scowling at the place where the ghost had been. Then he said aloud, to no one in particular, "It's cold out here," and went back inside.

Back in the misty reaches of time, when the forests were untamed, and the sea was a monstrous barrier to travel, when the climate was colder and wetter, and the highest passes were covered in snow for most of the year, an advanced civilization had flourished in these mountains. Archaeologists, with unusual good sense, called them the Matkans, because that's what they called themselves. The Matkans had developed a crude writing system, and from the records that survived, scholars had been able to piece together a detailed description of their—even by classical standards—extraordinarily boring culture. Their music, for example, had never progressed beyond the penny whistle. They had produced tons of artwork, nearly all depictions of sea captains, sad-faced clowns, and kittens with big eyes. Their drama consisted entirely of watching a woman spin a big wheel with letters on it while trying to complete a mystery phrase. The Matkans would have been well and deservedly forgotten, had it not been for their roads.

They built great roads. This hadn't been discovered until fairly recently, for the Matkan roads had been long overgrown. But once the first one was found and excavated, more discoveries followed, and the archaeologists learned that those roads led to more roads, and those to more roads, thousands of miles of them, stone paths that extended through nearly half the continent. Big deal, some might say. Lots of civilizations built roads. But the Matkans went all the way, building a complete traffic system, with passing lanes, cloverleafs, and metered parking.

Then the Matkans disappeared. Their civilization vanished. They left no clues to their disappearance, which did not prevent scholars from writing learned papers about it. Some said that climate change had destroyed their agricultural base, others that a murderous slave trade had caused them to leave their homes and flee into the forest. A few believed they had slowly poisoned themselves by eating a strange new sweetener made from maize, and a handful of the really dippy scholars claimed that the Matkans were so advanced that they had attained a higher plane of existence and transcended into beings of pure light. The truth, however, was that the Matkan civilization broke down because of the roads.

"You never take me anywhere," a Matkan woman would say to her husband. "I am so tired of being stuck at home with the kids, while you're out chopping wood. At least you get to see the other woodcutters. And now there's this new road running right past the hovel, so you can't say it's too far."

The husband would think it over for a while and agree. "No use paying all those taxes on roads if we don't use them. Beside, there's this gadget for the cart I've been meaning to try out. Called an axle. They say you can hitch an ox to the cart and get it up to three, maybe four miles per hour."

"Now don't drive too fast," the woman would caution. "You'll get us all killed."

"I won't," the husband would lie.

And so they left. First a few, and then more and more, until finally the whole society had packed their belongings, in carts or barrows or on their backs, to follow the roads. They never returned. Their destinations are unknown. Some say their descendants are still traveling, never stopping, searching for that ultimate, and unachievable, utopia—a district with good public schools *and* low property taxes. Left behind, their homes, public buildings, and temples fell into ruin. They collapsed and were covered over with grass and shrubs until nothing but a few half-buried chunks of stone remained to betray their existence.

Except the Temple of Matka.

It was still cold the next morning, and a bit misty, too, when Pollocks and the prince set out for the Temple of Matka. The guards at the gate saluted, but Charlie thought he noticed a tinge of disrespect in their manner. Most of the castle was still asleep. Pollocks was bleary eyed himself. "You're the one who said we should get an early start," the prince reminded him.

"Yes," his aide conceded. "Force of habit. It's what I always said to your father. We never actually did it." His stomach was grumbling. They had left before breakfast, when the cooks were still asleep. "There's a coffee shop along the way," he noted. "Perhaps we could stop for a muffin and a café au lait?"

"Hmm?" Charlie had been lost in thought. "We can eat when we get to Matka."

"Yes. Fine with me," said Pollocks. "I can wait. Whenever you're ready." The horses jogged on, past spring flow-

ers, budding trees, and the occasional roadruner.* They
were each leading a second horse, for the road, though well
paved, was steep. He tried again a little later, when they
stopped to change horses and the sun was full up. "It's just
that the high priestess is, so to speak, high. You have to treat
her with courtesy and respect. And it's often been said that
hunger can make a person short-tempered and irritable."

"That doesn't happen to me," the prince said absently.

Not so anyone would notice, Pollocks refrained from
saying. He was searching his mind for a tactful reply when
Charlie asked, "Pollocks, is there an acting troupe in
Damask?"

Pollocks brightened. "His Highness wishes to go to the
theater? An excellent decision. No, Damask doesn't have a
resident theater company, but right now there is a show in
town called *The Fishmonger's Wife*. It played for months in
Alacia. I can arrange seats for you if you like. The tickets
are seventeen shellacs, so they'll cost you a ponce. I saw it,
and it's great. It's about a fishmonger, you see, and he mar-
ries this woman with enormous . . ."

"I don't want to—wait. The tickets are seventeen shellacs but they cost twenty?"

"By the time you add the reservation fee, the handling
fee, the convenience fee, the parking fee, and the nonvol-
untary donation for new theater construction, they're up to
a ponce each."

"I don't want to see the play, Pollocks. I want to see an ac-
tor. Find the stage manager and bring him up to the castle."

Pollocks immediately looked worried. "The dungeons
are getting pretty full, Your Highness, what with all the officials you've jailed for bribery and corruption. If you're

---

*A bird with an incredibly hard beak that pecks strange glyphs into the rocks along-
side the roads and—oh, quit groaning. It's just one pun for Robert Asprin fans. (Asprin doesn't use footnotes, though.)

going to start arresting actors, we're going to have a crowding problem."

"I'm not going to . . ."

"Not that anyone would object, I'm sure. They're actors, after all. But I'm not sure they've done anything bad enough to be jailed with the nobility."

"Pollocks," said the prince patiently. "Find out who runs that acting troupe and bring him to me. I'm not going to arrest him. I just want to talk to him."

"Yes, Sire," the aide said doubtfully.

They stopped again on the edge of Lake Organza. It was a beautiful lake, deep and blue, whose smooth, clear waters reflected the deep green conifers on its banks, and the snowcapped mountains that rose around it. Snow melt and mountain streams fed it from three sides, and on the side facing Noile, a sparkling waterfall dropped eighty feet to become the Organza River. Normally the valleys of Noile were shrouded in cloud and drizzle, but today was unusually clear. Charlie found he could follow the twists and bends of the turbulent river all the way down to Noile's capital city, and he could even see the sails in the harbor beyond it.

Directly across the lake, in the shadow of the steepest peak, were the domes of the Temple of Matka, flanked by coffee shops. For untold centuries it sat empty, abandoned, and ruined. Then fifty years ago the Cult of Matka, whose monks worshipped a mysterious seeress, suddenly appeared and moved in. The young sorcerer Thessalonius, who had set up shop in Damask about the same time, began to pay visits to their high priestess. Word spread of her amazing prophetic powers. Her fame grew. Now, despite the steepness of the road, a steady stream of pilgrims made their way to the temple and up the stairs.

They let their horses drink from the lake. Charlie pulled a sheaf of weather predictions from his pouch and studied them. They did not make him happy. He looked up, toward the ridge that separated Noile from Damask. "Pollocks, what does that cloud look like to you?"

The older man smiled, as if at a favorite memory. "Well, Your Highness, I would say it looks like an elephant."

"What? No, I meant . . ."

"Or an aardvark. Yes, it has a snout like an aardvark."

"I'm asking if . . ."

"But it's backed like a walrus."

"Pollocks!" snapped the prince. "What are you going on about? I just want to know if you think it's going to rain."

"Oh. Pardon me, Your Highness. I thought you were playing a game." Pollocks studied the cloud. "No, I don't think it is going to rain. At least not in Damask."

"I feared as much. And try to stay focused, will you? I'm not a child or an idiot. We haven't played that game since I was six years old."

"You were much more fun to be around then."

"I'm sure." Charlie turned to study the mountain that lay between himself and Damask. The smooth, green slope held a single scar, not yet healed over with vegetation, where the dirt had been scraped away to expose the rock. Periodically someone would get the idea of diverting the Organza River to Damask. Charlie shook his head. The hardest chisels bounced off that granite, and there were miles of it to tunnel through. All the resources of the country could not bring the river to Damask. He looked up suddenly. "Who is this?"

Three men were riding up the road from Damask. They were not pilgrims. They ignored the temple. Instead they rode directly for Charlie in a disturbingly purposeful way. All three men were young, only a little older than Charlie, and they were stylishly, almost foppishly dressed. Even their horses had braided manes. But there was nothing foppish about the swords they wore, or their grim expressions. Two of the men hung back, letting the third, a man with a pale complexion and a ponytail, take the lead.

"Oh dear," said Pollocks. "Trouble."

"He looks familiar," said Charlie. "Who is he?"

"Young Albemarle Gagnot. The son of Lord Gagnot. The son of the man you jailed for selling the grain reserves."

"Somehow I don't think he is here to plead his father's case."

"I expect that is exactly what he is here to do. And probably somewhat more forcefully than we would prefer. Your Highness . . ." Pollocks took the young regent's arm. "I think, with a bit of diplomacy on your side, we can salvage something from this situation. Young Gagnot is an officer in the Damask Horse Brigade. And he's quite a popular officer. This is a very influential troop—all the wealthy young men of the city are either in it or vying to get in it. Albemarle would be a good man to have on your side."

"And a dangerous man to have as an enemy?"

"Most decidedly, Sire." Here Pollocks hesitated, then pushed on. "You may not be aware, Your Highness, that the people of Damask feel that your rule is—how shall I put it—a bit heavy-handed. After all, corruption has long been a part of Damask politics. They were not expecting you to sweep the floor as clean as this." The three men on horseback were quite close now. "I'm not saying there is cause for an uprising, Your Highness, but if there was . . ."

"Gagnot would be the one to lead it?"

"He could certainly bring a lot of armed men against you."

"Thank you for that evaluation, Pollocks," said Charlie. "Now it's clear to me how I should treat this man."

"Ah, good." Pollocks let out a breath of relief.

The prince watched Gagnot dismount, leaving the other two men behind, still on horseback. They favored Charlie with uneasy, tentative smiles, but Gagnot's expression was one of clear distaste, as though Charlie was a fly he had found in his soup. Charlie had seen that look before, on men born into wealth and privilege, and women of extreme beauty, when forced to deal with someone they considered a social inferior. Gagnot stopped a dozen feet in front of the prince, but did not look at his face. Instead, he addressed his words to a point somewhere over Charlie's shoulder. "Your Highness." Here Gagnot paused to adjust his gloves. "I will be brief. I insist that my father be released immediately."

Pollocks leaned close to Charlie. "Reassure him, Your Highness. He's an arrogant young man, certain to defend his family's honor. Explain that his father is merely being held for investigation, that you're sure nothing will come of it, that he's being treated well . . ."

"Gagnot," interrupted the prince loudly. "Your father is a criminal and a thief. I intend to see him tried and hanged."

Pollocks put his face in his hands.

Gagnot's face instantly flashed from disdain to anger. His hand went to his sword. The prince ignored this and stepped forward, his thumbs tucked into his waistcoat, his hands well away from his own sword. "Lord Gagnot is a disgrace to his king, to his country, and to his class." He stopped in front of the younger man. "Have I made myself clear, Abe?"

Gagnot was not an original speaker. He spoke as if he was reciting from a book. "You have offended me, sir."

"Oh, really?"

"I say I am offended, sir. Are you calling me a liar?"

"Uh-huh. Right," said Charlie. The question sounded strange and stilted, but Charlie knew what Gagnot was up to. He was following an ancient formula called "giving the lie." It allowed him to challenge Charlie to a duel while still claiming to be the injured party. Charlie had no patience for it. "Forget it, Abe," he said. "I am too busy to play such games."

Gagnot scowled at him. "You cannot deny me satisfaction, Your Highness. You are not a gentleman by birth, but even a *bastard* king holds noble rank. You can't claim I am above your class."

"I wouldn't dream of making any such claim."

"Don't disgrace yourself by demanding some arcane weapon, either. You have your sword and I have mine." He turned toward the two seated men. "You have met my friend Dunswitch, I believe." The rider on the right nodded to Charlie. "Lord DeCecco has agreed to be your second, should you ask for one. The man on the left inclined his head to Gagnot and Charlie. "He is not related to me in any way, and has no business dealings with me or my family." Gagnot faced forward again. "So you see—oof."

He had made a mistake. Those who had seen Bad Prince Charlie in action knew better than to take their eyes off him. He hit Gagnot in the pit of the stomach, causing the young noble to double over. A second punch to the head knocked him to the ground. Gagnot cursed and spun over on his back, reaching for his waist. Charlie kicked him in the side. Gagnot curled up in pain. The Bad Prince did not fight cleanly.

DeCecco hesitated, but Dunswitch spurred his horse forward. In an instant Charlie stepped back from the fallen man, and had his own sword out. "Get back," he snapped. The rider stopped his horse. "So it is a duel you want? Let me remind you of something. A duel is an affair between gentlemen, to settle a point of honor. *I have no honor* and care nothing for it. I said I will not duel and I will not." He paused, to collect the hostile looks of the other men. And then gave them his own grim smile. "But I will *fight*."

He feigned a slash at the rider, causing his horse to rear up, then turned back to Gagnot. His opponent was on hands and knees, trying to clear his head. "Get up, Abe. We're going to fight. No seconds, no rules, no challenge, no field of honor, no *Code Duello*. Just a plain, ordinary fight with swords."

Gagnot rose with unexpected swiftness and drew his sword. But Pollocks inserted himself between the two men. "Lads, lads! You cannot fight here, nor duel, either. You are in Noile. You have no rights in this land. Put away your swords, or we'll all be jailed."

"Tchah." Gagnot tried to step around Pollocks, who kept himself between the combatants. "We're alone here. No one is watching."

"You are on the grounds of the High Priestess of Matka," warned Pollocks. "She sees everything. She knows everything." He pointed to the temple complex across the lake. "Her power is great, her influence is without limit. We dare not violate the peace of this sacred ground."

Everyone except Charlie looked toward the temple. Dunswitch and DeCecco exchanged glances. Even the horses gave nervous snorts. Gagnot kept his sword up, but stopped trying to circle Pollocks.

"Put it down," said Pollocks. "You can't help your father if you are in prison."

That was enough to end the fight. Perhaps Charlie's antagonists let themselves be persuaded, or perhaps they were reluctant to risk injuring the elderly man, or perhaps they merely succumbed to a quite natural disinclination to charge onto a naked blade. "The old man is right," said Dunswitch. He rode up to Gagnot and leaned over. "A fight here will gain you nothing. There are better ways to rid ourselves of this bastard king." Behind him, DeCecco nodded.

Gagnot frowned, but eventually thrust his sword back into its scabbard. Dunswitch brought him his horse. Tight-lipped, he climbed into the saddle. Charlie, ignoring them all once the challenge was met, had already mounted his steed and was riding away without a backward glance. Pollocks hastened to catch up with him, guiding his horse close enough to grab Charlie's arm. "Your Highness, do not let them ride off like this. A generous gesture now would do much to help affect a reconciliation later. Otherwise, I truly fear that these men can contribute to a revolt against your rule."

Charlie looked thoughtful. "Do you really think that will happen, Pollocks?"

"I do."

The prince turned his horse around. "Gagnot!" he called. The other three riders stopped to listen. "Gagnot, it is my intention to seize your estates and sell them to pay off your father's debt. You will be ruined. Consider yourself warned."

Gagnot's back stiffened. He started to turn around, but the other two men seized his arms and whispered to him. Eventually they rode off without looking back.

Pollocks was making groaning noises into his beard. He looked at Charlie, wild-eyed. "Are you mad? To create an enemy like that? You must be mad!"

"Nothing like a walrus," said Charlie mildly.

"What?"

"That cloud. You said it looked like a walrus. It doesn't look anything like a walrus."

In spite of himself, Pollocks looked up. "Well, of course it doesn't look like a walrus *now*! When we started talking it looked like a walrus. Very like a walrus."

Charlie was riding again toward the temple. The sun was over the mountains now, giving the gray domes a silvery sheen. "Look, there are coffee shops. Come on, I'll buy you a cup."

"No coffee for you! You're irritable enough already."

"Hey, we're in Noile now. We can get chicken salad. Or even a custard." They left their horses with a stable hand and joined a line of tourists. Charlie hid his regal insignia. Although he had no authority here, he wanted to see how the common people were being fleeced. "So what does this High Priestess look like? Have you ever seen her?"

"I had that privilege when I accompanied your father

the king on trips here. Exotic, mysterious, and beautiful are words I would use to describe her, both in appearance and in temperament. But you will soon find out for yourself."

"When is my appointment?"

"I have not made one for you."

"What? We came all this way and they don't even know we are here?"

"Rest assured, Your Highness, they know we are here. Surely you would not think her much of a seeress if she could not predict a visit from a regent prince."

"I won't think her much of a seeress whatever she does. When it comes right down to it, you know, I'm a skeptical sort of guy." Charlie hesitated before going on, realizing that a man who had just spent the previous evening talking to a ghost might have difficulty establishing himself as a skeptic. He hedged a little bit. "Okay, I've heard the stories. People *say* she knew things about them that she couldn't have known, things they didn't know themselves."

"Those aren't mere stories."

"Come on, Pollocks, you know that most of that stuff is a swindle. They just tell you stuff you want to hear. Or they give predictions that are so general they could apply to anyone."

They reached the front of the line. Pollocks shook out a container of yarrow stalks. A monk studied them and handed him a slip of paper. It read, *Address your problems early to obtain the best results.*

"Good advice," said Pollocks.

"Common sense," said Charlie. "That's the soothsayer's stock in trade. Either vague generalities or something incomprehensible. That's my preference, actually. If someone is going to give me silly fortunes, I like them to be the totally cryptic kind. You know, stuff like, 'the wise search their hearts for inner strength' or 'the path of despair leads to the river of wisdom.' "

"Cryptic sayings often gain meaning as one gains experience."

"Hey, that's good. You could write your own rice paper slips."

"Why don't you try one, Your Highness?" Pollocks led the prince to a fountain, where small, hollow clay ducks were tumbling over a waterfall, then bobbing up in a turbulent pool. Tourists were standing around the edge of the fountain, tossing in coins, and trying to grab a clay duck. The area around the fountain was ankle deep in shards of broken pottery.

"How do you choose?"

"Make an offering to the High Priestess, Your Highness, then just grab one. It's totally random."

Charlie flipped a coin into the pool and quickly scooped up a clay duck. He placed it on the ground, then smashed the duck with his boot. Bending over, he found the little slip of rice paper that had been inside.

" 'The wise search their hearts for inner strength,' " he read. " 'You have an appointment with the High Priestess at noon. The monk to your left will lead you to the High Priestess. Please be prompt.' "

Charlie looked to his left. There was a man in monk's robes only a few feet away. He looked at the fountain again. Dozens of clay ducks were passing over the waterfall every minute. Baffled, he past the slip to Pollocks, who looked at it and clucked his tongue.

"Noon," he said. "I wonder if the meeting will include lunch."

Charlie walked all the way around the fountain. "There is no way a particular duck could have been directed at me. And the slip contained the exact phrase I just told you. And even if someone had overheard me and taken down my words, that clay duck must have been fired days in advance. Impossible."

"The High Priestess sees all. Not all seers are charlatans, Your Highness. Only yesterday *you* desired Thessalonius to predict the weather."

"You only meet one man like Thessalonius in a lifetime. And he never made predictions like this. This is just a conjuring trick, Pollocks. I don't know how they do it, but it's still a trick. Here." The prince extracted another coin from his pouch, looked around until he was sure no one was watching him, then casually dropped it in and grabbed another duck. "Let's see if they can do it again." Pollocks followed him as he carried the duck away from the fountain, crouched down, and cracked it on the pavement. He read the slip and shook his head.

"What?" said Pollocks.

" 'No, you won't be having lunch. Just some wine and a cheese plate,' " Charlie read aloud.

Pollocks looked at the paper. "It also says that 'the path of despair leads to the river of wisdom.' "

"Yes, I caught that."

"And we still have some time until noon. Good. Come, Your Highness. You must see the ceiling of the Great Hall. It is magnificent."

He led Charlie down a granite walk, flanked with small, bubbling fountains and flowering olive trees. They went up a broad stairway to a colonnaded entrance, but there had to buy tickets and stand in line before they could enter the Great Hall. Charlie had heard, of course, of the ceiling of the Great Hall of the Temple of Matka, the masterwork of the artist Domenicelli. Pollocks told him even more about Domenicelli, his humble beginnings, the stroke of fortune that earned him the commission to decorate the huge domed ceiling of the enormous Great Hall, the years of planning, and the construction of the special scaffolding so that Domenicelli could work almost single-handedly. He concluded with a description of the acclaim Domenicelli received when his masterwork was revealed to the public, finishing his story just as he and Charlie reached the door. "This is it. The masterwork of a master artist. There is nothing like it in the Twenty Kingdoms." Pollocks pushed open the door. "Magnificent, is it not?"

Charlie craned his neck. "It's wallpaper?"

"Exactly. It's hard enough just to do a flat wall. Can you imagine how difficult it was to wallpaper the inside of a dome? Cutting and pasting the strips so that the pattern matches on every single edge, putting them all up without a single bubble or crinkle? A lot of decorators would have just given up and painted the damn thing."

"Right."

"He didn't waste any, either. When it was all finished he only had two rolls left over, and he was able to return those to the store and get a credit slip."

"Let's go see the High Priestess," said Charlie.

They found their guide, still standing by the fountain. He led them back to the Great Hall, but this time they went through a side door, bypassing the line of tourists, and down a short flight of stairs, where another burly monk guarded a thick door. He consulted a list.

"Prince Charlie, Regent of Damask," said Charlie, without waiting to be asked. He showed them his signet ring.

The two monks nodded. The one with the list turned to Pollocks. "And you?"

"His Faithful Family Retainer," said Pollocks, showing his FFR card. The guard unlocked the door. The guide led them down a twisting passage, rough hewn out of rock, so narrow that their shoulders brushed the wall on both sides. It was dim. Only a few candles burned in widely spaced alcoves, and a few shafts of sunlight fell from above through small ventilation holes. There was a distinct smell of burning herbs and sandalwood incense, that grew stronger as they continued. The shafts of sunlight abruptly cut off, which told Charlie they were underneath another building. Sure enough, the passage led to another set of stairs, with another door, this time unguarded, at the top. Their guide paused with a hand on the knob. "The High Priestess of Matka," he murmured, and gestured them through.

They were in a round room, again with a domed ceiling. It had no windows, but a dozen candles were spaced along the wall, lending the room a soft, ethereal light. A door at the far side was covered with draperies. Smoke wafted up from vents in the floor. The scent of incense and burning herbs was overpowering. In the middle of the room was a granite boulder, about waist high, with a flat top. On this rested a strange chair of a type Charlie had seen only once before, essentially a bag filled with dry beans. A young woman sat in the lotus position, cradling a stringed instrument. Charlie wasn't sure if it was a sitar or a zither. She raised her hand. Pollocks dropped reverently to one knee. "The High Priestess," he whispered.

The girl studied the back of her hand, then the front. She made a fluttering motion with it. "Oh wow," she said. "Listen to the colors."

"What?" said Charlie.

He strode forward until he could see the girl clearly. She was slim, with light brown skin, and straight black hair that fell to her waist. She wore an ankle-length cotton skirt, a choker of tiny beads, and a shirt with gaudy splotches of color. Her face was round, her eyes were almond shaped, her teeth were straight and white, and her eyes were jet black, although it was hard for Charlie to tell because her pupils were so dilated. She strummed a few chords and murmured, "Like, the whole room is in harmony with the music."

Pollocks came up behind him. "You see, she's called the High Priestess* because she's usually . . ."

---

*My friends reminded me that Jasper Fford uses puns *and* footnotes. They also said he's better looking than I am. Hmmph!

"I get it," snapped Charlie. "I get it, okay? Don't run it into the ground. Dammit, Pollocks, you brought me all the way up here to meet a stoner?"

"Don't underestimate her until you hear what she has to say."

"Fine. I'll hear what she has to say and then I'll under-estimate her."

"The smoke is the breath of the earth. She inhales it to expand her consciousness and become one with the uni-verse. It allows her to see the interconnectedness of all things. Here." Pollocks rummaged inside his pouch and came our with a greasy paper bag. "You should make an offering. Try these salted corn chips."

From behind the curtained doorway came the sound of low voices, perhaps chanting. The girl plucked the sitar, producing an atonal melody that might charitably be called music. The prince took the bag with some reluctance. He walked to the edge of the rock and held it out. Presently the girl focused on it. She took the bag from Charlie, poured some of the yellow chips into her hand, stuffed them into her mouth, and crunched them for a while. Then she swal-lowed, gave Charlie a big smile, and said, "Hey, thanks. I have got the munchies like you wouldn't believe."

"Can I get you anything else? Some cherry wine, a se-rape?"

"No, I'm fine. So, Charlie—do you mind if I call you Charlie?"

"Go ahead. And you are?"

"Xiaoyan Yang. But just call me Xiao. So, Charlie, you are the Prince Regent of Damask, soon to be crowned, or so everyone thinks, but you hold many secrets, am I right?" She didn't wait for an answer, but changed her focus to a point over his head and continued. "I see the paths, Char-lie. There are many paths open to you, and it is important that you choose your path carefully. For the High Priestess of Matka can foretell, but she cannot compel. You control your own destiny. Your future depends on the choices you make. Should you choose one course of action, your future will end badly, but if you choose another, you will be really, really screwed."

"Uh-huh. You're harshing my mellow, Xiao. Do any of my possible futures end happily?"

Xiao stared into space for a long time, silent and motionless. In fact, Charlie had just about concluded that she had zoned out, and was getting ready to take his leave, when she suddenly looked at him again and shrugged. "Sorry, no. Badly and disastrously, that's all I see." In a quick, lithe movement, she hopped down from the boulder and patted him on the shoulder. "Bummer, dude. I feel for you." She took him by the hand and led him to the curtained doorway. "Let's get a brew. All this smoke dries out my throat. Pollocks, wine is your tipple, right?"

For a woman who seemed totally spaced only a moment ago, she seemed remarkably sharp all of a sudden. Charlie made a mental note that once again Pollocks seemed to be correct—this was a girl he should not underestimate. He was even more surprised when they passed through the curtained door. For Xiao had an immense staff.

The curtained door led into a long room that contained row upon row of desks. The walls were lined with maps of the Twenty Kingdoms, and great stacks of file folders were piled everywhere. In contrast to the smoky room Charlie had just left, this one was brightly lit and full of people. Each desk not only had a monk sitting at it, but two or three more standing around it, talking in low but intense voices. The monks at the desks were furiously writing on little slips of rice paper, then passing them to the standing monks for review and discussion. The standing men had their arms full of notebooks and clipboards. They did not stay long at one desk, but came into the room through another door, stopped briefly at a number of desks to give information and review the predictions, then went back out.

Xiao waved a hand. "This is where it all comes together."

"This is where you really make the predictions?"

"Oh no. I, and the other priestesses, make the predictions back there in the smoke room. Here, these men take a simple, straightforward extrapolation into the future and turn it into ambiguous mush. Right, Li?"

"Right," said the monk. "Here's one from a merchant who's invested heavily in a trading ship. It hasn't come back. He wants to know if it's going to return or if he's going to suffer a heavy loss."

"So," said Xiao, "we tell him something like—let me think—'difficulty in the beginning leads to ultimate success.'"

"Right," said Li. "If the ship doesn't come in, he'll interpret that as the difficulty in the beginning and he'll have hope for the future. If the ship does come in, he'll interpret that as the success, and the difficulty was getting the money to make the investment. Either way, we're right."

The prince looked disdainful. "The man would have to be a fool to take this stuff seriously. He should take one look at an answer like that and know you haven't the slightest idea of what happened to his ship."

Pollocks and Xiao and Li all looked surprised. Pollocks said, "But, Your Highness, they do know."

"Sure," said Xiao. "We saw the ship delayed by unseasonable storms. It should reach port in another ten days."

"But if you know the fate of his ship, why don't you just say so?"

"Because we . . ." Xiao started to speak but was interrupted by a voice from another desk.

"Excuse me, Priestess Xiao, but we need your input here."

The voice came from a group of men who were gathered around a desk in a corner. They were going through some open files. Pencil sketches of an attractive young woman lay on the desk. The monk who had called Xiao over had written out a number of rice paper slips, then crumpled them up and dropped them on the floor. "It's about that woman Demesne. She was here two months ago. She wanted to know if the man she was seeing was the right one for her."

"A common question for women to ask," explained Xiao. "And one we definitely have to answer in an ambiguous way. It's an unanswerable question, after all. We can see if they're going to get married. We can see if they're going to stay married. But who can say, even if a couple stays married for fifty years, that they are 'right' for each other? So we tell them something like, 'if he is not as he should be, there will be misfortune.' "

"We didn't bother to look into her future more deeply," said the monk. "It's such a common question. A month later she was back."

"And she had a completely different boyfriend. We gave her another vague answer."

"And now she's back. Same question, different boy."

"She must like your answers," said Charlie. "You're getting repeat business."

"Uh-huh," said Xiao. She drummed her nails on the monk's desk. "Okay, give her a little more information. Tell her I see whips, chains, baby oil, and leather wrist cuffs in her future."

Pollocks made a face. "Is that true?"

"Of course."

"Is she on the giving end, or the receiving end?"

"Oh, she knows the answer to that already. She just doesn't know she knows it. That's why she keeps coming back looking for answers." Xiao took Charlie by the arm. "Come with me, Your Highness. Your retainer can wait here." She led Charlie down a quiet hallway. "You have questions for me, and I have much to discuss with you." At the end of the hallway, two more monks guarded another heavy door. They nodded silently to Xiao and opened it for her. Charlie followed her inside. It took him a moment to realize, with some surprise, that he was in her bedchamber.

It was decorated in a way that was embroidery-intense. It held a large, low bed with an embroidered coverlet, embroidered cloth hanging on the walls, and an oil lamp with an embroidered lampshade hung from the ceiling. An intricately embroidered dressing screen separated a third of the room from the bed. There was a low, round table of highly polished dark wood, but no chairs. Around the table were sitting cushions—embroidered, of course. A single candle in a carved soapstone holder burned in the middle of the table. It sat on an embroidered cloth trivet. Surrounding the candle, spread out across the table, was Xiao's equipment for reading the future.

There were two crystal balls—a large translucent white one about the size of Charlie's head, and a smaller, fist-sized one with a pink hue. It was set on top of a leather carrying case, embroidered with the words *Palm Divinizer III*. Spread around it were a deck of tarot cards, a book of the I Ching (with both yarrow stalks and an assortment of coins for generating hexagrams), a black onyx scrying bowl half filled with water, a pair of empty teacups with wet leaves in the bottom, a basket of fortune cookies, an astrological chart, and the early edition of tomorrow's newspaper. Standing at the end of the table was a water pipe, a bulbous contraption of glass and beaten copper, with silver trim. It was unlit, but a linen bag half full of herbs leaned against it. Charlie presumed these generated the same smoke the priestess breathed in the oracle room.

Xiao gestured at the table. "Choose your method, Your Highness. I am an expert in all forms of divination."

"Really?" Charlie looked her up and down. "How can you be an expert in anything? You're no older than I am, and it took me this long to learn that that I know very little."

"One needs no training," the young woman said solemnly. "The methods teach themselves to those with true understanding. For one gifted with the sight, all sources of information are accurate. Except for the newspaper, of course."

"Right," said Charlie, equally solemn. "Then my favorite method of divination is goat entrails." He waited for a reaction and, when he didn't get one, added, "You can read entrails, can't you? Good. Just call for the entrails of a freshly slaughtered goat and we can get started."

Xiao looked at him with her hands on her hips, not certain if he was ridiculing her. Charlie looked back with his best deadpan expression. Finally Xiao shrugged, opened the door, and said to one of the monks, "Sing, bring me a platter of goat entrails."

"No goat entrails today, Miss."

"Sheep entrails? Pig entrails? Any other type of entrails?"

"Fresh out of entrails."

"Well, what have you got that's close?"

"We've got some nice barbecued spareribs."

"Those will do. Send them along."

"You get two vegetables with that."

"Coleslaw and black-eyed peas."

"Coming right up."

Xiao closed the door, crossed in front of him, and disappeared behind the screen. "Excuse me while I slip out of these clothes." The long skirt and tie-dye blouse were flipped over the screen. While she was undressing Charlie cracked one of the fortune cookies and read the slip of paper inside. It read, *Made from butter, salt, sugar, flour, egg whites, natural and artificial flavorings. Dicalcium phosphate added to preserve freshness.*

He watched the shadowy motion behind the screen. "How long have you been doing this? You must have started very young."

"Two years," said Xiao. "I became High Priestess when I was sixteen. Not so young."

Charlie was surprised. "Pollocks said my father had been getting advice from you for many years."

"He was seeing former High Priestesses. I was a lay priestess then, and before that I was an acolyte. I was brought here when I was twelve."

"What happened to the old ones?"

Xiao stuck her head out from behind the screen. "Nothing happened to them. When we turn eighteen, we are retired from the job. We leave the temple and return to the Old Country. In fact, we are banished from the kingdom, never to return, nor even to contact anyone here again, on pain of death." Her hand scrabbled on a vanity table until she found a makeup brush, then pulled back.

Charlie thought this over. "Because an independent adult priestess would be too dangerous, is that it? Because of all the secrets you've learned?"

"Correct. Do you want tea or coffee, Your Highness? I almost forgot you gave up drinking."

"It wasn't hard. The beer in other countries is awful. I don't know how people can drink it. Horrible, bitter stuff. For some reason Durk's is the only brewery that makes good . . . glup!"

He made a series of sounds that indicated his heart was trying to climb out of his throat, and his tongue was beating it back down only with difficulty. For the Xiao that stepped out from behind the screen was completely naked.

It is a well-known feature of the Twenty Kingdoms that all their princesses grow up to be beautiful. Something in the milk, one presumes. Xiao was not a princess and she was not from any of the Twenty Kingdoms. Nonetheless, Charlie rapidly concluded that if she was the type of girl the Far East was exporting these days, the babes they kept for domestic consumption must be super indeed.

She was slim and narrow-waisted, with small, high breasts. An intricate tattoo encircled her navel. Every trace of body hair had been shaved away, and her smooth skin, coated with a scented lotion, gleamed in the candlelight. She held a bottle of almond oil, which she proffered to Charlie. "Would you mind terribly doing my back?"

Charlie took the bottle in a daze. Nothing in his life had prepared him for a sight like this, but he was not a man who let control of his wits slip away for long. Indeed, he had almost got his voice back when Xiao turned around, letting the backs of her thighs brush against the front of his, and stretched her arms behind her head to lift her hair out of his way. This action lifted her breasts even higher, a sight which once again forced Charlie's vocal cords into paralysis and caused most of his neural pathways to shut down. Like a sleepwalker, he took the bottle, poured some oil into his palm, and began rubbing it onto her shoulder blades. Smooth little muscles rippled under his hands.

Eventually the fog in his brain began to lift. A light, musical voice penetrated into his eardrums. He realized that Xiao was talking, that she was describing to him just what the gift of "sight" was supposed to be.

". . . multiple universes," Xiao was saying. "Divination implies predestination, which contradicts the idea of free will. But if you accept the multi-universe idea, the paradox is resolved. Every decision that we make, every choice that confronts us, results in a new universe splitting off. Our journey into the future involves blindly choosing a path that leads through the many possible futures. But a priestess of Matka can see the paths."

"Uh-huh," said Charlie. He had reached the small of her back, and was wondering if he dared lower his hands to her bottom. The smooth, round globes were already well oiled. Momentarily, he let his hands rest on her hips.

Xiao squirmed sensuously beneath his hands. "Mmmm. Now you know why we cannot give unambiguous answers to the question we are asked. For once you have seen your own future, the possible universes collapse into one. Your path is now determined, but that may not be the path you would have chosen. Our answers are couched so that all those who seek the path are always left with a choice. Do you understand, Your Highness?"

"Sure," said Charlie. He had slid his hands around her waist, to her smooth, flat stomach, and was now letting them drift toward her thighs.

Xiao suddenly turned within his arms and faced him. Her nipples grazed his chest, causing his pulse to add another ten beats per minute. Her face was turned up toward his, her eyes closed, her lips wetly parted. "It's wonderful to think of it," she whispered. "An infinite number of possible universes, all different, means there are infinite possibilities for all of us. Anything can happen."

Her lips were only inches from his. Charlie's hormones had wrested control away from his brain, and he spoke automatically, without thinking. "Not really," he murmured, bending his head so his own lips approached hers. "It's more likely you would have a converging series, where each successive universe is only infinitesimally different from the last one."

Xiao stiffened in his arms. She pushed against him and backed away. "Infinitely converging series?" she said, eyeing him suspiciously. "You talk like an engineer."

"Who, me?" Charlie tried frantically to recover from his gaffe. "No, not at all. Converging series? Just a phrase I picked up. I know nothing about math. I studied—um—art history. Yes, I'm an art history major. When I graduate I'll be *completely unemployable*, I swear!"

Xiao's face softened, but the moment had been ruined. There was a knock at the door. She quickly wrapped herself in a loose robe of patterned silk, and answered it. Sing came in, wheeling a cart with plates, utensils, and covered dishes. He left without saying a word.

"Ah," said Xiao. "Now we shall see what the future holds for you." With quick, practiced motions, the movements of someone who had done this a thousand times before, she scooped up the bag of herbs, poured just the right amount into the water pipe, tamped them in with a small brass rod, and lit the pipe from the candle. She took a long, deep drag on the mouthpiece, and held the smoke in her lungs for so long Charlie started to get concerned. Then she blew it out through her nostrils and said, "Oh wow, like, let's get started, okay?" Without waiting for an answer, she took the cover off the largest dish. It contained a plate of pork ribs, lightly coated with tangy sauce. Xiao uncovered a second dish and frowned. "Potato salad? I asked for—wait a minute." She turned her attention back to the ribs, stared at them for a long while, looked over her shoulder at Charlie, then perused the ribs once more. A few moments later she threw the lid back on the dish, stalked over to a pile of cushions, and sat down, facing away from Charlie.

Charlie waited while the silence stretched out. Eventually he said, "Something wrong?"

"No," said Xiao. She folded her arms across her chest. "I'm fine."

"Well, good." Charlie waited some more. "So what did you see?"

"Nothing."

"Right." Charlie hadn't expected anything else. He still clung to the slight hope that she'd take off her clothes again, but the situation no longer seemed to be moving in that direction. "So I guess I'll just be going."

"Who is she?" said Xiao.

"Who is who?"

"Red hair. Green eyes. Expensive clothes. What is her name? Your captive. The woman you're holding prisoner."

"Catherine? Um, she's not exactly a prisoner. She sort of agreed to stay there."

"And you like her, right?"

The prince thought for a while before he spoke. "There are some political issues to be resolved," he said carefully.

"My personal relationship with Lady Durace is exactly that—personal. It is not a matter for discussion."

"No one can see into a woman's heart," said Xiao. She pointed at the plate of ribs. "I see things that will *happen*. I cannot tell you why." Now she faced Charlie, and her pretty lips were curled with scorn. "So don't talk trash with a High Priestess of Matka. I know what you want to know. You want to know if you will make it with her, isn't that right?"

"Maybe," said Charlie. He had talked about Catherine with his uncles, but they were family. He was less willing to bandy a woman's name about with a girl he just met. "Are you saying you can tell me that? Whether I should press my suit, or if I'm just wasting my time?"

"It is a mistake to couch your questions in that way," said Xiao. "You give yourself only two choices when truly, the paths are many."

"Oh, for goodness' sake," said the prince. "More double-talk. Xiao, give me your hand.

Xiao looked surprised, but lifted up a slim arm. Charlie took her hand and, in one swift motion, jerked the surprised girl to her feet. He brought his other hand around and delivered a stinging swat to her bottom. "Ow!"

Charlie pushed her back down. "Okay," he snapped. "That's enough of that. I have run out of tolerance for nonsense. I didn't ride all this way for the view. I rode here for an answer, and I want it right now, and I don't want a vague, ambiguous display of dissembling. I want a straight, simple yes or no."

Xiao scooted away from him. "Ask your question, then! You want to know about your girlfriend, I'll tell you about your girlfriend. Rest assured you won't be pleased with the answer. Catherine Durace is . . ."

"I want to know," interrupted Charlie, "if we will get rain in Damask this summer."

"What?" said Xiao.

"You heard me. Rain. We need rain. Are we going to get it? A lot depends on it. What I'm going to do in the next few weeks depends on whether we get rain."

Xiao made no attempt to conceal her surprise. "You don't want to know about your girlfriend?"

"I want to know about a lot of things, but first I want to know if the people of Damask are going to get enough rain to sustain a harvest. I've got responsibilities. I've got decisions to make and what I decide depends on our chance of getting rain."

Xiao stood up. She took Charlie's hands, and when she spoke, her voice had become much softer. "Your Highness, to get the answers that you seek, you must learn to ask the right questions. The answer to that is not what you need to know."

Charlie dropped her hands. "More nonsense. I don't have time for this. I want to know if my people's crops are going to get enough rain. Just give me a straight answer, dammit! Yes or no!"

"All right, then fine! Don't listen to me. The answer is no! No, the crops will not get enough rain. No, no, and no." The High Priestess tied her robe tightly shut and flopped back down on a pile of cushions. "No! Is that unambiguous enough for you? Is there any part you don't understand?"

"No. Thank you. That's what I needed to know. And now, if we're through here, I must be getting back." Charlie started for the door.

"No, we are most certainly not through." Xiao got up. "You are such a jerk. You don't deserve this, but I have to give it to you anyway." She disappeared behind the screen and came out with a small object dangling on the end of a thin gold chain. "Here, put this around your neck."

Charlie took it and looked at it. It appeared to be a tiny bit of crystal, wrapped and secured to the chain with gold wire. He handed it back. "Thanks, but I'm not really into jewelry."

Xiao refused to take it. "Do you have to argue about everything? Put it on. It's a getting-out-of-a-tight-spot device. I can't tell you how it works, but . . ."

"But when the time comes, I'll know," Charlie finished for her. "I understand how a getting-out-of-a-tight-spot device works, thank you very much." He held it to the lamplight and looked at it with distaste. "'But what does it do?'" he mimicked, "says the hero to the wise old sage. 'Oh, I can't tell you,' says the wise old sage to the hero, 'but when the time comes, you'll know.'" He swung the crystal on its chain and caught it. "I could never understand why the wise old sage just didn't tell the hero what to do."

"That's just the way they work," said Xiao. "Don't look at me that way. I didn't create the damn thing. I'm just passing it on to you. Take it, for goodness' sake. You're playing a risky game. You know that. If anyone in the Twenty Kingdoms needs a getting-out-of-a-tight-spot device, it's you."

The prince had to admit there was some logic in this. Reluctantly he put the chain around his neck and slipped the crystal under his shirt. "There's one more thing," said Xiao. "If you ever need to use the getting-out-of-a-tight-spot device, don't lose the chain. Be sure to save the chain."

Charlie pulled the chain back out and looked at it. "Why? What's special about the chain?"

"Nothing. It's just a very nice gold chain. Pure gold. You can wear it afterward. Like, if you go to a nightclub, you can leave your shirt unbuttoned and show it off." She saw Charlie's expression. "Or perhaps not. Maybe you can give it to a friend. The point is, just don't throw away a good gold chain."

"Right," said Charlie. He put the chain and crystal under his shirt. "Thank you for the interview. How do I get out of here?"

"Follow me," Xiao walked swiftly and Charlie followed

behind, watching her bottom swing with no little feeling of regret. Eventually they exited the building, onto a terrace with chairs and round tables with umbrellas. Pollocks was sitting with some monks, sipping a glass of wine and looking over Lake Organza. He stood when they approached. Xiao walked right up to him. "You didn't tell me he was an engineer," she said accusingly.

"He only took a couple of semesters," said Pollocks, "and he didn't do that well."

"And that he's in love with another girl."

"Whoa, how time flies," said Pollocks, looking at the sun. He grabbed the prince by the arm. "We really need to get started, Your Highness. It's a long ride back." He hustled Charlie away. "Your Holiness, thank you for your hospitality," he called back over his shoulder. "She likes you," he said to Charlie.

"And who do you think you are now, the Faithful Family Matchmaker?"

"If she didn't like you, she wouldn't be upset about Lady Catherine."

"I'm not an idiot, Mr. Lonely-hearts. I can figure that out."

"I just thought I'd mention it. What prediction did she make for you?"

"We need to find Thessalonius," said Charlie.

But the famous sorcerer was not to be found. In the days that followed, the weather continued fine. Which is to say, it was not good at all. Most years the occasional summer thunderstorm would make it through the mountains, and thus keep Damask from being a total desert, but this year gave nothing but warm days and sunny skies. Oh, once in a while there would be a light shower, just enough to lower the dust and raise hopes, but serious rain was not forthcoming. The few streams that trickled down from the mountains grew smaller and smaller as the snowcaps melted away. Duck ponds and stock ponds shrank. Farm gardens withered. More commoners left their farms and attached themselves to the public works projects, even as Charlie cut the grain allotment and instituted water rationing. Discontent grew. Muttering in the ration lines increased to grumbling and then to complaining out loud. Revolution was in the air.

The Minister of Agriculture, one Lord Dumond, a close friend of Lord Gagnot, came to Charlie with a proposition. He had been exchanging messages with his counterpart in Noile. Noile had a grain surplus, but Damask had no money to buy it. The Noile minister thought he could arrange to send food if Damask gave up its sovereignty and rejoined Noile.

Never! the prince regent declared, pleased that the nobility was considering the idea. He reported the conversation to his uncles, who were equally pleased. Various lords were raising troops of their own and that was a good thing, because they would undoubtedly fight with one another and create the sort of internal division that would justify foreign intervention. Still, Charlie would need to spark the fire, and the tinder of revolution was not quite dry enough.

He grew haggard. At dawn each day he was out on his horse, checking that the grain was being equitably distributed, and carefully tabulating the remainder in the silos to make sure none was being siphoned off. He inspected the public works projects to verify that the foremen were treating their workers fairly. He skipped meals and worked late into the night, either in the small office connected to his suite or the large office near the throne room, calculating food allotments, issuing directives for the public works projects, or reviewing the books of each government ministry. Each audit was invariably followed by throwing one or more officials into the Barsteel, on charges of corruption. And each arrest was followed by even more resentment, as each and every corrupt official invariably complained that

everyone did it, everyone had always done it, and he was
only being singled out because the prince regent wanted a
larger share of his gains.

Pollocks got more and more nervous as the tension outside the castle increased. He drank less, because the wine
no longer sat well on his stomach, but smoked more. His
pipe burned almost constantly. His concern increased
when Charlie again showed an interest in the theater. A
new troupe arrived in town. Charlie sent a message to the
manager. In reply, the manager delivered to the prince regent an invitation to the opening night party. Charlie was
holding the invitation when he called the FFR to his office.

" 'Misleading Ladies,' " he read from the buff card. "Is
this a comedy? It sounds like a burlesque."

"No, Sire. It is a whodunit. A murder mystery."

"So someone is murdered on the stage?" It was a silly
question but Pollocks realized that Charlie was merely
thinking out loud. "Are they poisoned, by any chance?"

"Poisoned, stabbed, bludgeoned, strangled. There is a
wide variety of death in murder mysteries, Your Highness.
The challenge is for the audience to guess who the murderer is. Both of your uncles are rather fond of this type of
drama."

"Are they? Really? But if the victim is murdered on
stage, where is the mystery? Doesn't the audience see who
the murderer is?" Charlie saw Pollocks mentally gear up
for a long explanation, so he waved the question aside.
"Never mind, Pollocks. We'll find out when we get there.
Accept this invitation."

"Very good, Your Highness." Pollocks, who loved the
theater himself, was delighted. He only hoped the prince
did not intend to audit the box office. Nonetheless, he
arranged with Oratorio to provide extra security for the theater, and dissuaded the prince from sitting in the royal box,
arranging for Oratorio and Rosalind to sit there instead.

"We'll be able to see better from a rear box," he told

Charlie. "The forward boxes are really designed for fashionable people to show off their clothes."

"Wow!" The prince was leaning forward, almost falling out of the box. "Are those girls?"

Pollocks glanced at the stage. "Ah, yes," he explained to Charlie. "Until fairly recently, women were not permitted on the stage. Women's parts had to be played by boys. As this illusion is difficult to sustain, except in the case of very young characters, the playwright would insert some reason why the woman had to disguise herself in men's clothing. This allowed the woman's part to be played by a boy pretending to be a woman pretending to be a boy. All the great playwrights did this. Indeed," he continued, warming to his theme, "the entire history of stage drama can be understood as the pursuit of reasons for putting women in men's clothing."

He paused to take a sip of wine, then leaned forward in his seat. In the royal box, an earnest young man had buttonholed Oratorio and was speaking into his ear. Pollocks frowned when he saw the young man was Albemarle Gagnot. The last curtain call was announced and Gagnot disappeared.

He realized that Charlie was asking him a question. "You seem to have a pretty good knowledge of the theater, Pollocks. Were you ever in a play yourself?"

Pollocks cleared his throat. "In my youth, Your Highness, yes. I was involved in a few theatrical productions. Strictly amateur, you understand, nothing professional. But I must say we did garner a few outstanding reviews from the local critics." He did his best to sound modest, but it was obvious to the prince that he was quite proud. "I once played the role of Violento—that's Martin's best friend, the one who gets killed—in *Martin and Marianne*."

Even Charlie was familiar with *that* play. It was one of the most famous romances in the literature of the Twenty Kingdoms. *Martin and Marianne* were young lovers from rival, feuding families. Overcoming great obstacles, they

managed to marry and consummate their love in the first
two acts. The rest of the play was then taken up with their
arguments over which set of in-laws they were going to
visit for the holidays. "Was it an all male cast, in those
days?"

Pollocks stroked his beard, indulging in fond memories.
"No, Your Highness. By then times had already changed.
Now women tread the boards as expertly as men. And this
is a boon to modern playwrights. They are now free to take
advantage of women's dramatic range, to create fuller,
deeper, more rounded characters, to place actresses in roles
that completely delineate the female experience, social
dramas that explore women's place in society and bring to
light their failures and triumphs. They never actually do
this, of course. Mostly they just still try to get women in
men's clothing."

"Why?"

"Because they figured out that the men in the audience
will pay good money to see pretty women in pantaloons
and hose."

"Oh, right." Charlie was watching the lead actress, a
pretty woman who was dressed in pantaloons and hose to
conceal that she was the daughter of the woman who had
been kidnapped by pirates. "It seems a bit unfair to the
women in the audience, though."

"Well, there's a new style of play being developed, in
which the male leads are in drag. I'm told that women find
them hilarious."

But to Pollocks's disappointment, the prince sat through
the whole performance without showing the slightest bit of
interest in the plot, merely giving the actresses the same attention that every other young man gave them. Afterward
he accepted an invitation to the opening night party. The
cast presented him with a gift—a ceremonial dagger in an
engraved case. Charlie thanked them, stuck the dagger ab-

sently in his belt, and spent the rest of the evening in quiet conversation with the stage manager.

And that, apparently, was that. The next day was business as usual. He announced a plan to institute a standardized system of weights and measures to Damask. Pollocks objected. "The nobility already dislikes you. Now the merchant class has also turned against you. Standardized measures make it harder for them to cheat their customers."

Charlie pretended to be surprised. "Really? And how do the customers feel about this?"

"Well, I suppose they don't object, but the working class is even more angry with you than the merchants or the nobility. Ever since you issued that decree banning discrimination on the grounds of religion. Every priest and monk in the country has been riling them up against you." Pollocks relit his pipe from a candle and took small, nervous puffs on it. "I honestly don't see why. Religious toleration is not that unusual in the Twenty Kingdoms."

"Countries don't have freedom of religion because people *want* freedom of religion," Charlie explained to him. "They have freedom of religion only when there are enough competing religions that it keeps any one of them from gaining enough power to trample the others. The faithful themselves are opposed to religious freedom."

"Then why give it to them? Your Highness, if I may make a personal observation, you don't seem to have a friend in this country. Surely it cannot be pleasant to be so widely hated."

"I don't care what other people think of me," said Charlie, but his voice faltered toward the end of the sentence. It wasn't pleasant. But he couldn't explain his reasons to Pollocks.

He continued to work through the long summer days, stopping only for the occasional visit with Catherine.

She must be lonely, he told himself. *And bored.* Certainly, she had a spacious suite, but she was all alone in there, except for the constant attendance of her personal maids. And Rosalind, of course. And visits from Oratorio. And her other friends. And members of her various clubs, charities, and societies. And the steady stream of visits from Damask's nobility, who called frequently to pay their respects and console her over her loss of liberty. In fact, Charlie had to book as long as three days in advance to get an appointment. But he visited as often as he could. Because, he reminded himself, she was obviously bored and lonely.

"It's all going to plan," Catherine told Charlie. "Stop looking so worried." They were in her chambers. She pushed a teacup into his hands. Charlie sipped it without tasting it. Catherine had just finished hosting a meeting of the Damask Ladies Garden Society. They filed out as Charlie entered, each one giving him a look of hostile disapproval. Charlie took it stone-faced.

"It needs to go faster," Charlie said. "Our food stocks are too low. What is Fortescue doing? Autumn is almost here. If he waits too long, there will be snow in the passes and he won't be able to get food over the mountains."

"Scone?" asked Catherine. Charlie shook his head. "Toast? Charlie, autumn is a long way off. Fortescue has to make certain that conditions are stable inside Noile before he takes his army out of the country. And over here, the people aren't going to revolt until they have a leader to inspire them. Packy and Gregory are working on it. Give them time."

"I just don't want them to suffer any longer than they have to. People who are malnourished are more susceptible to disease. If we get an epidemic through here we'll be in serious trouble."

"They're hungry, Charlie. They're not starving. We've all been through bad times in Damask."

"I don't like to see people hungry, either."

"I don't like to see *you* hungry, Charlie. Have some toast."

"No, thanks."

Catherine stood beside Charlie and put her arm around his waist. An electric shiver went down his spine. She was wearing white sandals and a flowery summer dress. It had ruffles along the bottom and lace across the bodice. It looked very light and cool. The prince felt very hot. "Charlie," she said gently. "There are a lot of people out there. And you're only one man. Skipping your own meals isn't going to feed them."

Charlie sighed. "I guess you're right." He allowed her to lead him to the tea table, where he spread some cream on a scone with his new dagger. She stood beside him and stroked his chest while he ate it.

"We have a plan. You're doing everything you can— Charlie, what's this?" Catherine undid a button and slipped her hand inside his black silk shirt. Charlie felt her fingers move across his chest. Her fingers were warm. The whole room felt warm. "A gold chain? Why Charlie!" Catherine gave a merry little laugh. To Charlie it sounded like notes from a silver flute. "I never figured you for the type of man who wore jewelry." She twisted the chain around her little finger.

Charlie swallowed some tea. "The High Priestess of Matka gave it to me."

Catherine's hand stopped moving. "Really?" she said. "The High Priestess?"

"Um, right," said Charlie, with the sudden feeling that he had said something wrong.

"You *beast*!" cried Catherine. She let go of the chain and threw herself to the floor as the door handle clicked. "You beast! *I'll never marry you!* Never, do you hear! I don't care what you do to me!" She lay in a heap, sobbing brokenheartedly as a maid entered. Silently the girl cleared the cups and rolled away the tea table, all the time looking coldly at the prince, who stood dumbly with an ornate dagger in one hand and a prostrate girl at his feet. As soon as the maid left and the door shut firmly behind her, Catherine bounced to her toes. "How does she do her hair?"

"Who?"

"The High Priestess, silly. What was she wearing?"

"Nothing that I can remember."

Catherine stepped back, folded her arms, and looked at the prince with narrow eyes. "Is she pretty?" she asked, in a way that clearly indicated there was a right and a wrong answer to the question.

"Oh, I suppose some men would find her attractive."

"Humph." Catherine mused on the reply. "The Temple of Matka has been around for a while. I guess the High Priestess must be pretty old by now."

"She's nearly retirement age."

"Ah. Well, then." Catherine buttoned Charlie's shirt back up, seeming to let her fingers linger over his skin. "It's a pretty chain, Your Highness, and very thoughtful of her, I'm sure, but I really don't think gold jewelry suits you. Just one woman's opinion, of course."

"I value your opinion," said Charlie, who had never worn jewelry and did not think any of it suited him.

"Have you considered silver? I think silver looks so much better on a man, especially a man with dark eyes and dark hair." She reached up a hand to stroke Charlie's hair. Charlie thought his heart was going to burst.

"Perhaps," she continued, "we could go shopping together in Noile and I could help you pick some out."

"In Noile?"

"When this is over, of course. I expect to spend some time in Noile. You'll be banished from Damask, but you can still go to Noile. I know you'll be studying in Bitburgen, but surely you'll have time to visit." Both hands were stroking his hair now. Her green eyes, wide and beguiling, looked into his. "You will come to see me, won't you?"

"I won't be returning to Bitburgen right away," he said, although up to this moment he had been planning to do exactly that. "I was going to spend some time in Noile myself. I—um—have business there."

"Wonderful! It's a date then." She gave him a brief hug. All too brief, in Charlie's opinion. "Pollocks tells me he's trying to get you interested in the theater. Do you like opera? They have a wonderful opera company in Noile. I'd love to introduce you to it."

"I'd like that," said Charlie.

"We should also see the . . . oh!" This was in response to another knock at the door. In a flash Catherine was across the room, her face flush, her hair disarrayed. "You animal!" she hissed, as Oratorio entered the room. "Is there no limit to your depravity?"

"Um, Sire?" said Oratorio, trying to give Catherine a sympathetic look without letting Charlie see it. Catherine waited until the knight had his back to her, then began giving Charlie seductive smiles.

"What do you want?"

"The wizard Jeremy sends a message. He said they did what you asked. He said that you said it was important and that you wanted to know right away."

"Hmmm? Uh, right," Charlie told him. He was finding it hard to concentrate. Catherine had her lips parted and was running her tongue over her teeth. Charlie forced his attention back to Oratorio. "Collect Pollocks and tell him to meet me there. Don't let anyone else into the wizard's tower. And you," he told Catherine, doing his best to keep up the pretense, "you'll submit to my will, or else. I've been patient so far, but my patience is not without limit. Ha-ha!" He finished with what he hoped was an evil laugh. Catherine's face showed nothing but anguish. Until Oratorio left the room. Then she blew Charlie a kiss and shut the door.

❧ ❧ ❧

The prince bounded up the stairs to the sorcery labs, turned the corner to Thessalonius's office, and came to an abrupt, and astonished, stop. The stone around the door was sintered and cracked from heat. The heavy wooden door was charred around all four sides, with a blackened hole burned clear through where the lock was once set. A puddle of cooling brass was all that remained of the bolt. The brass hinges, although twisted, were still intact, and the door sat cracked an inch open. Oddly enough, at least to Charlie's mind, there was no trace of smoke, or even a burned smell. Down the hall he could hear a woman crying.

Jeremy came up behind him. "He really didn't want anyone to get in there," the wizard said. "That was one hell of a protective ward. Tweezy said it was much stronger than anything he used before. There must've been a lot of energy bound up in it. When it finally cracked, all the energy was released. At least, we hope it was all released. We haven't tried to go inside yet."

"So it could be hazardous? You want me to go in first?"

"Well, Your Highness, it *was* your idea. But no, I merely wanted to point out the danger."

"Who is that crying?"

"Tweezy, Your Highness. *She's not hurt,*" he called, as Charlie took off down the hall at a run.

At the laboratory door he could hear Evelyn's voice. "Tweezy, it's okay. Don't worry about it. It will grow back in no time. It will look just as good. Maybe better." He pushed the door open. Evelyn was bending over the younger girl. Tweezy was sitting in a chair, looking at herself in a hand mirror. Her face was streaked with tears. The mass of blond curls now looked like a scouring pad that had been used to clean a cast-iron pot after a meal of black bean stew.

"It's summer," Evelyn continued. "Short hair is nice in the summer. It's so much cooler. And easier to take care of."

Tweezy cried harder.

Jeremy caught up with Charlie. "She wasn't hurt, Your Highness. There's a little redness, but it will fade away by tomorrow. Mostly she was just frightened. We rolled her in a blanket and put it out right away."

"You were expecting this?"

"No, but all professional sorcerers must know first aid and emergency preparedness. Safety is our number one priority."

"Uh-huh." Charlie put a hand on Jeremy's shoulder and pulled him back down the hall. "There's a salon in town, isn't there? Kind of an expensive, ritzy place? Not just for hair, but other things. Manicures and facials and all that girl stuff?"

"Are you thinking of Tiffany's Soirs, Your Highness?"

"Maybe. They also sell these kind of weird fizzy bath bombs that all the babes are crazy about?"

"Yes, that's the place. Tiffany's Soirs Salon for Women. I know the name because Evelyn and Tweezy talk about it all the time. Of course, they could never afford to go there." He shrugged. "I offered to show them how to make fizzy bath bombs right here in the lab for a few pence, but they said these were different."

"Right." Charlie reached into his pouch and came up with a handful of silver shellacs. "Send her there. Hair style, makeover, the whole works. In fact, send them both there. Give them the day off with pay."

Jeremy took the coins and looked at them with astonishment. "Why, Your Highness, this is extremely generous. I know the girls will be very happy. Tweezy will forget all about her fright when she hears this. I know they won't be able to thank you enough."

"Uh, no. This isn't from me. Tell them it's a gift from Lady Catherine."

Jeremy looked surprised again, but said, "Even better. They love Lady Catherine."

"Everyone does," Charlie said with a faint smile.

Down the hall, Charlie heard footsteps. Pollocks stopped at the door to Thessalonius's office, and was trying to peer through the crack. "Your Highness, are you in there?"

"Pollocks, wait!" Once again, Charlie ran down the stretch of corridor. "Don't go in yet!" He skidded to a stop in front of the Faithful Family Retainer. "I'll go in first."

The older man gave him a disparaging look. "Good Lord, what an ego. Very well, Your Highness, I shall stand aside while you have the honor."

Charlie gently prodded the door with his foot. It swung open about a quarter of the way, and then stuck. He craned his head to look inside, but saw only a section of stone wall and a bookcase. Cautiously, he slipped a foot inside. He heard a rustle and snapped his head around. Jeremy was standing behind him with a fire blanket.

The prince turned back and slid his entire body through the door. He looked around. The others heard him say, "I don't believe this."

"What?" Pollocks and Jeremy said together. Charlie stepped aside to let them come through.

"This. This is a sorcerer's private office? What about, you know, the sorcery stuff? The racks of little bottles with strange homunculi growing inside? The window with the brass telescope and the astronomical instruments? The ancient scrolls? The mortar and pestle, and the bubbling black cauldron, and the raven in a cage?"

"I suppose every sorcerer has his own style," said Pollocks.

Thessalonius's office was as clean and spartan as a military barracks on the morning of an inspection. In the middle of the room was a plain desk of light wood. In the middle of the desk was a sheet of foolscap, a quill, a penknife for sharpening the quill, and a tightly capped bottle of ink. On the corner was a lamp. The desk held nothing else.

The rest of the room was storage. The wall to the left of the desk was solid bookshelves. The books stood up straight by themselves, without bookends. Only a few of them looked old. Thessalonius seemed mostly interested in the latest editions. In back of the desk a pair of windows looked out on mountain peaks. A stretch of low shelves under the windows held scrolls, each tightly rolled up, each in its individually labeled cubbyhole. The wall to the right was taken up with floor-to-ceiling filing cabinets. Leaning against them was a rolling ladder for reaching the highest drawers.

And that was it. There was nothing magical about the place, nothing that indicated it belonged to a renowned sorcerer. Charlie stepped deeper inside the office and turned to look at the wall behind him. His eyes caught a few tiny holes in the mortar, and a few places where the stone seemed a slightly lighter shade of gray, but aside from that it was blank and featureless. He slid open a desk drawer, then opened all of them. All were empty.

"I just . . ." The prince paused to collect his thoughts. "I've been away for a few years, but I just don't remember Thessalonius being this kind of a neat and methodical guy."

"He wasn't," said Jeremy. "Then all of a sudden he got into these modular storage systems. He spent days looking through catalogs from some Nordic kingdom and taking measurements. And this was the result."

"I don't know," said Pollocks, turning around slowly. "There's nothing really wrong with it. It just seems that magic and Scandinavian blond furniture don't go together."

"I preferred the natural beeswax finish myself, but this is what he chose. It all arrived in pieces. We spent weeks sanding and staining and assembling it. By the time we added up the total cost, he could have purchased finished furniture for the same price."

"What did he do with all his sorcery things?"

"He moved his equipment and experiments into the main lab, where they really should have been anyway. But Evelyn insisted that we get rid of the raven. She said it was trying to eat her caterpillars."

"Evelyn really likes those caterpillars, eh?"

"We all have our hobbies."

Charlie let him talk while he circled the room and looked at the shelves carefully. The drawers and scrolls were carefully labeled, but the labels were all numbers and abbreviations, so they were no clue to the contents. *There must be an index somewhere,* he thought. Aloud he said, "Jeremy, did he have any special equipment for predicting rain?"

"Just the basic equipment, like we have in the lab. Thermometers, barometers, wind speed indicators, and crystal balls. The same stuff all weathermen use."

"Hmm. All right, Jeremy. Thank you for your help. Pollocks and I need to spend some time in here. I'll call you if I need you."

Jeremy nodded and withdrew. Charlie said to Pollocks, "He's gone."

"Thessalonius?"

"He packed up and left. He didn't plan to come back, either. He tidied everything up and took all his personal belongings. Look." Charlie pointed to the squares of light gray on the front wall. "He took his diplomas and certificates."

"Then what are we looking for, Your Highness?"

"Whatever we find that looks important," said Charlie, not wanting to commit himself to more than that. "Some clue to his whereabouts. Some indication of what he was working on. Any of his weather predictions. Antidotes to poison."

"Antidotes to poison?"

"It's a long story. Never mind. We'll do the filing cabinets first. You start from that end and I'll start from this end."

Both men pulled open cabinets simultaneously. Each grabbed a handful of files, lifted them out, flipped them open, stared at them in disbelief, and then looked at the other with resignation. Charlie put his back in the cabinet and slammed the drawer shut.

"They're in a foreign language," said Pollocks. "Not one that I can read."

"I know," said Charlie. He untied one of the scrolls and spread it on the desk. He gave it a quick glance and let it curl back up. "I should have expected this. It's Chaldean. The ancient tongue of Babylonia. The standard language for sorcery, magical notation, and recipes containing eye of newt and tongue of dog."

"Can it be translated?"

"I imagine Jeremy can read it, and maybe Evelyn." Charlie stepped back and looked at the cabinets. "But it will take months to do even a quick analysis of all this, and it's likely that we'd end up with nothing but his expense accounts. Are they all this way?"

Pollocks pulled open a few more drawers, took out a few files at random, and scanned them. "I'm afraid so, Your Highness."

Charlie also pulled out a few more files. He put them back. "This isn't going to . . . Wait, what's this?" He carried the last file to the desk and looked at it carefully. It consisted of several large sheets of vellum. Each unfolded to cover almost the entire desk. They were crisscrossed with light blue lines.

Pollocks looked over his shoulder. "It's the plan for the sunken road project."

"Yes. It's exactly the same, except the notes are in Chaldean, the sorcerers' language. Why would the Royal Sorcerer be interested in a public works program?"

"Why did he want to eliminate the chickens? Thessalonius was interested in a lot of things."

"There's nothing magical about building a road. It

wouldn't be much of a public works project if it wasn't labor intensive."

"But if he approved of the project," Pollocks said brightly, "then perhaps it is a good thing that you are going ahead with it."

Charlie considered this. "Right. He was supposed to be able to predict the weather. If he was predicting a drought, he might have anticipated the need for a public works project."

"Exactly. Or . . ." Pollocks hesitated.

"Or what?"

"Or he might have been expecting a war, Your Highness. A good system of roads is essential for moving men and equipment around quickly."

Charlie thought this over. The flat plains provided a great field for armies to maneuver. Would a network of sunken roads provide breastworks and trenches for battle? He didn't have the military experience to judge that. He sat back in the sorcerer's chair, hooked a leg over one arm, and swiveled to look out the window at the snowcapped mountains in the direction of Matka. "Pollocks, set up a meeting with my uncles."

❧ ❧ ❧

Xiao walked through the temple complex, her white robes wrapped around her slim silhouette, her long black hair flowing behind her. She knew she was being watched by the tourists, so she kept a calm, serene expression on her face. Inside she was seething.

What had she done, she railed at herself. How could she have been so stupid? What kind of way was that to act in front of the boy? Acting jealous, getting into an argument with him. What did he think of her now?

What she really needed to do now was talk it over with a bunch of other girls. Or at least one other girl. But there were no other girls she could talk to at the Temple of

Matka. Cili was two years younger than Xiao and wouldn't understand. Zhang was two years older and had already left. She had finished her term as High Priestess and had gone back home. But that, Xiao vowed, was something she would never do.

She climbed a set of outside stairs and paused on a flat rooftop, turning her face up to let the sun bathe her skin. She became aware that the background noise from below had faded away, and when she looked down she saw a crowd of people—pilgrims, tourists, and monks—watching her. She lifted her arms in a gesture of blessing and the people bowed their heads. She turned away with a sigh.

That was the problem right there. She could never go home, not after this. Here she was a High Priestess. At home she would once again be the property of her family. The money she brought back would be taken from her. They would sell her to a husband and then she would be his property, under the rule of her mother-in-law.

No. She wouldn't do it.

She stopped at a doorway. It opened to a stairway that led down to a windowless room. A monk sat beside the door, his legs crossed in the lotus position. He smiled at Xiao and nodded, but she didn't enter right away. Her mentor did not like the light. The sun was nearly overhead. Xiao waited beside the monk for a half hour, until the sun had shifted a little, and the doorway held a bit of shadow. Then she went inside.

Just as she reached the bottom step a candle flared. Her mentor, the man who had taught her everything she knew about prophecy, was sitting on a low chair. He wore the same robes that the rest of the monks wore, and his cowl was pulled over his head, leaving his face in deep shadow. Nonetheless, she could sense he was smiling, because she knew that he knew what had happened, and she didn't find it amusing at all.

"Did it go well?" he asked.

Xiao felt a burning in her cheeks. But she kept her voice level and professional. "I did as you instructed."

"Very good. Did you do anything else?"

Now Xiao knew she was turning red. She was grateful for the dim light. "He's . . . so different from what I expected."

"But not in an unattractive way, I suspect."

"Um, no. But he seems rather irritable."

The man in the blue robes laughed. "Oh, I wouldn't worry about a few rough edges. Women have their way of smoothing a man out."

What did he mean by that? "What do you mean?"

The smile in his voice disappeared. He actually sounded embarrassed. "Um," he said. "We won't get into that now."

Xiao pushed the subject out of her mind and got right to the heart of the matter. "Is he a real prince?" It was her key concern. This was what she had been promised for doing her part.

"Prince enough for you, my dear. He's a gentleman, and that counts more than rank."

He was right, Xiao acknowledged. That was what really counted. As a priestess of Matka, Xiao was treated with respect. But once she left here she would just be a common girl. That wasn't too bad in the Twenty Kingdoms. A woman could have her own money here and even own property. But she would still be a commoner and have to bow and scrape to the upper classes. She didn't want to go back to that.

The way out, of course, was to marry a gentleman and become a lady. Of course, Xiao knew those stories about common girls marrying highborn men were strictly fairytales. It almost never happened. *But it could happen,* she thought. *I will make it happen.*

Yes! she told herself as she walked back to her room. If she just had another chance. If she just controlled herself this time. She wouldn't snap at him. She would be calm and agreeable next time. But what had possessed her to take off her clothes in front of him. Had she gone crazy? Boy crazy? Xiao had heard the term "boy crazy" before, but she had always thought it was just an expression. Yet even now she remembered the warmth of his hands on her shoulders, could still feel the delicious tingle that enveloped her body when her breasts touched him.

She looked at herself in a mirror. "Pull yourself together," she told the reflection. "He will be back. And this time you will control yourself. You will be totally cool."

⚜ ⚜ ⚜

"A Weapon of Magical Destruction?" said Packard. "Well, Charlie, I can't say I'm surprised." They were back in the same conference room where Charlie had accepted the post of prince regent. It was late in the evening. The summer sun was red on the horizon, casting long shadows into the room. Candles were already lit. A decanter had been set out, along with glasses. None of the men were drinking. Charlie was pacing the floor. As he passed in and out of the shadows in his black clothes, he seemed to fade away and reappear. Packard found it a little unsettling. "Sit down, Charlie. Relax."

"We'd heard rumors," said Gregory. "We knew the king had Thessalonius working on some big project. So now we know it was a WMD. That's very troubling."

"Damn right it is," said Charlie. "I have no objection to seeing Damask get absorbed back into Noile. But I don't like the idea of him getting his hands on a WMD. According to the ghost, this thing could wipe out a whole army in one shot. It could destroy an entire city in a flash. Can you imagine what Fortescue would do with a weapon like that? He wouldn't be satisfied with consolidating Damask and Noile. No country would be safe, not from a man with his ambition."

"Do you really think he'd use such a weapon?" asked Packard. "He's ambitious, we all agree, but he's also pragmatic. He's not an evil overlord, after all. My understanding is that this WMD is a one-time event. If he ever used it, the retaliation from the other kingdoms would be devastating."

"Every weapon that's ever been invented has been used eventually. Anyway, just having a weapon hanging over all our heads, like myriad swords of Damocles, is horrific enough. We need to find it before he gets here."

"We'll find it. We'll bring in more sorcerers. We get a bunch of temps who read Chaldean to go through Thessalonius's files. We'll get a task force of sorcerers to investigate the construction of a WMD, to try to guess how big it is and what it looks like."

Charlie looked out the window, where the fields were slowly, but surely, browning up. "We've got a time constraint," he reminded his uncles. "Our food reserves are going fast. We don't want to invite Fortescue in before we find the WMD, but we can't wait too long, either. How is the revolution going?"

"Excellent, Your Highness. You'll be pleased to know that your loyal subjects really hate you."

"Good, good. Are they ready to revolt?"

"Not quite. We're still organizing and arming them. We have to be subtle about it, you understand, and pretend we're working behind the scenes. And we're still working on setting them up with a leader to inspire them."

"Good. Whom did you pick? No, let me guess. Abe Gagnot, by any chance?"

Both Packard and Gregory looked surprised. "Very good, Charlie. How did you know?"

"He just seemed like a good choice. Military experience, lots of friends, lots of influence, and forceful enough to hold attention. He's also a bit hotheaded and he bears me a personal grudge."

"You did very well in creating that situation, Charlie. He'd certainly like to see you deposed. However, he also bears a certain amount of innate loyalty to the crown and to

Damask, that is yet keeping him from taking action. We're working to overcome those scruples."

Charlie thought this over. "Yes, well, we wouldn't want a revolutionary who is too easily swayed, anyway. We don't want someone who is going to double-cross us in the end." He drummed his fingers on the hilt of his dagger. "I suppose that when the time comes, I could order his father to be executed."

His uncles exchanged glances. "Execute Lord Gagnot, Charlie?"

"No, no. Of course I wouldn't actually do it. But the threat of it would force his hand."

"That's certainly a possibility, Charlie," said Gregory. "We'll let you know if it comes to that."

"He has plenty of incentive already," said Packard. "What with his father in jail, the potential confiscation of his family estates, and his love of Catherine Durace. All it requires are a few more gentle nudges from us and a little judicious whispering in his ear, and he'll think an insurrection was his own idea."

"Mmmm," said Charlie. He seemed to suddenly have taken a great interest in the view from the window. He spoke with his back to his uncles. "So Lady Catherine is acquainted with the situation?"

"Oh yes. She and young Gagnot were quite an item while you were away at school. Now she's making sure he knows how unhappy she is supposed to be. But I expect you knew this. That's why you chose Gagnot to set up as an enemy, isn't it?"

"Um, right," said Charlie. He continued to look out the window, watching a pigeon fly from a balcony across the courtyard. A man stood behind it, hidden by shadows. Charlie frowned slightly, but when he turned back to his uncles, his expression was cheerfully bland, the benign face of a card player who has been dealt a very bad hand. "All part of my clever plan."

"Don't take too much on yourself, Charlie," warned Packard. "You'll wear yourself out. We'll find this WMD for you. You can trust us."

"I know I can." Charlie headed for the door. Before he reached it, he stopped to pose his uncles a final question. "What I can't figure out is why Dad wanted such powerful magic to begin with. He was not a good man by any means, but he wasn't warlike. What was he going to do with it?"

"In many ways, your father was a difficult man to understand," said Gregory. "Don't worry about it, Charlie."

The prince nodded and left the room. Immediately Packard bolted the door behind him. "I don't believe it," he exclaimed. "All my life I've heard it said, countless times, but I never thought that it would turn out to be true."

"What?"

"That *honesty is the best policy*. Here we've been pussy-footing around for months, trying to find the king's WMD without letting Charlie know, and now he just ordered us to look for it."

"That will certainly make things easier. We can do a proper job of it now." Gregory reached for the decanter, poured two glasses, and sipped one thoughtfully. "We'll start with a room-to-room search of the castle and its environs. We'll examine Thessalonius's files. We'll . . ."

There was a coded knock on the door—two taps, followed by three. Packard unbolted it and allowed Pollocks to slip in. Then he bolted it again. Gregory was looking sternly at the Faithful Family Retainer. "Pollocks, we're very disappointed in you."

"I'm sorry to hear that." Pollocks was breathing hard, as though he had been running up stairs. He made an attempt to look contrite, and managed to convey the impression for a full three seconds before giving up on it. He tried to look around Packard to see if there was wine on the table. His eyes brightened when he saw the decanter.

"You were supposed to stop Charlie from finding out about the WMD."

"I thought he was successfully distracted, Sire. He never mentioned it to me. It was the ghost that told him, I take it? Very difficult things to anticipate, ghosts."

"You should have persuaded him not to visit it."

"He didn't seem interested. He refused every summons to see the ghost, at least when I was present. I don't know what caused him to go out that night."

"Now, Gregory, there's nothing to be gained by recriminations," said Packard. "As it turns out, Charlie wants us to find the WMD for him, so it all worked out for the best."

"That's true," said Gregory. "Pollocks, go through the king's appointment books. Make a list of everyone he saw in the weeks before his death. We'll interview them all."

Pollocks nodded.

"How are things going with Lady Catherine?"

"Very well, Sire. I wouldn't say she has our prince regent completely twisted around her little finger, but he's at least three-quarters twisted."

"Very good. I want you to continue to keep an eye on them. Full reports, daily.

"Yes, Sire."

"Is there any way you can manage to hear what they are saying? He trusts her more than he trusts us, I suspect. A boy is likely to tell his girlfriend many things he won't tell anyone else."

"Eavesdropping will be quite difficult, but I'll see if I can manage something."

"Very good. You may go, Pollocks."

Once again Packard unbolted and then re-bolted the door. When he and Gregory were alone again he said, regretfully, "What a shame about Charlie. I do hate to break up a fine romance like that."

"True, but on the other hand, a romance that ends tragically makes such a good story. Women enjoy such things.

There's no need to feel sorry for Catherine. She will not mourn him long."

"I hope," said Packard, "it will be the same with Fortescue." He took the second glass from Gregory, tossed it off, and set it on the table. He walked to the window, the same one Charlie had been looking through, and opened it to feel the cool night air on his face. A motion caught the corner of his eyes. He stuck his whole head out the window and craned it around to see the south tower, now little more than a shadow in the uncertain twilight. But he was certain he saw motion.

"Come here, Gregory," he said. "What is Catherine up to now?"

❧ ❧ ❧

It was a daring, if somewhat short-lived, escape.

On top of the south tower a heavy beam of oak had been securely fastened to the stone. The end of the beam extended over the edge of the tower, and from it a stout block-and-tackle had been attached. From this arrangement a wide woven basket had been lowered to the window of Lady Catherine Durace.

Into the basket she climbed, and there is no denying that this took a bit of nerve. For although the scheme had been well thought out and much discussed among the small cadre of conspirators, the job of actually crawling out a window, in the dark, and sliding her delicate bottom into a small basket suspended on a narrow rope some fifty feet above the ground, was not a task for the faint of heart.

But she made a stirring sight as she descended. She wore a dark wool dress for concealment and to protect herself from the chill night air, but a playful breeze whipped the skirt up around her thighs, showing an enticing length of creamy skin glowing in pale moonlight. The men below stared in appreciation. For, indeed, there were men below. Albemarle Gagnot was waiting with a half dozen companions. Their faces were concealed within their cloaks, and the hooves of their horses had been wrapped with burlap to muffle the sound of horseshoes. They carried dark lanterns with the windows cracked open to release only narrow beams of light. The beams followed her down the wall, and when she arrived on the ground they bathed her in light from three sides, as though she were on a stage lit by foot-lights. Perhaps it was because of this theatrical effect that Catherine, after slipping out of the basket, immediately responded with a bow and a curtsy.

Her rescuers nodded in silent approval. Rosalind, watching anxiously from above, withdrew her head and shut the window. Gagnot stepped forward and took Catherine's hand. She gave him a warm smile. His men closed their lanterns once again and moved toward their horses. No one spoke. It was quiet except for the whisper of the night wind, the sound of muffled footsteps, and the gentle rustle of cloaks and harnesses. Alas for Catherine's intrepid band of supporters, the silence did not last long. It was broken by a voice from the shadows, the voice of Bad Prince Charlie. He said, "Nicely done, my lady. Very nicely done indeed."

The effect on the men was reminiscent of Lord Galvin's experiment when he touched an electrode to a frog's leg. They jumped. Jolted into action, the drew their swords and opened their lanterns to shine on the prince.

He was unarmed and underdressed, without his jacket or his sword. But he ignored the weapons pointed in his direction and merely walked past Catherine to tug on the rope behind her. "I'm so glad you didn't cut up the linens to make this."

"I thought about it, Your Highness," replied Catherine sweetly. "But they were such nice linens I couldn't bear to damage them."

"I'm sure we could all have a long and fascinating discussion about bedclothes," cut in Gagnot. "But Lady

Catherine has another engagement tonight, so if you'll excuse us, Your Highness." He motioned for two of his men
to bring up the horses. The rest crowded around Charlie
and made threatening motions with their swords.

Charlie was unfazed. "Now," he said loudly. And then
more lamps went on.

They went on in a wide semicircle around Gagnot's
men and were accompanied by a clatter of drawn swords.
They belonged to the palace guards and they were twice as
loud because there were twice as many as Gagnot's men.
Other lights went on in the tower windows, to silhouette the
archers standing behind them. It was as neat a capture as
anyone could wish for, until the prince totally spoiled the
effect by barking, "Arrest them."

It is one of the curious anomalies of the military life
that the enlisted soldier will hesitate to obey a senior officer. He will obey his junior officer. A lieutenant will let a
general overrule his captain, but the enlisted man, if given
a direct order by a general, will often hesitate until the order is confirmed by his lieutenant. Thus it was that when
the palace guards were told by their prince regent to arrest
some armed men, they took no action. Oh, they didn't dis-
obey exactly. They closed in, moved around, waved their
swords, and generally acted threatening, while they waited
for Oratorio to show up and tell them what to do. And Oratorio was not to be found.

"Oh, for God's sake," snapped Charlie. He grabbed one
of Gagnot's men, pushed the cloak off his face, and found
it was Dunswitch. "Give me that." He snatched the sword
from his hand and turned to face Gagnot. "Abe, a fortnight
ago you challenged me to a duel. Very well, I accept. Let's
have it out now."

"Agreed!" said Gagnot. "Your tyranny has gone on long
enough. Someone needs to remove you and it might as well
be me." He attacked with his sword, Charlie parried his

stroke, and the clash of blades rang in the clear night and echoed off the surrounding walls.

But they had only that one strike and parry before Catherine stepped between them. (And this was also a gutsy thing to do, to step between two men swinging steel.) Both Abe and Charlie stopped themselves short and lowered their swords. "Boys, boys," she said soothingly, looking from one to the other. "Put away your swords, please. There is no need to fight."

"We're fighting over you," Charlie told her, "and I can think of no better reason to fight."

This was a pretty good line, romantic and dashing, and it angered Gagnot no end that he could not think of anything to top it. "She made her choice, Charlie," he said. "She's coming with me."

So it seemed that the situation had reached an impasse, one that could not be resolved without blood being shed, and it was fortunate indeed that Oratorio chose that moment to arrive, a little out of breath, on the scene. "Stand down, all of you," he ordered, and the Royal Guards obeyed. "You!" he told Gagnot's men. "Put your weapons on the ground. Now!" and they too obeyed, except for Gagnot himself. "Your Highness," he said to Charlie. "Please excuse my delay."

"Arrest them all," Charlie told him. "Put Catherine back in her room and see that she stays there this time."

"Your Highness," said Oratorio in a low voice. "Before we take action, your uncles would like a word with you." He lifted his lantern so that Charlie could see Packard and Gregory standing behind him.

Charlie was having none of it. He was red hot with anger and jealousy. He turned back to Gagnot, fully intending to continue the fight. Gregory had to push his way through the guards and grab his arm. "Not now, Your Highness," he hissed into Charlie's ear. "We're not ready yet."

Packard, too, had grabbed Catherine and guided her outside the circle of listening ears. "He's right, Charlie," he told the prince, after Gregory hustled him away from the soldiers. "We're not prepared. Fortescue isn't prepared. And he wants an uprising, not a private duel. You're putting our whole plan in jeopardy."

"I'm putting the plan in jeopardy? What about her! What were you doing?" he demanded of Catherine. He pointed to Gagnot. "And what is he doing here?"

Catherine smiled with perfect serenity. She started to speak, but Gregory interrupted. "I'm sure our Catherine has a perfectly reasonable explanation," he said. "Which she'll explain later," he added, cutting her short as she started to speak again. "The point, Charlie, is that while Catherine's cooperation is helpful to the plan, she is not vital to it. *You are.* If Gagnot kills you in a duel now, it is all over. If you kill Gagnot, you'll set us back weeks. It may be even longer before we can have a rebellion. And we can't wait that long. People are already hungry, Charlie. You said so yourself."

It was easy to see that they had found the right key to unlock Charlie's attitude. "Oh, all right," he conceded reluctantly. "Oratorio, get them out of here." He waved his arm to encompass all the conspirators. "Get them all out of here. Gagnot, too. Send them home. Tell them if they try any stunt like this again, it will be the Barsteel for them all."

⚜ ⚜ ⚜

It was several hours before Charlie had an opportunity to vent his feelings, after the intrepid band of would-be rescuers had been escorted back to town, the guards reassigned to their posts, and Catherine returned to her suite. The prince was seething with anger, but Lady Catherine was not the least bit cowed. She told him quite firmly that, while she would be pleased to explain everything to him in good time, she would first have to change out of her traveling clothes and brush her hair. And before that, she needed to have a bath. And before that, a light meal, as the night air had given her an appetite. And while she was talking she was guiding Charlie toward the door, until he soon found himself standing outside her suite with the door bolted behind him and an order for the kitchen in his hand.

He was returning some time later when a very nervous Rosalind stopped him in the hallway. He tried to go around her but she blocked his path. "Your Highness?"

Charlie nodded impatiently.

"I'm Rosalind Amund, Your Highness. Lady Catherine's lady-in-waiting."

"I know who you are."

"I just wanted to say that none of this was Lady Catherine's fault. The escape was my idea. I planned it all and talked her into it. I'm the one to blame. She had no part in the conspiracy."

"You talked her into climbing out a narrow window into a rope basket fifty feet above the ground without giving her a reason?"

"Um, yes. It was a—it was to be—a girl's night out. You know, have a few cocktails, do some window shopping, the usual thing. She was surprised as anyone when Gagnot showed up."

"I see. You planned this all by yourself?"

"Yes, Your Highness. No one else at the castle was involved."

"No one? You were up on the roof working that winch by yourself?"

"Um, yes."

"An enthralling tale. I'm completely convinced." Out of the corner of his eye, Charlie saw Pollocks approaching. He motioned for the family retainer to stay back and addressed Rosalind severely. "Go to your room, Miss Amund. I will decide on your punishment later."

Rosalind departed with her head bowed. Charlie motioned for Pollocks to approach. "Pollocks, what was that all about?"

"I must say the young lady shows a great deal of loyalty to her friend."

"Do you think Lady Catherine put her up to it?"

"Oh no. I think she was sincerely trying to shift the blame onto herself."

Charlie looked past him to see Oratorio approaching. The Captain of the Guard came to attention and saluted smartly. Charlie sighed. "What now, Oratorio?"

"A word with you in private, Your Highness?"

"You can speak in front of Pollocks."

"Very well, sir." Oratorio took a deep breath. "I want to confess, Your Highness."

"I didn't take you for a religious man, Oratorio. However, there are priests in the city who are good at that sort of thing."

"I meant about the escape attempt, sir. Lady Catherine's escape. The truth is . . ." Here Oratorio paused to clear his throat. "Err, the truth is that it was all my idea. I planned the whole thing. I persuaded Lady Catherine to leave her rooms. She did not even know that Gagnot and his men would be waiting below."

"I see."

"I got the idea from a trick we once used at the fraternity. We had these two girls in our dormitory, you see, and it was after hours, and we had to smuggle them back out. So we let down a rope . . ."

"Get to the point, Oratorio."

"I've come to tender my resignation and accept my punishment, Your Highness."

"Oh for God's sake. Oratorio, come to my office tomorrow. We have a lot to discuss. For now, you're dismissed."

"Yes, sir."

"Wait. Come back. Do you know Miss Rosalind Amund?"

"Sir?"

"Place her under house arrest. She is not to leave the castle. I want her guarded at all times."

"Yes, sir. I'll arrange it, sir."

"See to it yourself, Oratorio. Don't delegate this assignment. I want you personally by her side."

Oratorio seemed at a loss for words. Charlie could almost see the confusion of thoughts running through his head, until finally the guardsman simply said, "Yes, sir," spun around, and departed.

Charlie watched until he turned the corner, then turned to Pollocks. "What are you smirking about?"

"I was merely reflecting that not too long ago, someone made a remark about *me* playing matchmaker."

"Shush, Pollocks. I suppose you also want to take sole credit for this night's escapade."

"Not at all. In fact, I have an alibi. I was playing cards with five friends at the time of the incident."

"What? You showed up right after me."

"I was making a joke, Your Highness."

"Oh. Explain it to me later. I'll see if Her Ladyship is taking visitors now." He entered the prisoner's suite.

Catherine was a clever girl—Charlie was always prepared to admit that—clever enough to delay their meeting, until after the prince had had the chance to talk things over with Pollocks and his uncles, eat a good meal, and generally let his anger cool down from a rolling boil to a mild simmer. Even this residual heat quickly dissipated when Catherine greeted him at the door with a kiss.

She was now in her nightgown, a satiny, shimmery thing that caught the moonlight coming through the still-open window. Her long red hair had been brushed to gleaming smoothness, and her lips and nails were glossy pink. The remains of a dinner tray lay across the coverlet. She pulled Charlie across the room to sit next her on the bed, where she arranged his arm around her waist. "That was so sweet of you to challenge Abe to a duel over me, Charlie. You looked very dashing running around out there with a drawn sword. But you really don't need to put yourself in any danger on my behalf." She kissed him again on the cheek.

"What?" said Charlie. "What was that all about? Catherine, why were you going out the window on a rope? I know this has been difficult for you, being cooped up here, but you can leave if you've had enough. Just tell me."

"Oh, Charlie." Catherine snuggled next to him. The remains of Charlie's anger disappeared in a blood pressure surge. "Of course I had to try to escape. It's all part of the act. The public would lose respect for me if I didn't make at least one attempt. They'd think I wasn't suffering enough. A failed escape makes me into a tragic heroine, one who is worthy of their support. It's good publicity."

She drew back to look at his face. The expression Charlie returned was still one of incomprehension, so she started again. "Charlie, look at it from the point of view of a Damask resident. Consider what they see. A naive young woman of high birth—myself—is arrested, and thrown into a tower. Nightly she is taken against her will by an evil prince. Of course they are shocked. Of course they are outraged. Their hearts go out to the poor girl. At first, anyway.

"But after a while, the shock and outrage wear off. Word gets out that her accommodations are quite comfortable, even luxurious. They know she is well fed even while their rations are being cut. And the women, *especially* the women, can't help but notice that the evil prince, while undoubtedly evil, is rather good looking." Catherine slipped a hand inside Charlie's shirt. She began drawing little circles on his chest. "So she has to try to escape, you see." She gave her head a gentle shake, so the soft red hair brushed against Charlie's face. "Or the women might begin to wonder if she's really enjoying herself. They could start to think that it wouldn't be so bad, perhaps, to be ravished by an handsome prince. Even if he's evil." Somehow her lips had gotten close to Charlie's ear. He felt her soft breath on his neck. "Evil, evil, evil," she whispered. She took his ear-lobe between her moist lips and gently nibbled on it. "Such a bad, bad prince."

"But," said Charlie weakly. "What about Gagnot?"

"Oh, Abe is the person we need to convince most of all. He'll be leading the insurrection, you know. I had to put on a good show for him. It's important that he, most of all, believe I'm really in trouble. He's not very politically minded, but he'll want to save me."

"Yes," said Charlie. Some of the heat came back into his voice. "What about you and Gagnot? I understand that you and he had an understanding?"

Catherine drew back and looked at him. "Why, Charlie! Are you jealous?"

"Me? No, of course not. I just don't like being kept out of the loop. If you're going to do something like this, you need to keep me in the full picture."

"I didn't want to bother you with my plans when you are working so hard, Charlie. And it was better for you to be truly surprised. That way you didn't have to pretend. Anyway, there was nothing for you to know. There was never anything between Abe and myself. He is such a foolish boy. He was willing to believe everything I told him."

"Some guys are like that."

"He isn't really my type. Abe has never been out of Damask. He doesn't have your worldly wisdom, Charlie." Catherine moved back next to Charlie and rested her head on his shoulder.

"Oh. Well, I don't like him anyway. And if he knew your plan, he shouldn't have let you climb out an upper window. That was dangerous. You could have been hurt."

"The element of danger made it more realistic. The air of desperation it conveyed made it more poignant. Anyway, it was my own idea. But thank you for being worried about me."

"It was all your own idea? Totally? Oratorio and Rosalind each told me it was their idea."

Catherine laughed. "Did they really? They are such darlings." She hugged him. "When this is all over we really must get them each a nice gift, for being so patient with us. Perhaps something silver for Oratorio and crystal for Rosalind. Noile has wonderful shops for that sort of thing. We'll gift wrap them and—oh!—we'll have them engraved. From the two of us." She looked into Charlie's eyes. "Won't that be fun?"

It seemed to Charlie, under those circumstances, that there was nothing in the world he'd rather do than spend time with Catherine, even if it meant shopping. But he had work to do and plans of his own to make. With much reluctance, he left her and went off to summon Oratorio, find Pollocks, and talk to his uncles.

"Perhaps you should bring her a gift," said Pollocks.

"Catherine?" said Charlie. "I bring her gifts all the time."

"I mean the High Priestess. That's who you're going to see, isn't it?"

Charlie gave him an irritated look. "I'm not courting her, Pollocks. This is state business. I'm returning to the Temple of Matka because I want to question them about the WMD. If Dad was visiting her regularly, and she really is a seeress, then she ought to know something." Two stable hands each handed him the reins of a saddle horse. He threw his pack over one and checked the harnesses of both.

"She's a woman. It wouldn't hurt to bring a gift." Pollocks pointed to the chain around the prince's neck. "She gave you a gift on your last visit. You need to reciprocate."

"I don't know what she would like. And I don't have time for shopping."

"I took the liberty of having some fizzy bath bombs sent

up from the city, Your Highness." Pollocks brought a box from behind his back. It was already wrapped in silver paper, with a pale green ribbon. Charlie took it with reluctance and tucked it into the pack. He saw Pollocks looking at it.

"Now what? I suppose you want me to write a note to go with it?"

Pollocks cleared his throat. "Ah, I also took the liberty of writing a note for you."

"Oh really? Something slushy and romantic, no doubt?"

"Just a few lines of poetry." Pollocks produced a quill and ink bottle. "If you wouldn't mind adding your initials."

Charlie dug the box out, but hesitated with his quill over the card. "She gave me a gold chain. Fizzy bath bombs don't seem quite adequate."

"A few moments ago you weren't going to bring anything at all. Now you're criticizing my choice of gift?"

Charlie seemed like he was about to speak, but then closed his mouth, signed his name, blotted the ink with his cuff, and put the box back in his saddlebag. He mounted his horse, but hesitated before starting. "Pollocks, I won't claim to understand how women think . . ."

"No man understands how women think, Your Highness."

"But this could backfire on me. She might later feel I've been leading her on, when I have no romantic interest in her."

"No?" Pollocks looked at him speculatively. "None at all?"

Charlie had a momentary flashback, of Xiao stepping from behind the screen, her skin oiled and gleaming in the candlelight. "No."

"I understand that once you get to know her, she has a nice personality," said Pollocks. "Very caring and supportive."

"Supportive, right." Charlie thought of Xiao's breasts, high and firm, and the way her bare bottom had brushed against his thighs. He tried to push the vision of her body

out of his head, but all that replaced it was the remember-
ance of her dark eyes, the way she looked at him, and the
lilt of her voice when she spoke. "I don't care."

"I'm told she's kindhearted, cheerful, outgoing, and
likes children and pets."

"Then we have nothing in common."

"They say opposites attract."

"Shut up, Pollocks." The prince mounted his horse and
gave it a little spur. It fought the reins at first, but soon settled
into a steady pace, with the second horse in the string following calmly. Pollocks had asked Charlie to assign himself
some bodyguards, saying that feelings against the prince regent were running high enough that protection might be
needed. Charlie had decided to travel light and rely on fast
horses to outrun trouble. Very shortly he passed a group of
workmen repairing a stone bridge over a streambed, one of
the public works projects. They looked at Charlie resentfully,
which was a good thing. But the streambed was dry, which
was a bad thing. He rode up into the mountains, where the
scenery changed a bit. The snowcaps had receded, and the
streams were milky with melt water. He looked grudgingly at
the water as it flowed away from Damask. He changed
horses every hour, with no stops to rest, and got to the temple
a little earlier than on the previous visit, passing the old tunnel entrance again, skirting the edge of Lake Organza, whose
cold, clear waters reflected a cloudless blue sky, and again he
looked off to the coast, with Noile Harbor in the far distance.
This time, when he rode to the front steps, there were no
crowds. To his surprise a number of signs around the entrance made it clear that the Temple of Matka was now
closed to visitors. Yet two monks were waiting to take his
horse, and a third monk to lead him to the High Priestess.

"You're late," said the monk.

"Huh? I wasn't aware that I had an appointment."

"You didn't. But the High Priestess knew you were
coming, of course."

"If she predicted I would come, she should have been able to predict what time I would arrive."

"She did. But you are late. You should have gotten here earlier."

Charlie had never been able to win an argument with a monk.

This time they took him to a temple building with a roof garden, floored with terra-cotta tile, where Xiao was sitting on a cushion in the lotus position, with her eyes closed and her head bowed. She was wearing a caftan. Charlie was disappointed. Although he told himself he was here strictly on Damask business, he had still rather been hoping she'd take him to her room and do the naked oil thing again. The High Priestess did not look up as he mounted the stairs. When his shadow fell across her she murmured, "Oh, man. Like, I need a toke."

A monk was standing behind her with a handful of rice paper slips. "Just a few more to go." He held a slip toward her.

"The answer is no," said Xiao. Her eyes were still closed. "No, her husband isn't cheating on her. Of course he's lost interest in her, she's gotten as big as a house, what did she expect?"

The monk looked at the slip. "Ah, perhaps we should provide something a little more cryptic for this one?"

"Oh, give me those." Xiao snatched the rest of the slips from him and held them to her forehead. "Yes, no, no, yes, Tuesday, yes, no, bottom drawer on the second cabinet, no, no, no, yes, it was thirsty." She crumpled the slips and handed back a wad of paper. "There. If they can't handle the truth, that's their own problem."

"I see Your Worship is tired." The monk bowed and withdrew. "We can resume later. In the meantime, His Highness the Prince Regent of Damask is here." He bowed toward Charlie and descended the stairs.

Xiao bounced to her feet and in a moment was in Charlie's arms, hugging him tightly, and when Xiao hugged, she tended to put her whole body into it. Charlie once again had the feeling his brain cells were punching out on the time clock and taking an extended lunch break. Xiao did not have the regal bearing, the fine features, or the classical beauty of Catherine Durace. But she was certainly cute enough, and when she wriggled her lithe little body against him, the prince found it difficult to think of any other woman, or even to remember why he was there. He wondered if she was wearing anything under her caftan.

It wasn't until she stepped away from him that he was able to collect his thoughts. "I need your help, Xiao."

"You want to know about the Weapon of Magical Destruction," said Xiao promptly. She was still holding his hand. She didn't let go of it.

Charlie, of course, was surprised and not a little taken aback. He tried not to show it. "You know about the WMD? Yes, of course you would know. I expected that. That's why I came up here. But you know that already, right?" Xiao was looking at him with her head cocked, giving Charlie the feeling that he was babbling. "What I mean is, you're a seeress. You knew that I knew that you would know. Right?"

"Either I'm still stoned or you are," said Xiao. "What are you going to do with a Weapon of Magical Destruction?"

"Destroy it. I don't like any weapon a prudent man can't run away from."

"Good answer. But since you can't find the WMD anyway, what difference does it make?"

"Because I don't want anyone else to find it, either. So how about you just fill up your bong with your magic herbs, wave your hands around your crystal ball or whatever kind of hand-waving you do, and tell me where it is?"

"Sorry," said Xiao definitely. "Can't help you."

"What! What do you mean?"

"Your secret lies behind a door that is closed to me."

Charlie gave her a narrow look. Once again Xiao had

made the transition from air-head to coolly calculating in a suspiciously short span of time. "What happened to all that seeing-the-paths stuff you told me last time?"

"There are some paths I cannot travel. Thessalonius is a powerful and clever sorcerer. If he chose to hide something, he would hide it not only from sight, but from all other perception as well."

Charlie zeroed in on this. "You talk about Thessalonius as if he were still alive. Do you know that for a fact?"

Xiao thought for a while. "Thessalonius has also closed the door on his path. I would not be able to find him, either."

It sounded plausible enough. That didn't mean it was true. When you lived with the wealthy and powerful, you heard plenty of lies. Charlie had learned early in life that all the best liars were totally convincing. "I won't push it," he said finally. He let go of Xiao's hand. "If you say you can't see the future of the WMD, I'll accept that. But what about the king? He was coming up here on a regular basis. What did you talk about?"

We talked about you, Xiao managed to keep herself from saying. "We talked about the future of Damask."

"Didn't he say anything about a super weapon?"

"Not to me."

"But you could do your seeress stuff and find out what he was up to, right?"

"That's in the past. I am able to see the future. The king is dead. His path has ended."

"So has mine, it seems like." Charlie looked for a chair, didn't find one, and finally sat down on a low wall than ran around the edge of the roof garden. Small red maples in barrels were scattered around the tiles. Strange herbs grew in wooden planters. "I've reached a dead end. It was a waste of time coming up here."

"Not quite," said Xiao. She took both of his hands and pulled him to his feet. A light breeze had sprung up, blowing wisps of her long black hair across her face. She tossed her head to fling it back. It swirled around her in a dark cloud, to settle softly around her shoulders in a most alluring way, an effect that no doubt took months of practice to achieve. "There is still something for you to learn."

"There's always something to learn," said the prince. "Life is a continuing education, and nature is the world's classroom. Et cetera, et cetera. But if you don't mind, I'd just as soon dispense with the philosophy and move along with the prognostication. If you can really do the things you say, you must have known what Dad was doing. You must have seen something about a WMD. Some little clue. Something that could give me a hint."

"There is nothing I can say. Now follow me." She was walking backward and pulling on his hands, her eyes always looking into his, weaving her way through the potted trees without looking at them.

"Why don't we go to that room with the smoke and candles and zither music? Maybe that will help."

"It won't. Besides, I'm off that stuff now. I need to get my head straight before I leave."

"You're leaving?" Although he couldn't explain why, Charlie felt a pang of loss.

"I told you I was nearing retirement age. Too long have I listened to the people here, and too long have I realized their secrets. Such knowledge becomes a burden too heavy for one person to hold. Even now, a ship waits in Noile Harbor to carry me away from these lands."

"Uh, right. You mentioned that before. I guess I wasn't expecting you to leave so soon." Xiao let go of Charlie's hands and turned to walk down the stairs. Charlie followed her. "So, you're having a little going away party, I guess? I brought you a gift, did I mention that?"

"This way." Xiao opened a door at the bottom of the stairs. "Enter here. At the end of the corridor is another door. It is unlocked. Enter it. When you come back I will be gone."

Charlie looked inside the door. The corridor was long and dark. He couldn't see the far end. "Great, we're getting mysterious again. Before I go in, I want to know—"

His words were cut off by Xiao's kiss. She flung herself into his arms and pressed against him as though she were trying to wrap her body around his. Through the thin material of her caftan he could feel every inch of her, and he knew at once that she really was wearing nothing underneath it. Her small round breasts were flattened against him so he could feel her nipples digging into his chest, and her soft, rich mouth was slightly open to cover his own. She held the kiss just long enough for the heat of her body to penetrate his clothes, and then she pulled away and said, a little breathlessly, "I just wanted to make sure you were still wearing your getting-out-of-a-tight-spot device."

Charlie was also breathing hard. He pulled the chain out from under his shirt and looked at the little charm. "All you had to do was ask."

"I like my way better."

Charlie internally conceded that he liked her way better also. Aloud, he said, "And what is this supposed to be good for?"

"Sorry," said Xiao. "That I cannot tell you. But . . ."

"When the time comes, I'll know. Yeah, yeah, right."

"If you know the answer, don't ask the question of a seer. You're just wasting her time and your own."

"Seers and sorcerers. Everything they say is a waste of time. Why can't you both just give straight answers? The seeress could say, 'Three weeks from now a man will hold a sword to your throat.' The magician could say, 'Here, take this getting-out-of-a-tight-spot device. Activate it and the sword will melt.' Or whatever it does. Then we all know just where we stand."

"Listen," said Xiao. "I could give you all sorts of complicated stories about how if you knew the device would let you win a swordfight, you'd be getting into all sorts of swordfights that you'd normally avoid, and thus you'd choose a path you wouldn't have chosen. But the simple answer is this: It's magic. You can't figure it out with logic. The sorcerers just make them that way and sorcerers are all strange people. Who knows what's going on inside their heads?"

Once Charlie thought about it, it didn't seem that strange. He knew there were writers who proudly wrote incomprehensible books and musicians who wrote cryptic songs. "All right," he said finally. "I suppose sorcerers's spells don't have to make sense."

"Promise me you'll keep it with you," Xiao said.

"I promise."

"I'm a High Priestess of Matka, remember. You don't want to break an oath to a High Priestess."

"I said I promised, okay? Obviously you think I'm going to get in some sort of tight spot. If you could just give me a hint . . ."

"At the end of the hallway," Xiao reminded him, pointing down it, "there is a door."

"Yeah, I remember." The prince hesitated, trying to think of something more to say. "Okay, well, I guess this is goodbye then."

Xiao gave him a quirky little smile. "The door. Go."

"Right. I'm going." Charlie stepped into the corridor. He stopped to look over his shoulder. The High Priestess was gone.

Before entering the corridor, he paused for a few minutes to let his libido cool back down, and since he also had the suspiciousness quickly learned by anyone holding a government post, he jammed a stone in the frame to keep the door from closing behind him. There was, indeed, another door at the far end of the corridor, although by the time he reached it, the darkness was deep enough that he was groping his way along the walls. He found the handle by feel. As there was no light coming under the door, he presumed that whatever lay behind it was also in darkness. He was wrong. Behind the door lay a thick black curtain, and once he slipped past that he was in a room that was well lit with wax candles and even had a small fire burning in a grate. Many of the candleholders had been taken down from the walls and put on a table, because a man was sitting there working over a pile of papers.

He looked up as Charlie entered, but did not rise, merely acknowledging the prince regent with a nod of the head. He was a big man—even sitting down he looked big—with powerful arms and shoulders. Charlie identified him as someone who had spent his boyhood wielding a sword, and his manhood directing other men to wield swords. His beard was shot through with gray and close-cut in the military style. He'd cut the insignia off his military tunic, and the stripes off his wool twill riding breeches, and then tried to conceal them all under a faded green traveling cloak. Charlie had never seen him before. He recognized him immediately.

"General Fortescue," he said.

Fortescue nodded. "Prince Regent." Charlie was surprised at how old Fortescue was. Then he checked himself. *No, I know he's only thirty-six. But decades of battle have aged him.* Like his beard, Fortescue's hair was also streaked with gray, and the lines in his forehead were prematurely deep. He held up a slip of rice paper and pondered it. "Amazing what these women can tell you."

"You mean their prophecies make sense to you?"

"Always. Unfortunately, half of the time they only make sense after the fact. When the battle is over, you read them and say to yourself, 'Damn, I misinterpreted this. Now I understand what it really means.'"

"Right."

"They so often have a certain ambiguity to them. Of course, I don't want to blame the girl because I fail to interpret her words correctly. She gives us what information she has. It's up to us to make use of it."

"Right."

Fortescue stood up, stretched, then poured himself a goblet of brown liquid from a green bottle. "Port wine, Your Highness?"

"Thank you, General." Charlie knew that protocol meant he had to accept. To refuse a drink might imply that he thought Fortescue was trying to poison him. "So you've been coming here for a long time?" He accepted a goblet and took a tiny sip. The general drained his own glass and filled it again.

"Of course. But I keep my visits a secret. My opponents also visit the Temple of Matka, but it gives me an advantage if they don't know that I know what they know."

Charlie had to take a moment to decipher this. "Right."

Fortescue sat back down. Charlie selected a chair and sat across the table from him. The general produced another slip of paper and showed it to Charlie. "But the High Priestess prophesied that we should meet. And when I heard you were also here, I thought it was important that we do so. I've paid a good deal of money to your uncles, Your Highness, with more yet to be paid. I'm sure they are honorable men, but—well—sometimes the message conveyed is not the message that is received." Fortescue tossed off his port and smiled at Charlie, his words and gestures conveying that hearty, man-to-man, let's-skip-the-rigmarole-and-put-our-cards-on-the-table attitude that helped build confidence among his officers. It would have had the same effect on the prince if Charlie had not heard his father, time after time, use the same tone with visiting dignitaries he was trying to con. "It is worth the cost, of course, for nothing is more expensive than war. But I wanted to make sure that you were comfortable with your role in this."

"I appreciate your taking a personal interest, sir." Charlie felt his way carefully through the conversation. "My uncles are fomenting civil unrest even as we speak, and I have succeeded in alienating the nobility. Under the threat of losing their holdings, they will be more than pleased when you step in and remove me. And without means to feed the unruly mobs, they'll be happy to have you restore order."

"Good man. I'll have plenty of men standing by. In a situation like this, it's important to go in with a good show of force. One's opponents are not inclined to resist when they know from the start that resistance is useless."

"I'll remember that, sir. Now what about food? The situation is getting dire. There won't be much time."

"No fear. The grain wagons will be right behind the troops." Fortescue chuckled. "We're bringing it in on military supply wagons, at first, and issuing the troops with extra rations to distribute. It creates the impression that the soldiers are sharing their own food with the civilians. Then the population feels more kindly toward their occupiers."

"Clever," Charlie agreed. He didn't care much how the people felt about their rulers as long as they didn't feel hungry. "Then I think it's just a question of playing our game out to the end."

Fortescue nodded. "Of course, there's also the issue of the WMD."

"Ah," said Charlie. He nodded, as though the general's words had not taken him by complete surprise. "Well, I do admit that I'm not quite . . . not quite certain how a WMD fits into all this."

And he thought, *Be careful, Charlie. You nearly confirmed to him that we have a Weapon of Magical Destruction. Fortescue's been at this game a lot longer than you have. That's why he contrived to meet you when your uncles weren't around. Packard and Gregory wouldn't have made slip like that.* He wondered how Fortescue had learned about it. From Xiao? But Fortescue must have known about it before he came.

Still, it put him on his guard. "I mean," he continued, "the whole point of this charade is to avoid a war. We want to minimize fighting. Avoid it all together, if we can. So I don't see that there's any need to bring in a WMD."

"Of course, of course," said Fortescue heartily. "We want minimum casualties all the way around. A little insurrection, a show of force, parade the troops, we look the other way while you flee the country, and then we get to work on reunification. As long as the weapon is surrendered peacefully, I don't anticipate any problems."

"Yes, right." It seemed to Charlie that the room had gotten chillier. "Uh, General? You seem pretty well convinced that we actually have a Weapon of Magical Destruction."

Fortescue chuckled again and poured himself another glass of port. "You're not going to try to hold out on me, are you, Your Highness? That would only cause trouble for everyone."

"No, I wasn't going to hold out on you."

"My people have been very concerned about this. A lot of sorcerers in a lot of kingdoms have spent decades trying to trigger large-scale magical reactions. None of them ever achieved the slightest bit of success. But all of ours agreed that if anyone could do it, it would be Thessalonius.

"Then the man withdraws into seclusion. His assistants take over his day-to-day work. He orders a bunch of strange supplies—materials that our people say could only be used for a WMD. And finally he disappears. Now what are we supposed to think?"

Dammit! Fortescue, Charlie realized, was telling him that Noile had spies in Damask, probably right in Damask Castle, and Charlie had better not try to bluff him. "Thessalonius might have taken a holiday."

"Oh, it's all just guesswork and circumstantial evidence, I admit. We probably wouldn't worry so much if you hadn't come into the picture."

"Me?" Charlie was becoming more confused by the minute.

"Your reputation for cruelty has preceded you. After all, you *are* Bad Prince Charlie."

"I can explain that," said Charlie hurriedly. "The truth is that I *asked* her if she wanted dessert and she said, 'No, I'll just have a bite of yours.' So I ordered . . ."

"The mere thought that you might have access to a WMD has been keeping a lot of people awake at night. If I didn't believe that you would turn over the WMD, I would have to take it by force. At the very least, I would have to launch a preemptive attack to prevent you from using it first."

"That won't be necessary." At once Charlie understood why his father had hidden the WMD, and why Thessalonius, if he was still alive, had gone into hiding. Did Damask have spies in Noile? It had never occurred to him to ask his uncles. "But I can understand your concern. That's why I think the best course of action would be for Damask to destroy the WMD. Then neither side would have to worry about it being used against them."

The general apparently found this amusing. He responded with yet another hearty chuckle. Charlie, who always did have a low threshold of irritability, was starting to find them annoying. He wondered how much port Fortescue had drunk. Charlie's personal point of view was that a man should be clearheaded and sober when making decisions that might require killing large numbers of people.

Fortescue refilled his glass yet again. "A most interesting idea, Your Highness. But surely you don't need to be told that the capture of your Weapon of Magical Destruction is really the whole point of this exercise? It is, in fact, the keystone of my future plans."

"It is?" Charlie decided that, diplomacy-wise, he was playing out of his league. He resolved to cut the meeting short at the first opportunity, before he agreed to something he didn't want to agree to. "I thought the point of this

exercise was to reunify Damask and Noile without the nobility kicking up a fuss about losing their independence."

"Damask will be a burden to Noile. It occupies no
strategic position, it can't support itself without aid, its
leaders tend to be selfish, corrupt, and shortsighted even by
the standards of nobility. And even a small occupying force
will be costly. And a diversion of men and materials that I
can better use elsewhere. Only the capture of the WMD
makes this exercise worthwhile."

"I see," said Charlie, who was not sure that he did.

"Now, if your uncles had simply sold it to me, they
would have looked very bad when the time came to put it
to use. They would have been thoroughly vilified. It would
have been impossible for them to live in Damask. But if the
weapon is captured, you see, then no one is to blame. Oh,
you will get blamed a little, but then you're not the type to
worry about your reputation, are you?"

"But why would you put it to use?" Charlie strove to
keep the desperation out of his voice. "Noile has been pacified. Damask is being turned over to you. Who would
you . . ."

"This is the chance of a lifetime, Charlie." Fortescue
dropped the formal title. He stood up, grabbed the port,
and drank deeply from the bottle. "This is a time when history will be made. The bordering states cannot risk their
people against such a weapon. We will expand our terri-
tory, far beyond what has ever been dreamt before. It will
be the birth of a new century for Noile. Our children and
grandchildren will thank us for this."

Oh no, thought the prince. *Not another one*. Not another
megalomaniac bent on conquest. What was it about these
military types? Did all that saluting and close-order drill
do something to their brains?

His expression must have made his thoughts clear to
Fortescue, for the general caught his look and immediately

began to backpedal. "Not that we'll ever actually use it," he hastened to reassure Charlie. "Certainly not. That would be terrible. We'll explain to our enemies that it would only be used as a last-ditch defensive measure, to prevent them from attacking us. Especially after we've attacked them first. Maybe we'd have to detonate one to prove we actually have it. And that we have the will to use it. Possibly a second one, to show them we can make more. But certainly no more than two. That assumes that once we have Thessalonius's WMD, we can duplicate it. But our sorcerers are confident of that."

"Sure," said Charlie. "Sure. But, you know, I don't think this WMD is really suitable for that kind of strategic defense. I'm not totally sure of my facts here, but Dad kind of explained to me that it was tricky and unreliable—and very expensive to maintain, he said—and really it would be better to just bury it somewhere and forget about it. Poor design, he said. Stay away from it."

"Ah yes." Fortescue gave Charlie a sympathetic smile. "We heard about this. Your father told you all about it, you say? You've been taking advice from ghosts?"

There was something in his tone of voice that put Charlie on the defensive. "It's a complicated world, General. And there are more things in it than can be explained by mere philosophy."

Fortescue moved aside a stack of paper to reveal a textbook. Charlie read the title upside down—*Introduction to Natural Philosophy*. The general flipped the book open and ran his finger down an index page. " 'Ghosts,' " he read. " 'Explanation of.' "

"Um, I was speaking figuratively."

Fortescue was still looking up the entry. He spoke absently. "With the WMD I'll consolidate my power, and, of course, my marriage to Catherine will resolve any remaining political considerations. Then . . ."

"Catherine?"

"Lady Catherine Durace. My fiancée. Surely she told you."

Muscles were knotting up in Charlie's neck. His left hand, still holding the goblet of port, grew white around the knuckles. "You're engaged to Lady Catherine Durace? Engaged to be married?"

"Hmmm? Oh yes. Her own idea, I understand. I must say I didn't think highly of the plan—I'm not really the marrying kind, although I'm told she is quite attractive—but her family made it clear that it was necessary to insure their support."

"Really." The knotted muscles had moved up from the prince's neck to his jaw.

"There have always been those troublemakers who call me a usurper, who don't appreciate what I've done for Noile. But as the House of Durace is in the line of succession for both Noile and Damask, this should quiet that sort of talk. A few people may have to be executed for treason, but that's a small price to pay for security."

Charlie stood up. "Nice meeting you, General Fortescue. I must leave. Dentist appointment. I totally forgot about it." He brushed past the blackout curtain, shoved open the door to the corridor and walked quickly to the outside exit. Halfway there he broke into a run. Outside he blinked in the harsh, cold light. He had to stand still for a minute to let his eyes adjust. Then he ran toward the stables, where he saw a pair of monks tending his horses. They stood back and stared at him as he threw on the saddles, fixed the harnesses, and took off, with the horses' hooves throwing little showers of pebbles. And he rode in a hot, bright fury all the way back to Damask.

The warm summer day was fading to a still summer night. Intermittently a puff of breeze stirred the flags over

Damask Castle, but mostly they hung limp until the color guards lowered them, and the laundry hanging outside the washhouse dripped silently without flapping. In the east block, a room full of senior officials grew murky, despite the open windows, as they puffed on their long clay pipes, discussed the issues of the day, and took advantage of the still air to blow smoke rings. In the wizard's tower, Jeremy practiced with an illustrated monograph and a small pipe of his own, trying to teach himself to blow the fancy shapes that wizards are expected to produce. Evelyn and Tweezy, in the supportive manner of apprentices everywhere, helped by making insolent remarks. Over the kitchens, the smoke from the chimneys rose straight into the sky, while down in the courtyard, the lamplighter was having a particularly easy time of it getting his wicks to ignite. He did not see a hooded figure cross the courtyard behind him and slide quietly into a stairwell.

The role of Faithful Family Retainer put Pollocks in a convenient position. He carried enough rank, and was close enough to the throne, that he could be introduced at court. Yet the job required enough personal service that no one would think it unusual to see him going up a service stairs. Although when going about this particular errand, he had always been careful not to let himself be seen.

The pigeon lay quietly in an inside pocket of his coat. The new breeds, he often reflected, were amazing birds. In the hand they were quiet and docile, easy to conceal. You could walk right through a crowded meeting with one under your jacket and no one would be the wiser. Once in flight they were amazingly fast. The first time he had been given a carrier pigeon, Pollocks had worried that hawks would get it. The mountains were full of hawks. But ninety percent of the birds got through. And these newest breeds would even fly at night.

He went up the central tower. There were small windows that let in the fading light, but when he was on the opposite side of the tower from the setting sun, he had to feel his way along carefully. There was little risk here—it was a relatively modern castle, as castles go, not some crumbling old structure, and the stairs were uniform and well made. Sending the message, Pollocks considered, was not the dangerous part. The dangerous part was writing the message. He wrote them out first in longhand, and when he was satisfied that they were tightly written, concise, and correctly spelled, he copied them onto a rice paper strip, and rolled it up, and wedged it into the message capsule, and then burnt the original in the grate. Even though he locked the door, he knew there were maids and guards and other people who had passkeys. He was always fearful that someone would come in and wonder why he was burning papers. He never relaxed until that part was done.

He rounded a corner. It was a relief to get back into the sun, even when there was not much left. He paused on a landing, one that had a small, locked door. On the other side, he knew, was a small balcony that overlooked the east wall. He would have to move quickly, once the door was open, lest anyone below look up. They would be looking into the setting sun, so that light would help conceal him, but still he didn't want to reveal himself longer than absolutely necessary. From his left outer pocket he took an iron key and unlocked the door. From his right inside pocket he took the pigeon. He nestled it against his chest and stroked it for a moment, admiring its graceful form. This one was named Tomaso, from a character in a Bardwell drama, a part Pollocks had once played in his youth. But Pollocks hadn't named it. They were already named when they came to him. All carrier pigeons had names, like racehorses. What baffled Pollocks were the breeds. He had been told this was a dark checkered pied white cock. Indeed it was dark and checkered, so how could it be pied and white?

No matter. Against a darkening sky it would be impossible to see. Pollocks checked that the message capsule was secure on its leg and stroked it one more time. It cooed almost inaudibly and fluffed its feathers. He turned the key in the door, pushed it open a sliver, and put his eye to the crack. The balcony was deserted. All looked clear without.

But behind him there was suddenly the sound of metal sliding against metal, and the stairwell burst into brightness as dark lanterns were opened. This was followed by the slick hiss of metal against leather as swords were drawn. Pollocks didn't even turn around. "Damn," was all he said, as he shoved the door open and flung the pigeon into the night.

"Damit! Stop him," called a familiar voice, and Pollocks heard behind him a clatter of footsteps up the stairs. At the same time another familiar voice ordered, "Get him!" and there was a clatter of footsteps *down* the stairs. Two men shoved past Pollocks at nearly the same time, and stumbled onto the balcony, where they stared into the sky. The pigeon had already vanished.

"Falconers," said Packard. "Send for the falconers. Get the peregrines after it."

Gregory shook his head. "They don't fly at night. Let it go. It doesn't matter now. We don't need the message." He turned around and looked at Pollocks. "We have *him*."

❧ ❧ ❧

Catherine had an explanation for Charlie. Catherine always had an explanation for Charlie. She toyed with some needlework and looked up at him with mild surprise. "Oh, Charlie, didn't Packard and Gregory explain that to you? I am *so* sorry. I thought you knew."

"No," snapped Charlie. "They didn't. And I didn't." The prince was pacing rapidly back and forth across her salon, one hand on the hilt of his sword, the other clenched tightly at his side.

"Oh dear. I can see how this must have come as a shock to you. But yes, I was betrothed to Bradley some time ago."

"Bradley! Who the hell is Bradley?"

"General Fortescue."

"Oh. Right."

"It is a political marriage, of course." Catherine rose and tried to take Charlie's hand. He pushed her away. "But it is so important, Charlie, for a stable reunification. It will give legitimacy to Fortescue's rule and that will make things so much easier for us."

"For us?"

"Bradley and myself."

"I don't like it," said Charlie. The sun was setting and the lamps had not yet been lit. His face was in shadow, so she couldn't see his expression, but his voice was harsh and unyielding. "I don't like the way any of this is going. Secret weapons and secret meetings and secret engagements. I didn't agree to any of this." He slammed his free hand on a table. "All those talks we had about meeting in Noile after this was over, and you never mentioned you were betrothed. Why didn't you say something?"

"Oh, Charlie." Catherine spoke as though a great light had suddenly dawned on her. "I didn't realize. Charlie, did you have expectations for us?"

The prince glared at her. He didn't answer.

Catherine stood next to him and put her arm in his. This time he yielded. She put her other hand up to gently brush his cheek. "You poor boy. You must feel terrible. Oh, how you must think I misled you. It's all my fault." She looked into his face. A tear slowly welled up in each of her eyes. "Charlie, can you ever forgive me?"

Charlie suddenly shoved her away. She lost her balance and fell down. "Charlie!"

"Quiet," snapped the prince. He drew his sword and whirled around the darkening room. "Who was that?"

"What?"

"I thought I heard a noise. Who else is here?"

"No one is here. I didn't hear anything."

"Someone is spying on us! There, behind the curtain!"

"No one is behind the curtain . . . Charlie!"

The prince drove the point of his sword through the draperies. He pulled it back viciously and stabbed again, and then a third time. At the third thrust he threw his sword on the floor and surveyed the curtain with grim satisfaction. Catherine shrieked and pushed his aside. "Have you gone mad? Do you realize what you've done?" She grabbed a handful of cloth and stared at the rents in horror. "Charlie, this is hand-tatted lace!"

"Oh no."

"Yes. This is very expensive cloth."

"They caught him."

He was looking past her, out the window, at the central tower. Catherine followed his gaze, just in time to see a bird fly off the tower and a hooded figure disappear back inside. "Who was that?"

The prince grabbed her arm. "I'll show you."

When they want to be charming, no one can be as charming as old men. They have had decades to learn what other people, deep inside, really care about, and they have had time to develop the skill of reading other people's expressions and interpreting the subtle nuances of voice and gesture. Charming old men know just what to say to make you feel good about yourself.

But the same advantages of knowledge and experience give sinister old men the ability to be really, really sinister. The ambiance of a dark stairway, a stone tower, and a setting sun added to the menace. And even if Pollocks was not intimidated by the mere atmosphere, Packard and Gregory were also backed up by a half dozen unsmiling guards. Even Oratorio, normally a friendly young man, was looking at Pollocks in a stern and unforgiving manner.

"And to think we trusted you," said Packard, which is

what people always say when they catch a spy. Of course, most people don't get much opportunity to catch a spy, so it's not like the phrase gets worn out from overuse. "You've betrayed us to Fortescue, haven't you?"

"No, my lords! Never." From the start, Pollocks had mentally conditioned himself for the possibility of being caught, and had prepared brave and witty answers to every anticipated question. But now he was in the grip of two guards, each holding him so tightly that agonizing pains were shooting up his arms and into his neck. It was difficult to maintain any semblance of cool.

"Who else could it be?" Gregory asked Packard. "Is Fortescue going to double-cross us?" He looked at Pollocks. "What did he tell you?"

"Nothing! I don't know anything about Fortescue!"

"Who is getting the message?"

"No one. I mean—um—it was . . . my recipe club. You see, every month you send out a recipe to your friends—this one was for amaretto cheesecake—and they send one back to you and—*aiieee!*" He ended with a screech as one of the guards holding him twisted his arm up behind his back. Oratorio frowned and motioned for the guard to ease up.

"Of course, it could be merely routine intelligence gathering by Fortescue's army," said Packard. "I'm sure he doesn't trust us any more than we trust him. It doesn't mean he's going to double-cross us."

"We'll find out," said Gregory. "We've got time. We'll make him talk." He looked at Pollocks and the most sinister part about it was that he wasn't even *trying* to be sinister. He was simply telling the truth. "You'll tell us everything you know. About the king, the WMD, Thessalonius, Charlie, Fortescue, all of it. If you have any secrets to betray, you'll betray them. You know that's true. After a few hours, you'll be begging to be allowed to tell us. Although you may linger on in pain for a few days after we're through with you."

"No," whispered Pollocks.

"Take him to the dungeons," Packard told Oratorio. "To the *Star Chamber*." Oratorio looked distinctly unhappy now, but he nodded to the two guards.

They didn't get far. From below there came the sound of a heavy door crashing open, the scrabbling of footsteps on stairs, and the prince rose into view, dragging Catherine behind him. He took one quick look at his uncles, the guards, and the restrained retainer and figured out the situation at once. "You!" he said to Pollocks. "A spy!"

"No!"

The prince let go of Catherine, who fell to the stairs, rubbing her wrist. He advanced on Pollocks with his fists clenched. "And to think I trusted you!"

"We said that already," interrupted Packard. "However, we'll make him tell us . . ."

"You betrayed me!" screamed Charlie. He sprang at Pollocks, shoving him up against the wall. There was a silvery flash of steel in lamplight, and the dagger was out of Charlie's belt and in Pollocks's chest.

The two guards let go of his arms and stepped back. Pollocks looked down in shocked surprise, at the red stain that was spreading across his shirt, at the haft of the knife that was still in Charlie's hand. His eyes rose to meet Charlie's. Then the prince pulled the knife back and Pollocks's eyes rolled back in his head. He sagged against the prince. Charlie dragged him across the landing and thrust him into Oratorio's arms. "Get rid of him," he said. "Throw the body on a dung heap. No burial for traitors." He stuck the dagger back in his belt and turned away.

Oratorio glared at his back. But he said nothing, merely hoisted Pollocks carefully over his shoulder and walked down the stairs. Two guards followed him. Charlie turned to Catherine. She cringed under his glare and pressed herself against the wall.

"Really, Your Highness, that was most unwise," said

Gregory. "Pollocks could have given us much useful information."

"Never mind. We don't need it." Charlie was still glaring at Catherine. "Just answer one question for me. Were you aware that our Lady Catherine Durace here is betrothed to General Fortescue? And has been for many months?"

"What?" said Gregory.

"Catherine?" said Packard

"That's what I thought." Charlie looked the rest of the guards over, then jerked his head toward the frightened girl. "Take her away. Lock her up."

Two of the remaining guards went to Catherine's side and gently lifted her to her feet. The other two took up positions to the front and rear. The entire group moved slowly down the stairs and to the exit door. Catherine turned her head, to cast a look of defiance at the prince.

"No," said Charlie. The soldiers stopped. "Not back to the tower." The prince spoke with his lips curled back from clenched teeth. "Take her to the Barsteel."

❧ ❧ ❧

"How could this have happened?" moaned Packard. He was sitting in their usual conference room with his hands in his hair. They had been having individual meetings with the kingdom's nobility, making sure everyone was in line with the program, and the table was now covered with an array of empty bottles—port for the conservatives, claret for the liberals. "We worried that Charlie might double-cross us and we were keeping an eye on him. We worried that Fortescue might double-cross us and we planned for that contingency. We feared that Thessalonius might turn up, or the king's ghost might give us away, and we allowed for that. But Catherine? She seemed so—I don't know—so agreeable."

"Smarter men than ourselves have been fooled by less

clever women than our Miss Durace," said Gregory, calmly raising his glass to the candle and swirling the claret. He tasted it with approval. "Don't blame yourself because you can't understand one of them. Their minds operate on a completely different level than ours."

"She's engaged to Fortescue. She's planning to become queen of Noile and Damask. Do you understand where that leaves us? She played us for fools! How can you be so calm?"

"Because if she wasn't good enough to fool us, she wouldn't have been good enough to fool Charlie."

"She didn't fool him. He found out."

"And he put her in prison. Relax, Packy. Nothing has changed. Have some of this claret. Might as well finish the bottle." Gregory was feeling confident. Each one of Damask's lords had begun assembling his troops. Each one had warned that Charlie had to be removed, and if Packard and Gregory could not persuade the prince to leave on his own terms, he would be removed by force. Packard had promised to talk to the young man but didn't offer much hope. Gregory had warned that the prince regent had his own guard and storming the castle was no simple feat. Casualties could be expected.

Packard accepted the bottle and refilled his own glass. "Dammit, I wish Charlie had not been so hot tempered. I wanted to know what the hell Pollocks was doing."

"He was carrying messages between Catherine and Fortescue. Isn't that obvious? What else could he have been doing? Too bad. We missed a good opportunity there. We could have used him to feed false information to Fortescue." Gregory leaned back in his chair. "Relax, Packy," he repeated. "Nothing has changed. Fortescue didn't intend to let Charlie live. He knows too much. We weren't planning to let Catherine live. She knows too much. Pollocks, it seems, knew too much also, and Charlie has solved that problem for us. We couldn't have let him live anyway."

"I can't relax, Gregory, and I'll tell you why. One, Fortescue's army is right over the border. He's coming in whether we're ready for him or not. That means we have no time left to find the WMD."

"So we fall back on the contingency plan. Take our money and sell out to Fortescue, just like we told Charlie."

"Right. Which brings me to point number two. We can't kill Catherine if she's engaged to Fortescue. He'd hunt us down and flay us alive. So she'll be his queen and from her point of view, *we* know too much. What kind of life do you think *we're* going to lead? I'll tell you. Uneasy, uncomfortable, and very, very short."

"Ah," said Gregory. He smiled, and put his feet on the table. "We are not going to kill Catherine. Charlie is going to kill Catherine."

Packard thought this over. "No," he said, shaking his head. He thought some more. "Yes. I don't know. You really think he'd do it?"

"No, of course not. He's still in love with her. He wouldn't do it even if he wasn't in love with her. We'll do it for him. We give the order, but we do it under his seal. He'll get the blame. Don't you see how well this works out for us, Packy? Actually, Charlie gave me the idea."

"To kill Catherine?"

"He suggested that giving an order to execute Lord Gagnot would force young Albemarle Gagnot to attack. Well, we know how the young puppy feels about Lady Catherine. It's bound to have the same effect. He'll attack Charlie right away so he can free Catherine. Alas," Gregory said, without showing real regret, "his attack will come too late to save her. And then, if Gagnot fails to defeat Charlie, Fortescue will finish him off. There is no way he can escape."

"I hope not. That young man is making me markedly uneasy. This is such a strange turn of events, Gregory. We chose him because he seemed like such a disinterested third party. I mean, he never even tried to make a claim for the throne. He never seemed to want anything, never had any goals. He'd just lay out that ironic coolness that so many of those college kids adopt. I never thought he would stab a man."

"I guess if you go around pretending to be an evil prince long enough, it starts to get to you."

"Of course, we're executing people and we're not evil."

"Yes, but that's different. It's the greatest good for the greatest number philosophy. We're not just doing this for ourselves. The Damask population as a whole will be better off when we're through."

"You're right." Packard picked up the empty bottle and studied the label. "This really is a good claret. Do we have any more of this? We'll have to be sure to pack it up and take it with us."

"We won't need to. I still think we'll be able to defeat Fortescue."

"Come on, Gregory. If we haven't found the WMD by now, we're not going to. The ghost didn't tell Charlie anything and it didn't come back. We guessed wrong. We'd have been better off going with Jason from the start."

"Impossible. We can hardly kill one of our own."

"Well, that's true."

"And I still think it will turn up." Gregory rose and yanked on a bellpull, summoning servants to clean the room. "A Weapon of Magical Destruction is, after all, magical. You know how those magical things work. It will turn up at the last minute, just in the nick of time. They always do."

Catherine suddenly found herself in quarters far different from what she had been used to. The cells of the Barsteel were not designed for comfort, nor did they provide it. They were little more than iron cages—despite the name, only a few had steel bars—with bare stone floors. One tiny window gave a view of a courtyard. It contained a chopping block, so Catherine did not spend a lot of time looking out. (This private courtyard was for the nobility, of course—common criminals were publicly hanged out front.) Even on the brightest days only a small amount of light penetrated the cell, and the dimness within contributed to the atmosphere of gloomy despair. The fact that the opposite cell was occupied by the Marquis de Sadness did not help Catherine's mood, either, as he was constantly making comments like "Nice dress. It reminds me of something I saw in Illyria two seasons ago," and "If you'd waited another week you could have gotten those exact same shoes for forty percent off."

The cells, though plain, were certainly secure. Visitors to Damask often commented on the quality of the public buildings, most of them simple and unadorned, but solidly constructed. That was because they had all been built as public works projects during previous crop failures. You could do a lot with cheap labor. Most of the cages were crowded—the marquis was now sharing a cage with Lord Gagnot and a corrupt city auditor—but, as the only female prisoner, Catherine had a cage to herself. She spent an uncomfortable night on the wooden bench that served as a bed, shaking on the thin wool blanket. It was too hot to sleep under the blanket—the shaking was from fear. By morning, however, she had a better grip on her emotions. "There is nothing to be afraid of," she told herself. "Charlie's upset, but he'll get over it. He's not really a bad person. That's why you chose Fortescue over him, after all." She tried to look on the bright side. She had bathed and dressed shortly before Charlie had her arrested, as she had been planning to receive guests that evening, so her face and clothes were still fairly clean. If she had visitors, at least she would look presentable. And surely she was entitled to some sort of court hearing, wasn't she? Fortescue's army was just over the mountain, waiting for their cue to occupy the city. Worst-case scenario: They would be here in a matter of days. She could wait it out. A guard showed up briefly to bring her a cappuccino and biscotti from the coffee shop downstairs. She ignored them, thinking, *I'll be out of here soon enough. I'll wait for a real breakfast.* That was before the guard returned with the executioner.

Catherine had never seen an executioner. She had never attended an execution—watching people being separated from their heads was not her idea of a good time. But she could recognize an executioner when she saw one—he was unmistakable in his garb of a loose black sweatshirt and pants, and a black hood that covered his entire face except for two eyeholes. The cloth covering his mouth was damp. He was not as big as she expected, and instead of an ax he carried a heavy scimitar. He barely looked at her. "Tomorrow," he said. "His Highness doesn't want to wait around on this one. Tomorrow, at dawn."

"Does it have to be at dawn?" complained the guard. "Why do you guys always have to do this so early?" The guard was one of the city soldiers, a new enlistee in the army, not one of the more professional castle guards.

"What does it matter?" asked the executioner sarcastically. "You got a date?"

"As a matter of fact, I do. Tomorrow is Sunday. I've got heavy plans for tonight and I figured on sleeping in tomorrow."

"You got a date? No kidding."

"A high-class babe, too," bragged the guard. "One of the ladies at the castle. But, look, it's summer. Dawn breaks about five A.M. Do you really want to get up that early? I thought that execution-at-dawn business was just a figure of speech."

"It's not a figure of speech. You think it's easy going around in this black stuff all day." The executioner grabbed the front of his sweatshirt and flapped the cloth. "Especially in the summer. Once the sun comes up, this hood really gets hot. Let's do it early, before the sun starts to burn." He turned to Catherine. "Better for you, too, Miss. If it gets too hot, you'll perspire and then your makeup runs and gets streaky and people think you've been crying. Better to go out when it's still cool and let people remark on how brave you were."

"We could do it in the evening," suggested Catherine. "I don't mind waiting."

"Can't." The executioner shook his head. "I've got to take my son to a ball game."

"And I'm supposed to be at my mother's house for dinner," said the guard. "Listen, can't you put it off a few hours? The courtyard is shaded most of the day. It really won't really get the full sun until past noon."

"Well," conceded the executioner. "I guess I wouldn't mind a little extra shut-eye myself. How about, say, nine-ish?"

"Ten," said the guard. "It's not going to take long, right? You can lop off her head and still beat the crowd for Sunday brunch."

"Ten it is," said the executioner. He shouldered his sword and followed the guard back down the stairs. "If you're taking a girl to brunch, try La Terrace. They do a good fixed-price menu, and it includes champagne cocktails."

"Champagne cocktails? I thought you guys drank Bloody Marys," said the guard. "Ha-ha." Their voices trailed away down the stairs.

"There's still Gagnot," Catherine told herself. "Abe will rescue you. You'll be out of here in no time."

⚜ ⚜ ⚜

"What is all this?" asked Charlie. He looked at the pile of metal on the table. Next to it lay thick folds of padding, along with a heavy, leather-bound book.

"Your armor, Sire," said Oratorio.

"This isn't my armor."

"I'm afraid it is, Your Highness. Your uncles ordered it to be painted black, about the same time they did your clothes. It suited your image, they said."

Charlie shook his head in exasperation. "At least the fit is the same."

"Yes, Sire. I checked it all. The pieces are all nearly the same as my own armor."

Gagnot's challenge had arrived within an hour of Catherine's imprisonment. Charlie sent his acceptance back by the same courier. The prince picked up the book. "What is this? The Code Duello, I suppose."

"No, Your Highness. The Code Duello is for the professional duelist. You're an amateur, so you would be governed by the Code Duellittante. I brought a copy for reference." Oratorio took the book and opened it to the contents page. "There's a good deal about giving the lie. There's the lie direct, the lie indirect, the lie incorrect, the lie invective—that's when it's accompanied by insult—and the lie subjective—when it's all a matter of opinion."

Charlie looked over his shoulder. "And the lie subjunctive?"

"I never figured that one out. The French use it sometimes. Anyway, who gives the lie determines who gets choice of weapons. The next chapter has to do with choosing your seconds, choosing your second helpings—that's for after-dinner duels—and choosing the second seating, for duels on cruise ships."

"How very thorough."

"The rules state that the challenge must not be delivered at night. The combatants must have a chance for their tempers to cool and, if drunk, to get some sleep. It must not be delivered before breakfast, because an empty stomach makes a man short-tempered. And it must not be delivered in the presence of a beautiful woman, for a man may feel pressured to accept the duel to impress the woman and not due to the justice of his cause."

"What about the presence of an ugly woman?"

"A true gentleman behaves as though all women are attractive."

"Yes, of course."

Oratorio closed the book. "There's plenty of reason for you to decline this duel, Your Highness. I'm sure Gagnot felt he had to issue the challenge when you accused his father of corruption. Not to do so would be tantamount to admitting his father's guilt. But you don't have to accept."

"I've already accepted, Oratorio. What do you think of the black plume?"

"I'm afraid that plumes are not really to my taste."

"Mine, either." Charlie ripped off the ostrich feathers. "I think we can do without those." He picked up the broadsword, hefted it, slid it out of its scabbard, examined the edge minutely, slid it back into its scabbard, then passed the whole assembly to Oratorio for inspection. The captain of the Guard drew it and swung it over his head and around his shoulders a few times. He made a face. "The balance is not particularly good, Your Highness."

"Nor is the steel. I was trying to support local labor, even though we don't have good armorers in Damask. I never expected to use the damn thing."

"Yes, they're mostly just for ceremony."

"And I'm betting that's all this is going to be. You know how these formal duels are supposed to go. Gagnot approaches with his entourage. I meet him with my entourage. Gagnot rides forward and issues his challenge. I ride forward and issue my acceptance. The judges inspect the weapons. The judges inspect the armor. The band plays. Everyone breaks for lunch. The ring is drawn. The judges inspect the ring. The *Code* is read out loud to the crowd. Our seconds are consulted. They confirm that we agree to abide by it. The band plays again. Everyone breaks for tea."

"I know what you mean, Sire. It's easy to challenge someone to a duel, but few combatants are all that eager for the actual hacking and slashing to start."

"And neither are we. Do you think he'll say, 'So we meet again' or 'This time we finish it'? I bet he will. It's just the sort of thing he'd say."

"I couldn't say, Sire."

The prince looked him over. "I know you're unhappy about Pollocks and Catherine, but the situation called for drastic action. Nothing changes for you. You're still responsible for the defense of the castle."

"I know my duty, Sire."

"How is Rosalind taking this?"

"Not well, Sire. She's been crying."

"She'll understand when this is all over. Listen, Oratorio, you know the situation. Surrender to Fortescue at the first opportunity. Make sure your men understand this. Don't try to hold the castle against his army, whether I'm here or not. There's no point to it. They're professionals. They won't mistreat you."

"Yes, Sire. The men have already been instructed."

"What time did Abe say? This isn't going to be one of those riding out at dawn things, is it?"

"No, Sire. We can expect him about mid-morning.

"What I'm counting on," said Charlie, "is that Gagnot won't be able to control his men. With the right amount of goading, his lines will break down into a disorderly mob. He doesn't have any experience in leading men in battle."

"Neither do we, Your Highness," said Oratorio.

Near the bottom of a steeply sloping mountain, on the outskirts of the port of Noile, a small hostel sat in the center of a small meadow. It was not a good location, because it was several hundred yards off the road, but it was the only piece of level ground in the area suitable for building. The surrounding woods gave it added privacy, and therefore it suited the monks of Matka very well. They booked all the rooms and slipped Xiao inside, disguised by one of their light blue hooded cloaks. She didn't much care for the secrecy, but she'd been in the prophecy business long enough to appreciate the need for mysterious ways. She stood at the window, watching the wagons and the rest of the monks continue down the road to the port. Trees blocked her view of the harbor, but that morning she had seen it from the top of the mountain. And she had seen the ship, with its signature light blue sails, that would carry her away.

"I'd like to go down with them," she told one of her guardian monks. "I haven't been to the city since I became the High Priestess. It would be nice to do a little shopping before I leave."

"Make a list of what you're looking for and I'll have someone pick it up before the ship sails."

"It's not the same, Sing. I could go down after dark. In disguise."

Sing shook his head. "The shops will be closed in the evening. And you're too difficult to disguise. With all of us around, people will be looking for you. A High Priestess has to appear with the pomp and ceremony appropriate to her station. You can't just walk into a tavern and order an egg sandwich. People will lose respect for the office."

"Mmm." Xiao left the window to flop down on the bed. She picked up a couple of trade books—*The New Divination Handbook, 101 Vague All-Purpose Prophecies*, and *Advanced Cold Reading*—flipped through them, and set them aside. "What time do I enter the city?"

"They're working up a schedule now. Not too early. Probably around lunchtime. Give the streets a chance to fill up. The advance team is working on it. We expect to have a pretty good crowd there to listen to your farewell speech."

"I have it memorized already. It's not very exciting, is it?"

"What do you mean?"

"Well, I mean I basically just say farewell, it's been nice knowing you, be good, now go in peace and believe in yourselves. Does this sort of thing really inspire people? Does it ever do any good?"

"No, but it's traditional. What else can you say? 'Goodbye, now go back to fighting each other'?"

"I want a toke."

Sing looked surprised. "No, Your Worship. We've been through all that. That's no longer part of your lifestyle."

"I know, I know," Xiao said. "I'm not going to *have* one. I just said I *wanted* one."

"Have you studied your dossiers?"

She gave the monk an exasperated look. "I already told you. I'm not going to memorize a thick file for every noble in Noile. Not just for a walk through town. The advance team is working up a crib sheet. All I want is a few obscure personal facts on each official I'm likely to meet."

The monk looked like he was about to disagree, but they were interrupted by a knock on the door. Another monk came in, with a deck of index cards wrapped in brown paper. He gave them to Sing, who gave them to the High Priestess. She unwrapped them and shuffled through them quickly but thoroughly. "Perfect," she told the men, favoring them with a smile. "I'll memorize these tonight. They're already convinced I know their past and their future. I just need to drop a few quips to reinforce the idea."

"These aren't really deep, dark secrets," said the second monk apologetically. "Mostly just gossip and public information."

"That's all she needs," Sing told him. "They already believe in her power. The High Priestess just needs to give their imaginations a little kick."

"But," said Xiao. "I would like the full, updated dossier on Bad Prince Charlie. The latest information we have on him."

Both monks looked surprised. "Why?"

"I'm just interested, that's all."

"He's in Damask. It's not like he's coming here for your speech. You've already said goodbye to him."

"Oh," said Xiao, "who knows what the future holds?"

❧　❧　❧

Not surprisingly, Catherine had another sleepless night. Most of it was spent pacing up and down in her cage, periodically going to the window to see if the chopping block, by some slim chance, had magically disappeared. It was still there, well lit by moonlight. She wondered if it had ever been used before. Beheading was the punishment for those accused of treason, and up until now there hadn't been much of a problem with treason in Damask. No other country cared to learn its secrets and no one outside of the royal family had a particularly strong urge to rule it. It was entirely possible that she would be breaking in a new block.

In the next cage, the Marquis de Sadness and Lord Gagnot had gotten into a prolonged argument over Gagnot's selling of the grain reserves, with the lord still maintaining it was his right to do with them as he pleased. The marquis had appealed to Catherine to support him. "The people are starving," he said. "They have no bread to eat."

"Oh, let them eat muffins," said Catherine crossly, for at this particular time in her life she was not concerned with anyone's problems but her own. But as soon as she spoke, she regretted it. She had a suspicion that the line might go down in history as her last words, and it didn't sound quite right. *Let them eat scones? Let them eat croissants?* No. *Let them eat doughnuts?* Definitely wrong. *Brioche?* No, that was just bread again. The word was right on the tip of her tongue and she couldn't bring it out.

She was still pondering and pacing long after the rest of the cell block had dropped off to sleep. She looked at the chopping block again. A cat was sitting on top of it. There were few rats in the Barsteel. There was not enough food lying around to attract them and a regular coterie of cats to discourage them from moving in. *Too bad*, thought Catherine. She would have liked to see a rat in her cage right now. She would have kicked its beady little eyes out.

She lay down on the bed, then got up again and went to the window. She decided she would stay up all night and watch the sunrise. It might be the last sunrise she would ever see. She was at the window for an hour before she remembered that it didn't face east. The sun wouldn't shine in her window until past noon. She wondered what was taking Albemarle Gagnot so long. Men! You couldn't count on them for anything. Sure, they were quick enough with the flowers and little gifts, but expect a simple task from them, like going to the greengrocer to pick up a head of lettuce, or breaking you out of an impregnable prison, and they had nothing but excuses.

Discouraged, she went back to the bed and sat down. She wondered if she should start crying. If she started now, she would be all cried out by ten and she could go to her death with a brave face. She decided against it. She couldn't do it now without waking the other prisoners, and they would tell the story, and she would go down in history as a weak woman. That would not do at all. She would just have to tough it out. Besides, Abe could show up at any moment and she didn't want her face to be puffy and red-eyed.

Time passed. It grew light outside. The other prisoners stirred. Catherine remained sitting on the bed, staring blankly at the floor, swinging one foot. A noise came from the stairwell, someone climbing up slowly. She frowned. The guard said he would be sleeping in. He shouldn't be here for hours. Were they going to bring her some sort of last meal? The stairwell door opened and she saw the black hood of the executioner.

At once the other prisoners were on their feet, clinging

to the bars. Lord Gagnot looked horrified. The Marquis de Sadness was licking his lips and breathing heavily. No one said a word. They watched silently as the black-clad figure unlocked the door to Catherine's cage. She remained sitting, staring at him in shock. "You're early," she said. "You're not due for hours."

He said nothing, merely pulling her to her feet and out of the cage. Numbly, she allowed him to lead her to the stairwell door. It wasn't until the door closed behind her that she offered some resistance. "No!" she said hoarsely, slipping her arm out of his grasp and shrinking back against the wall. "No! It's not time yet." One foot slipped on a stair. She fell on her bottom. Behind the eye openings, bloodshot eyes looked down at her curiously. "It's not ten o'clock. That's what you said. Remember? About ten. Tennish? Champagne cocktails?" She got back up, grabbing the front of the black wool shirt. "I still have time!"

In spite of herself, she started to cry. But at once she stifled the sobs and wiped the tears away on the backs of her hands. She was not, *she was not*, going to surrender her dignity in front of this man.

The executioner took both of her hands in his and gently raised her to her feet. For the first time she noticed how old his hands were, how veined and gnarly. He slipped one finger under the edge of his hood and tugged it upward. She raised her eyes to his face. A white beard appeared, slightly stained with wine, and then a mass of unkempt white hair, surrounding a wrinkled, kindly face. He smiled at her.

"Pollocks?" she said.

"Your bastard prince regent made a grievous error," Albemarle noted with grim satisfaction. He was fixing thick wool pads to his shoulders, while his squire fixed the plates of mail to his lower body. "The choice of weapons was his, yet he chose broadswords. I know full well he's never been in the heavy cavalry. It's unlikely he has any sort of experience in fighting with a heavy sword and shield. I doubt he'll even be able to stay on his horse."

Both Packard and Gregory nodded thoughtfully. They were in the armory of Gagnot's manor house. Packard was seated in the room's other chair. Gregory was standing and leaning on his cane. The walls around them were hung with a variety of weapons; mostly heavy sabers and cut-and-thrust swords, with a scattering of lighter blades; foils and épées and even a court sword. The lighter blades tended to be more ornate. Some even had jewels in the hilts. But the heavier steel was simple and functional. Gregory noticed they all had certain things in common. They were well oiled, free of rust, and sharpened to a wicked edge.

"I wonder," said Packard, "if he thought he would be safer fighting from within a coat of mail."

"If he did, he's mistaken," said Gagnot. "The armor he has is undoubtedly ceremonial. It's designed to look good, not for actually fighting. The protection it offers is secondary to that." He tapped the steel on his chest. "This is the real thing, designed to be worn in battle. And it's proved very effective in our training sessions. It's simple, it's functional, and it's tough."

"So you're certain you'll have no trouble defeating him?"

"No trouble at all."

"I can't tell you how much we regret this," said Gregory. "We had no idea things would come to such a pass."

"In a few hours his time will have passed. Right now my concern is Lady Durace. I wonder if we should try to force our way into the Barsteel and free her and my father now."

"Oh, I don't think that is wise," Packard said quickly. "They're probably safer there, protected against any street violence that might break out."

"But he might decide to execute her before the duel. I know his type. It's the sort of vindictive thing he'd do."

"Have no fear," said Gregory. "Remember, the whole city knows he's coming out to fight a duel with you. Charlie might give an order for an execution, but no one will carry it out until they see who wins the duel."

Gagnot looked at his clock. "There is still time. Perhaps I'll pay her a visit before I ride out."

"No!" Gregory said quickly. "That wouldn't be a good idea."

"Why not?"

"Well, you know how women worry," said Packard. "It would just upset her if she knew you were going out to fight a duel."

"Because she cares so much for you," said Gregory.

"Good point. I won't tell her about the duel. I just want to see that she is all right."

"You're already dressed. You won't have time to remove your armor and put it back on again. I'll tell you what. Packy and I will visit her and give her your assurance that you will force her release."

"I'd like to tell her myself," said Gagnot reluctantly. "But I suppose you're right." He picked up his helmet and stroked the feathers adorning the top. "What do you think of these plumes?"

"I rather like them," said Packard.

"What is this?" said General Fortescue.

"A gryphon," said the sculptor. He flattened the sketch on the table for a better view.

"I asked for a horse."

"I want to try something new."

"I commissioned you because you're the best sculptor of equestrian statues in the Twenty Kingdoms. I asked for a horse because I want a horse."

"I'm tired of doing horses. I want to expand."

"And what is this?" Fortescue flipped the sketch over and studied the next one in the stack. "A tiger?"

"Exactly," said the sculptor proudly. "It's symbolic. Riding the back of a tiger represents the problems you faced when you decided to restore order to Noile."

"I'm surprised that you didn't put me on a dragon. Or a unicorn."

The sculptor looked pained. "Those are so trite, General."

"And what's this? A giant dolphin?"

"An orca. You're riding the back of a killer whale, holding a trident. Think about it, General. It would make a great fountain. I'd design it so that you'd be rising out of a foaming crest of water. Of course, some people might find the killer whale imagery too bloodthirsty."

"I'm surrounded by wolves in this next one. That's not bloodthirsty?"

"Wolves have an undeserved reputation. They're actually intelligent creatures that care for their young and mate for life."

"Spare me. You do have some horse sketches, I presume."

Reluctantly the sculptor opened his portfolio case and extracted a second batch of sketches. He handed them to the general. "I just ask that you keep an open mind, sir."

"I think you're anticipating here," Fortescue said after glancing at the top sketch. "If the horse has one foot in the air, it signifies that the rider was injured in battle. If it has two feet in the air, the rider was killed in battle. I haven't been killed yet, and all my injuries, thankfully, have been minor."

"That's a popular myth," said the sculptor. "A lot of people *think* there's a code for equestrian statues, but there really isn't. You can visit a historic battlefield and it may seem that way, but it's just a coincidence. You can make the horse stand any way you want."

Fortescue looked at the sketches again. They were done

in charcoal on vellum. He was careful not to smudge the dashing figure with his sword in the air and his hair blowing in the wind. "That horse is huge. I've never been on a horse that big. I've never even *seen* a horse that big. What breed of horse is that supposed to be?"

"The artistic license breed. People want their heroes and their heroes' horses to be larger than life. They're so used to seeing statues with oversized horses that if I made the horse actual size, it would look like you were riding a pony. I've enlarged your muscles for the same reason."

"No, they look life-size."

"You're right, they do," said the sculptor hurriedly. "The statue will be a corrosion-resistant bronze alloy. The base will be locally quarried granite. The plaques will also be bronze."

"I've seen a few statues made from that new white bronze. Rather good-looking, I thought."

"You don't want that stuff, sir," the sculptor said definitely. "Too much zinc in it. Trust me. In a few years those statues will be dissolving in the rain."

Fortescue's aide-de-camp slipped into the command tent and came to attention. "Excuse me," Fortescue told the sculptor, handing back the sketches. He stepped outside, with the aide following behind him. His regimental commanders were waiting for him. The army was camped in a cup-shaped depression, surrounded by mountainous ridges. Trees lined the slopes. Tents, wagons, mules, men, horses, and small cooking fires filled the little valley. Even though Fortescue couldn't see beyond the ridges, he looked in the direction of Damask. It was, he knew, only a half day's march from there.

He turned around and surveyed the valley. The soldiers were not yet ready to assemble, but fires were being put out, horses were being harnessed, and tents were being struck. Except for General Chomley's regiment. Their tents would not be struck until the men changed into their parade uniforms. Chomley was looking grim. Fortescue chuckled. "Relax, gentlemen. Come inside and have a glass of port. We're not marching off to battle. This is a parade. We're being *invited* in. A mere show of force is all they will require."

"Yes, sir," they all said, but Chomley added, "Unless we're being crossed, sir."

"And that is why the other regiments are here. We have wagons full of food and the troops are there to guard the wagons and keep the supply lines open. That's our story and we're sticking to it. Everyone clear on that?" They nodded. "Good. Come inside and have a glass of port." Chomley followed him back into the tent. The other commanders followed Chomley. The sculptor had just finished packing his sketches back into his portfolio. Fortescue put a hand on his shoulder. "Do you know of the Prince Regent of Damask?"

"Bad Prince Charlie? Yes, General."

"Work up some sketches of a statue for him. The boy is getting a raw deal. I think he deserves a little commemoration."

"No problem, sir. Standing, sitting, or equestrian?"

"Oh, put him on a horse, I think. He's a young man, I'm sure he'd like to be remembered that way. Two feet in the air."

"Two feet?" Chomley asked. "Are you expecting the prince regent to be killed in battle, sir?"

"Not at all," said Fortescue. "That's just a coincidence."

"But . . ." said Catherine. "How—why—how did you—what?" A lesser woman might have fainted. Catherine Durace was not the fainting type. She thought fainting was only for women who wore their corsets too tight. Nonetheless, she felt, if she ever wanted to be the fainting type, now was the perfect opportunity.

She was aware, as was everyone else at the castle, that the king's ghost had appeared on the ramparts. She had seen Pollocks stabbed before her very eyes, had seen the bloodstain spread across his chest. And it was, after all, rather dim in that stairwell. So it was not unreasonable for her to conclude that a demon from Hell was leading her to her doom.

And when the demon reached under his tunic and pulled out a dagger, her blood froze in her veins.

"A stage dagger," said Pollocks, handing it to her. "See, the blade retracts into the handle. His Highness got it from an acting company. It creates a very nice illusion of being stabbed, especially in dim light."

Catherine took the knife with shaking hands. It had a bit of a cutting edge down near the hilt, but the tip was blunt. She pressed it against her palm. An immense feeling of relief came over her as the blade slipped smoothly and quietly into the hilt. When she looked at it closely, she recognized it as the dagger that Charlie had been wearing in his belt.

"We have to move quickly," said Pollocks. "Come on." He took her by the hand again and dragged her down the remaining stairs. At the bottom, he stopped to put the executioner's hood back on. Then opened the door slowly, stuck his head out, and looked both ways.

"Where are we going?"

"Back to the castle. It's time for Charlie to leave the country, and you're going with him. It's not safe for you here."

"It's not safe for me with Charlie! He wants to kill me!"

"Not so. Packard and Gregory signed the order for your execution. They arranged it so Charlie would get the blame. The streets are empty now. Let's run."

They dashed across the street and began making their way toward the castle, using the alleys in back of the buildings. "I'm still confused," said Catherine. "Charlie got that dagger weeks ago. How long have you been planning this?"

"We didn't plan anything. We're improvising. Charlie believes his uncles killed his father and he thought they might try to kill him, too. He got the dagger so he could fake his own suicide if his back was to the wall. Then, when he saw that Packard and Gregory were ready to torture me, he pretended to kill me. So he could get me out of the castle."

"Then you knew it was a fake dagger?"

"Not until he stabbed me with it. Fortunately, I've had some theatrical experience. I was able to improvise. This way." They broke away from the buildings and trotted around to the west side of the castle. Catherine had many more questions she wanted to ask, but the older man was slowing down and panting. She put her arm around him to steady him, until they reached the wall. He leaned against it, breathing hard.

She looked around. The west wall did not have a gate. Oddly, a string of horses, saddled and bridled, had been tethered to a stake in the ground. "How do we get in?"

Pollocks pointed upward. Almost at the exact same time a rope ladder dropped down from the parapets. Catherine looked up. She couldn't see anyone. "Where are all the guards?"

"There's just a minimum crew here now. The others are riding out with the prince regent to meet Gagnot for the duel. Now, up you go."

Catherine climbed the ladder with little trouble, musing that the day already had its share of ups and down and it was still early morning. At the top, slim hands grabbed her wrists and helped her over the wall. The hands belonged to Rosalind. She hugged Catherine tightly, while whispering, "I didn't expect I'd have to help you break *into* the castle."

"You'll still have to explain it to me. Let's give Pollocks a hand." They tried to pull up on the rope ladder, but even working together they lacked the upper body strength to lift the Faithful Family Retainer. He came up under his own power, lugged himself over the wall, and sprawled on the ground. "Oof. These wall are higher than they used to be."

"Too much wine and tobacco," said Catherine reproachfully.

"Please. I get enough of that from the prince." Pollocks turned his head toward Rosalind. "What about the man who is supposed to be guarding Lady Durace's cell?"

"He's still asleep. I gave him that sleeping draught at dinner last night. He won't be up for hours."

"Good." Pollocks climbed to his feet. "Follow me, ladies."

"Where are we going?"

"To the south tower." Pollocks took her hand and tugged her along the parapets. Catherine took Rosalind's hand.

"But that's where I was being held before!"

"That's why no one will think to look for you there."

"And you'll need to pack some clothes," added Rosalind. They got to the tower without being seen and started making their way up the stairs.

"Wait a minute!" said Catherine. "I just thought of something. Blood! Pollocks, when they carried you away, your chest was covered with blood. How could you do that with a fake dagger?"

"It has a reservoir in the hilt. You fill it with tomato sauce. When the blade is pushed in, the red stuff spurts out."

Catherine took out the dagger and tested it with her finger. "No, it doesn't"

"I had linguine for dinner last night. I guess I forgot to refill it."

"Oh. Okay."

"Acting out a death is not easy, despite what you may have been told," Pollocks continued, leading them down the hallway. "A lot of people think that all you have to do is roll your eyes and fall over, but it takes more than that to be convincing. You must, essentially, *be the dead person*." He reached the door to Catherine's suite and opened it. "I had to ask myself, 'What is my motivation for dying?'"

"Your motivation was that you were stabbed," said Charlie.

"Charlie!"

"Ignore him," said Pollocks. "He has no appreciation for the craft." The prince had Catherine's smallest suitcase open on the bed. He rummaged through her wardrobe, grabbed a handful of clothes, and threw them on the bed next to the suitcase.

"But, Charlie," said Catherine, confused once again. "I don't understand. If you're here, then who is riding out to meet Gagnot?"

⚜ ⚜ ⚜

Later, every one of the many spectators agreed that the duel started out splendidly.

It was a beautiful day for it. The sun was bright, but it was still early enough that the temperature had not yet begun to climb. Because of the drought, the ground was baked hard, so there was neither mud nor large amounts of dust to contend with. A light, refreshing breeze rippled the banners. The crowd surrounding the square was large. Many had deserted their jobs at the various public works projects to see the spectacle. A large percentage of them had brought rather disconcerting tools—pitchforks and sickles and shovels and large hammers. Many were in uniform—newly minted soldiers from the various regiments raised by members of Damask's nobility. They were armed with swords and spears. Far too many had, despite the still early hour, tankards of Durk's in their hands. Alcohol and weapons—always a good combination.

The bakers and pie makers stared ruefully at the crowd.

Because of grain rationing, they had little to sell. They sighed collectively over the lost opportunity.

The lower levels of the City Hall, which commanded the square, were filled with courtiers from the castle. The hall was surrounded by soldiers and bodyguards. Packard and Gregory each had a chair in front of a large casement window, which afforded an excellent view of the proceedings.

It had begun much earlier with the meeting of the seconds, the reading of the Code Duellittante, the agreement to the field of battle, and the inspection of the weapons, followed by a break for morning tea. A band came out and played traditional battle tunes—"Whiskey in the Morning" and "Sally Juniper." Everyone rose to sing the "Damask National Anthem," which had the same melody and lyrics as the "Noile National Anthem" except the word "Damask" was substituted for "Noile." (The budget had been tight in those days and funding for a good songwriter had been rejected.) Then the seconds left to rejoin their regiments and the crowd moved to the outside of the square and waited for the parade.

Gagnot's men rode toward the square from the south. They were a private regiment. Their armor was gleaming and spotless and made for show. Their helmets were plumed in bright colors. Their swords had elaborate hilts and even more elaborate scabbards. Their spirited horses had been meticulously groomed. The animals trotted briskly forward, enjoying the chance to parade. Their colors were bright silks that flapped briskly in the light breeze. Albemarle Gagnot rode at their head. He had his helmet off. Slung over his shoulder was a small canvas pouch on a thick leather cord. The crowd cheered for him as he rode past. He waved back. Behind him rode his seconds, preceded by the color-bearer, who carried a pennant with the Gagnot family crest.

The Royal Guard rode toward the square from the north. Their armor was military issue, polished to a dull gleam, lacking the eye-catching brightness of their opponent's armor, but sturdy and functional. Their swords had simple hilts of wrapped leather, and simple leather scabbards branded with the royal crest. Their mounts were stolid warhorses, who plodded steadily forward with the world-weary attitude of horses that had been around the block a few times and seen it all. Their leader was in black armor and kept his helmet on. Behind him rode the officers who would serve as seconds. The color-bearer carried the flag of Damask, and it was only because of this that the crowd did not boo the black rider. Though many hissed in low tones.

Both factions of riders advanced to the edge of the square and stopped. The square surrounded a circular green, which was studded with cherry and flowering plum trees. Both species had suffered from the drought and looked decidedly bedraggled. Gagnot signaled with his hand for his men to stay in place and rode forward, stopping at the center of the green. He watched the black rider across the green, expecting him to ride forward also. Instead the rider stayed in place. Gagnot tried to hide his uncertainty. Did the prince regent expect Abe to come over to him? Was that the correct thing to do? Or would he be demeaning himself by seeming to submit to Charlie's authority?

The black rider remained motionless. Behind him, his seconds lifted up the helmets of their faceplates and looked at him. Gagnot could tell they were as uncertain as he was. A mutter of discontent rose from the crowd, who were by no means contented to begin with. Gagnot made a hasty decision: He would ride forward, but with his men. They outnumbered the Royal Guards. Crossing the square would allow them to show their force. He was about to raise his hand to call his men forward, when the black rider flipped his reins and began to move.

Instead of riding forward, he turned to his left and rode *around* the square. He rode in front of the spectators, who glared at him resentfully, and he rode in front of Gagnot's own troops, nodding curtly to them as though this was an inspection! Gagnot seethed. The black rider crossed the other side of the square, stopped to consider a sweetmeat stand, apparently decided not to buy anything, and continued back to his starting point. Only then did he turn his horse onto the green and ride forward to meet Gagnot.

He stopped with his horse next to Gagnot's, so the two men were side by side. Gagnot glared at him. Two boys ran out, one from either side of the square, carrying the broadswords. Abe took his gilded and bejeweled scabbard and buckled it on. He waited while the black rider buckled on his own plain black scabbard, and while the two boys ran back to the street.

"All right, *Prince* Charlie. No excuses this time, and no one to interfere with us. Your foul reign has come to an end." He paused for dramatic effect. "This time we finish it."

The man inside the helmet made a snorting noise. Gagnot ignored it.

"Your Royal Guards are outnumbered by even my own men, not withstanding the fact that the other lords, with their regiments, have also turned against you. The commoners will not support you. Even if you defeat me today you cannot maintain your position. But you will not defeat me. You know that you cannot match my skill in armored combat.

"Nonetheless, Charlie, I am going to show you mercy." Gagnot reached into the small canvas pouch and withdrew a scroll. "This is a letter of abdication. Sign it and I will guarantee you safe passage across the border. My men will escort you. You have my word." He held the scroll out.

"I say, Abe, you know what this reminds me of?" Oratorio said cheerfully. He lifted up the visor to his helmet. "My initiation into the frat. They made us all dress up in girlie underthings, don't you know, and . . ."

Gagnot's howl of anger could be heard clear back to the castle.

❧ ❧ ❧

"Shush," said Charlie. Everyone stood still while he listened. A faint roar could be heard from the city. "That's it then. The revolution has started. Gagnot will seize the castle. Fortescue will be here tonight. We've got to get you out of the country." He yanked open a chest of drawers and started pulling out clothes.

"Charlie! Stop!"

"What?" Charlie turned around. Catherine and Rosalind were both staring at him in shock. He looked behind him. "What?"

"That's my underwear drawer. You can't handle a lady's unmentionables."

"Oh. Sorry."

Catherine took his hands and pulled him away from the bed. "Rosalind will pack those. But, Charlie, why do I need to leave? Abe isn't going to harm me."

"My uncles will. They're the ones who signed your death warrant. They never intended to sell out to Noile. They want to take it over. Sure, they'll reunify the two countries, but under Damask's rule. If they get to the WMD before I do, that's exactly what they'll do. And they don't want you in their way."

"The Weapon of Magical Destruction? You mean it really exists? You found it?"

"Tell her, Pollocks."

The Faithful Family Retainer nodded. "It's hidden in the Temple of Matka."

"Fortescue's camped in a shallow valley just over the border. If the WMD is detonated there, his whole army will be wiped out. Noile will be defenseless. Even Damask will be able to take it over, and our troops are already mobilized." He gave Pollocks a stern look. "If you had confided in me right from the start, Pollocks, all this could have been avoided."

Pollocks looked contrite. "I'm sorry, Your Highness. But we didn't know if you could be trusted. Perhaps if you had confided more in me . . ."

"Yes, well, what's done is done." The noise from outside was growing louder. He ran to the window. The others followed him. "They're coming here. A mob has formed. It's all like we planned."

"I'm largely responsible for that," said Pollocks. "It was news of my noble death that pushed their simmering resentment to the boiling point." He took a clipping out of his wallet. "I don't know if you saw this in the paper. *'The tragic and valiant death of the late king's Faithful Family Retainer has stirred the passions of every soul in Damask.'* 'Stirred the passions,' did you hear? That's what a good performance can achieve."

"Yeah right," said the prince. "You nearly gave the whole thing away with your cheesy acting."

"*You* nearly gave the whole thing away with the smell of garlic and oregano! What possessed you to fill the knife with marinara sauce?"

"I'm the prince regent! It's not easy for me to slip down to the kitchen without being noticed. I had to grab the first tomato sauce I could find."

"Gentlemen," Catherine interrupted. "They're heading this way. Do we have a plan, or what?"

"Your suitcase," said Rosalind, holding it up. Charlie took it from her. He led them out the door and back the way they came, stopping once to look in the direction of the city. There was a cloud of dust where horses' hooves had thrown up the dry dirt, and emerging from it they could see the gray-and-green uniforms of the Royal Guard, fighting a defensive retreat back to the castle. Already the guards remaining at the castle had thrown open the gate to let them in. Charlie nodded, then motioned for the others to follow him. He took them back to the west wall, where Rosalind and Catherine had left the rope ladder pulled up. He pointed to the horses below.

"Those are for us. Oratorio is just fighting a delaying action, keeping the mob from getting here too soon. But he's also trying to minimize casualties, so the guard isn't fighting too hard. Once he's sure we're away, he'll open the gates to Gagnot's men and surrender the castle. If he can slip away later, he'll catch up with you and escort you to Bitburgen. It's in a neutral country, and there are lots of un-attached young women going to the university, so it's a good place to lay low for a while and not be noticed."

"Where are you going, Charlie?"

"To Matka. I've got to destroy the WMD. I'll join you later in Bitburgen."

"Why Bitburgen? Why not Noile? Fortescue will pro-tect me."

Charlie shook his head. "I don't trust Fortescue, either. If he manages to get the WMD, he won't need you. You'll just be more competition. After this blows over, you can decide if you want to join him in Noile. Or . . ."

He stopped, swallowed hard, and looked at Pollocks. Pollocks discreetly turned away. Charlie took Catherine's hand. "Or you could stay with me," he said uncertainly. "It doesn't have to be Bitburgen. Any country, any city, I can take you there. Or we could travel. The Twenty Kingdoms, or overseas, even to the Far East. I've got plenty of money. It's all invested in . . . invested in . . . Hey, Pollocks? What did my mother invest her money in, anyway?"

"A chain of coffee shops, Your Highness."

"Really? Huh. Anyway, what do you think?"

Catherine took his other hand in hers. "Charlie, do you remember the night we went out to dinner?"

"I'll never forget a moment of it."

"Do you remember what we talked about?"

"Um, maybe I've forgotten that part."

"I asked you if you ever considered petitioning the Council of Lords to declare you legitimate, so you could inherit the throne of Damask?"

"Oh, right. I laughed, because it was such a silly idea. Ruling isn't really my sort of thing."

Catherine gave him a sad little smile. "No," she said. "It really isn't." She kissed him on the cheek. "Go now. Find the WMD. Don't worry about me. I know what I have to do."

"I'll see you later then." Charlie swung his leg over the parapet and was down the rope ladder in less than a minute. He untethered two horses, sprang onto one, and took off up the mountain road leading the other.

"We need to be going, too," said Pollocks.

"Wait," said Catherine. "Let him get a good start. Then if there are any pursuers, we can lead them off in the other direction."

"Ah. Good thinking."

"Or . . ." said Catherine. She stared after the retreating figure.

"Or what?"

Catherine was silent for a while, her brow creased in thought. She watched Charlie until he disappeared around a turn. "I really did think about marrying him, you know. Do you think Charlie would have made a good king?"

Pollocks looked at the now empty road. "I suppose," he said doubtfully. "He's smart enough, and he's willing to make unpopular decisions. But he is not an ambitious man."

"Sometimes a man just needs a woman to give him direction in life."

"Yes, that would be Charlie. He would do very well with the right woman. But King of Noile? His heart wouldn't be in it."

"No," said Catherine. She still had Pollocks's dagger

tucked in her sash. She pulled it out and toyed with it. "But I would make a good queen."

"I'm sure you'd have been very popular here in Damask."

"Noile, too."

"I suppose you would, but that's little more than a day-dream. It's not like Damask, where the line of succession is muddled. There are at least four people, perhaps five, in Noile who very definitely stand between you and the throne."

"Things can change," said Catherine. She held the dagger up to the sun. A bright line of light gleamed on the sharp edge near the hilt. "There might be accusations of treason. There might be arrests. It wouldn't be difficult to arrange. A few accidents, a few executions, and there I am."

Pollocks looked shocked. "It is true that those things can be made to happen, my lady. But our Prince Charlie would never do such things."

Catherine was leaning over the parapet, looking at the rope ladder stretching nearly to the ground, and at the re-maining horses grazing on the brown grass. "No," she said, almost to herself, and so low that Pollocks couldn't hear her. "He wouldn't." With her hands out of sight behind the stone, she sliced through one side of the rope ladder. "But Fortescue would." In a quick motion she severed the other half and watched it fall silently to the grounds. She tossed the dagger after it. It clattered on the stones.

"What was that?" Pollocks came up to her. He looked over the wall. "What! What happened to the ladder? What did you do?"

Catherine took off running.

She ran along the parapets, back to the main gate. Ros-alind, too surprised to follow, stayed behind. Pollocks tried to catch Catherine, but couldn't keep up with the much younger woman. She reached the front of the castle and

leaned over the top of the wall, trying to make sense of the
confusion below. A short, double line of the Royal Guards
had formed up in front of the gate. A dozen or so mounted
knights were riding back and forth in front of them, trying
to break the line, but held at bay by the foot soldiers' pikes.
Behind them circulated a vast and disorganized melee of
foot soldiers, foot guards, mounted guards, mounted
knights, and armed commoners, all shouting, shoving,
brandishing swords, threatening each other, and choking
on dust. In back of all that, a royal carriage with Packard
and Gregory had pulled off the road. Charlie's uncles stood
on the roof of the carriage, where they could get a better
view of the action.

Catherine took out a handkerchief and waved it, hoping
to draw attention. "Abe! Albemarle Gagnot!"

A mounted knight detached himself from the mob and
rode to the castle wall. "Lady Catherine?" The knight tilted
up his visor just as Pollocks arrived at the gate, so the old
man could clearly see that it was Albemarle Gagnot who
was looking at them. And it was Albemarle Gagnot that
Catherine was calling to.

"Abe, he's gone up the mountain road. Prince Charlie.
He's on his way to Matka. You've got to stop him!"

⚜   ⚜   ⚜

Charlie knew he was being pursued and had little time. He
rode his horses until they faltered and abandoned the last
one on the shores of Lake Organza, reaching the temple on
foot. It seemed deserted. The monks in their sky-blue robes
were gone. The bright silk banners had been taken away,
the fountains were still and sprinkled with dry leaves.
There was no smell of incense, no chiming of bells, no
eerie atonal music. The coffee shops were boarded up. He
was not surprised. He understood now that the so-called
Cult of Matka had completed its mission. But the Prince
Regent of Damask was not completed with his. Not yet.

He found the building where he had met with Fortescue, and the larger building with the oracle's rock, where the monks developed their predictions. He found Xiao's private boudoir. All of these rooms were empty, the furniture and tapestries stripped away. A cold wind blew through the empty corridors. The Temple of Matka had been abandoned once again. Already green shoots were growing up through the blocks of paving stone.

He's here, said Charlie to himself. *He's got to be here. He can't take it with him and he wouldn't leave it behind.* He ran back to the main gate and looked in the direction of Damask. A faint cloud of dust was rising over the mountain ridges. It was enough to tell him that the castle had been taken and the army was after him.

He ran to the main temple, under the great, pale gray dome. It, too, was deserted, and when he called "Thessalonius?" the words echoed off the stone walls. He pushed open the door to the Great Hall. It had no windows and, without torchiers or candles, was too dark to see. "Thessalonius, I know you're here." He stood in the darkness, listening. He couldn't hear anything, not breathing or movement, nothing more than the rustle of insects and the gentle hiss of the wind, yet he felt that indefinable presence that always exists when a second person is with you in a room. He was about to go back out and search for a lantern, when a spark was struck on the other side of the hall, and a candle sputtered to life.

The prince let out a breath of relief. He walked toward the light. From this distance he couldn't see the man behind the candle, but he was sure he knew who it was. "Hey, Thessalonius. It's me, Charlie. Where have you been hiding all this time?" When he got closer, he could see a figure sitting on a low chair, tightly wrapped in one of the blue monk robes, with the hood pulled close around his face. Charlie looked around for a second chair as he crossed the Great Hall. Not seeing one—not seeing anything, in fact, in the cavernous dark room—he settled to the floor to sit cross-legged. As he did so, the man in the robes casually set the candle on the ground, so that Charlie's face was illuminated while his own face remained in shadow.

"It's been a long time, Thessalonius," he started out. "How have you been?" The man in the robes didn't answer this, but acknowledged Charlie's presence with a nod. "I'm an idiot. I should have figured this out earlier," the prince went on. "Jeremy was right. You have more skill than anyone alive in predicting the weather. The whole history of the Twenty Kingdoms hasn't produced more than a handful of people who could make any kind of prediction with any kind of reliability. There's no way a whole succession of young girls would all be able to prophesy. If they were making accurate predictions—and they had to make at least a few, to keep the cult going—it was because you were feeding predictions to them. You started this place, didn't you? I should have seen that right away."

"People see what they want to see." The voice in the darkness was low, dry, and raspy.

"Yeah, maybe. Not all the time, though. I came here expecting to see a scam. I thought I was so smart. I didn't realize how brilliant you were. You were actually running an intelligence network."

The man in the hood let out a short, hoarse laugh. "Now don't pretend you figured that out yourself, young Charlie. Pollocks told you all about it, I'm sure."

"No, you're wrong. I did figure it out, after my second visit. I wasn't sure about Pollocks then. I didn't know whose side he was on, until my uncles caught him sending you a message by carrier pigeon. But running a string of spies in Damask—and I'm sure you have them in Noile also—was just supplementary information. The real beauty of this thing was that people came here and *told you their secrets*. Military secrets, business secrets, personal secrets, they told everything and *they even paid* to have someone listen. You had a whole team of people to compile the information. To top it off, you had a sequence of hot girls as priestesses. That made it perfect. Guys can't resist showing off their knowledge to a pretty girl. Dammit, I was doing it myself."

"You were a lot more careful than most men, Charlie. There have only been two men who figured out my little game so quickly. And while I'm sure you won't appreciate this comparison, your father was the other one. In fact, he's the one who really took my simple oracle cult and built an intelligence network around it. It allowed him to follow what was going on in Noile during the time of troubles. He was able to keep Damask independent without spending a lot of money on the military."

"Oh, I never said that my father was a stupid man. Just that I didn't like him. But he, or his ghost, told me something I do agree with. This project you've been working on. It's too dangerous to let it fall into the wrong hands. And there are no right hands for something like that. You have to let me destroy it."

There was a long silence. Charlie forced himself to keep quiet, to let the older man speak first, although he couldn't refrain from a nervous glance at the door. He didn't know how long he had before the army got here. Thessalonius finally said, "I've given my life to that project, Charlie."

"I know you put a lot of work into it, Thessalonius. But sometimes things don't work out the way we want them to. Think about the chickens. If you don't . . ."

"Shut up about the chickens!" The sorcerer's voice held a surprising vehemence. Charlie slid back on the floor. "All my life I've been hearing about the chickens. You make one mistake and they never let you forget about it."

"Sorry."

"Did it ever occur to you that maybe that was all to the good? That Damask is better off without chickens? Do you know how many people choke to death on chicken bones each year?"

"No. How many?"

"I don't know. But I bet it's a lot. And then there's feather allergies and avian influenza and . . . and . . . lots of other stuff."

"Okay, okay." Charlie didn't want to get the old man upset. "Let's talk about the rain. Can you make it rain or not?"

"Rain? What are you talking about?"

"Come on, Thessalonius. Don't be coy with me. You were building a rain-making device, right? That's why it had to be up here in the mountains, right? The WMD isn't meant to be a super weapon. Did you finish it? Can you make it rain? If you can, we have to set it off now, because two armies are on their way to grab it. The crops aren't going to last another week without it anyway."

"Charlie, if I could make it rain on demand I would be the greatest sorcerer who ever lived."

"Some people think you *are* the greatest sorcerer who ever lived. I asked Jeremy if it was possible for a sorcerer to make it rain. He said no. He said that the power in a single thunderstorm was greater than all the magical spells ever cast. Now, I know that for decades sorcerers have been talking about tapping into some tremendous source of magical power, something that would be used to make a super weapon."

"The infamous Weapon of Magical Destruction that everyone is searching for."

"Yes." Charlie allowed a touch of smugness to creep into his voice. "Except Dad would not have backed a weapons project like that. He had no interest in war or conquest. But he was always trying to get more water into Damask. Everyone knew you were working on a big, secret project. That had to be it. Something so powerful it could change the weather."

"Very reasonable." Thessalonius shook his head admiringly. "I must admire your deductive powers, Charlie. The way that you sorted out the clues and came to a logical conclusion is quite admirable."

"Thank you."

"It is, however, completely wrong. I haven't the slightest idea how to make it rain. It's quite impossible. I never even considered it for a moment."

Charlie lay back on the floor and stared in the direction of the ceiling, which was invisible in the darkness. For a long time he was silent. Eventually he said, "Okay, I'm not too surprised. I guess in the back of my mind I always knew that I was indulging in wishful thinking. I wanted a peaceful solution to our problems. And . . . I wanted . . . to think that my father had something better going on than building a weapon."

"Oh, I expect there's still room for cautious optimism."

"Yeah. I'm still going to make sure this WMD isn't going to be used. Not by Fortescue, not by my uncles, and not by anyone else." The prince stood up. "And Thessalonius, I'm getting you out of here. If you built one WMD, they can force you to build another."

"That is not going to happen."

"Don't be so sure." Charlie bent down and picked up the candle. "None of them are above using torture. And modern torture methods will make anyone—my God!"

He brought the candle closer to the sorcerer's face. "Thessalonius, what happened to you?"

The old man pulled back the hood of his robe and let it settle around his shoulders. Charlie almost looked away, shocked at the sight of the raw, peeling skin and deep, open sores. The sorcerer gave another brief, raspy laugh, a laugh that finally told Charlie the man was desperately ill, and wasn't going to live long enough to be coerced by anyone. "Powerful magic, Charlie. Dangerous magic. I learned about it the hard way. That's why no one else will try to make another WMD after I'm gone. And that's why it took so long."

"To do what?"

"To make it clean. The original WMD would have left residual magic."

"What do you mean? Can this be reversed? Thessalonius, we need to get you into a hospital."

"It means the area around the WMD and everything downwind would have been contaminated for centuries. It would have thrown up a cloud of magically impregnated dust. Nothing that it touched would have survived for long." The sorcerer took another long, raspy breath. "And no, it can't be reversed. I'm dying and no magic or medicine will save me."

"Where is it, Thessalonius?"

"Not to worry, my boy. I succeeded. It took my life, but eventually I figured out how to make a clean release. It can be used with no hazard of long-term contamination."

"So that's what the Weapon of Magical Destruction is? A cloud of poisonous dust? And you've eliminated that?"

"Totally eliminated it, yes."

"There's no chance at all of deadly magical contamination?"

"None whatsoever."

Charlie's relief was palpable. He let out his breath in a long, heartfelt whoosh. "That takes a load off my mind. I was terribly afraid of Noile using this on Damask, or Damask using it on Noile, or Fortescue using it on anyone, but if there's no longer any danger . . ."

"Just from the explosion."

"There's an explosion, too?"

"Oh, didn't I mention that? An explosion such as the world has never seen. An entire city leveled in the twinkling of an eye. An army slaughtered at the snap of a finger. Soldiers, civilians, men, women, children, dogs, cats, horses, birds, no one is spared. Even the earthworms in the ground will die. Ships at sea will burst into flame . . ."

"Enough!"

"And the beauty of it is that there is no contamination. You can wipe out a city in one day, and the next day you can move in and start building. No, wait, that's not quite right. You would have to wait for the firestorm to burn out. Say, a couple of weeks."

"There's a firestorm!"

"Oh yes. Anyone who survives the initial blast will perish in the firestorm. They don't even have to be close enough to burn. The updraft will be so strong it will suck the air out of their lungs."

"No it won't, because it is not going to be used," said Charlie grimly. "I don't care how clean it is. I'm going to destroy it. Now tell me where it is, dammit!"

"No need to shout, my boy. It's at the bottom of Lake Organza."

"What?"

"I promised your father I'd keep it in a safe place. It can't get much safer than that."

"At the bottom of the lake? Are we talking at the bottom of the lake for good, or at the bottom of the lake attached to a rope and buoy so it can be located and pulled up?"

"At the bottom of the lake for good. There is no marker. It is not coming up. There it stays."

"And no one can use it? Are you sure?"

"Oh, I could do something with it. But I'm not going to. And no threat of torture, or torture itself, will sway me." The sorcerer took another long breath, followed by a long raspy laugh. "There is nothing they can do to me that will outdo what I am suffering already. Death, my boy, will be welcome at this point."

"I'm sorry to hear that," said the prince, with as much sympathy as he could muster for a man who, in Charlie's opinion, had brought about his own demise. "But we're safe from the WMD. My uncles won't be able to use it against Noile. Noile won't be able to use it against Damask, or anyone else. You're certain about this? Why did you take such risks to complete it if you were just going to throw it in the lake?"

"Oh, you know how the mind of a sorcerer works, Charlie. We're always doing strange things."

"Stop laughing like that, Thessalonius. You're creeping me out."

The sorcerer stopped his raspy laugh. He looked at Charlie solemnly. "Your Highness, you have my most sincere promise—the sacred word of a dying sorcerer—that your enemies will never use that Weapon of Magical Destruction."

The prince eyed him warily. Charlie didn't trust people who sounded too honest and sincere. More often than not, it just meant they had a lot of practice lying. But he had nothing more to say to Thessalonius. He'd been repeating himself already.

"And now, Your Highness," Thessalonius went on. "I suggest that you leave this place. Right away. It is my destiny to end my life in this temple, but you have another path to follow. And speaking of paths, you should not take the one to Noile. It is blocked by General Fortescue's men."

"I can't take the road back to Damask, either. The whole army is after my head."

"They won't get it." Thessalonius broke into a deep coughing fit. When he recovered his breath he spoke on. "I have some small ability to accurately predict the future, Charlie. You know that. So I can confidently say that you will not be captured by Damask. Go ahead and take that road."

It seemed to be as good a choice as any. Charlie nodded. He walked back to the door of the Great Hall. At the doorway, he turned and looked back, at the single candle, throwing a small pool of light in the cavernous room, and the shadowy, hooded figure, a frail, sick man sitting in that pool of yellow light. He was about to say goodbye when the sorcerer blew out the candle and vanished into the cool, quiet darkness.

Charlie left the Great Hall and made his way back out of the temple. He wandered around the deserted grounds a little bit, tossed a few pebbles into an empty fountain, then left the temple complex and started walking along the shore of Lake Organza, in the direction of the Damask road. He now regretted riding his horses so hard and leaving them behind. He would have to round one up, or make his escape on foot. Though he didn't mind walking. It gave him time to think, for he was at something of a loss about what to do with himself.

The search for the WMD, and his attempt to prevent it from falling into the wrong hands, had occupied his thoughts and much of his time since the lecture by his father's ghost. That search was now finished. The danger was gone. But Charlie had not been the one to destroy the weapon. Thessalonius had flung it into the lake before Charlie even knew about it, so Charlie didn't even have a feeling of achievement at the conclusion of his mission.

He couldn't return to Damask. He'd done everything he could to compensate for the drought, with his water rationing and food rationing and public works programs. He had tried to minimize the suffering, and he thought he handled it pretty well, but he'd been chased out. Either his uncles or Fortescue had to finish the job.

Catherine was committed to General Fortescue. Charlie kicked himself mentally, and then kicked himself again for being infatuated with her. He should have realized she was just leading him on. "Dammit, you're not a teenager," he told himself. "You're twenty years old, for God's sake. How could you be such a fool?"

I should have spent more time with Xiao, he thought. Pollocks was probably right. She had seemed genuinely interested in him and he thought she would probably be fun to hang out with when she wasn't doing her seeress act. But Xiao was gone now.

Back to school, he decided. It wasn't a cheering

thought. The classroom had little appeal to him after the events of the summer, but he figured he needed the mental discipline. Lose himself in study. History, geometry, classical literature. Put politics and romance out of his mind.

He came to the end of the lake, where he and Pollocks had stopped to water their horses on his first visit, and where the pile of stone rubble from the old tunnel attempt remained. A few hundred yards away was the start of the road to Damask. Charlie was pleased to see one of his horses grazing by the trailhead, apparently rested now.

He walked toward the horse. He had gone only a few steps when a pair of riders came up the trail. Without hesitation they rode straight toward him. Charlie didn't worry at first. Hadn't Thessalonius already told him he would not be killed or captured by Damask troops? But they seemed to be riding toward him rather quickly, and with hostile intent. More riders followed them, exiting from the trail in twos and threes.

Charlie looked around for cover. The only thing that looked remotely defensible for a man on foot was the pile of stone from the old tunnel. He casually altered his direction toward it. Not casually enough, apparently, for the two lead riders angled their horses to cut him off.

Sorcerers, thought Charlie, *have been wrong before.* He ran.

The riders spurred their horses.

Charlie almost made it. The first rider drew his saber and reached Charlie just as the prince reached the base of the rock pile. A heavy saber moving at the speed of a galloping horse delivers a fearsome blow, but Charlie was a strong young man and managed to parry it with his own sword. The force was still enough to knock him off his feet. He scrambled back in time to dodge the second rider and deliver a wicked slash to his thigh as he rode past. By the time the first rider wheeled his horse around, Charlie was on top of a boulder and able to strike at eye height. A clash of swords was all that resulted.

He scrambled to the top of the heap. The rock pile was soon surrounded by a circle of mounted soldiers. Had they attacked on foot, Charlie would have been dead in a minute. But a diffusion-of-responsibility situation developed. No one could ride a horse up the pile of loose rock. Yet each man knew that he, personally, had an advantage while he was on a horse. No one wanted to be the first to dismount and climb the rock to face Charlie's sword.

This sort of standoff can last indefinitely, usually until an officer shows up to order men up the hill. And, unfortunately, an officer did show up. Then more officers, and more soldiers, until a pretty sizable force of men surrounded Charlie. From his vantage at the top of the heap, he saw Albemarle Gagnot emerge from the trailhead.

Damn, he thought. He worked out a quick, desperate plan in his head. He would wait until some men dismounted and formed up to assault the hill. While they were still at the bottom, and not expecting him, he would charge them with his sword drawn and attempt to slash his way through their ranks. Then he would leap onto one of their horses and gallop away at full speed.

This plan gave Charlie the longevity of a pint of pilsner at Oktoberfest, but he couldn't think of anything else. He looked toward Gagnot again, and was surprised to see that he hadn't moved. He wasn't even looking at Charlie. He had stopped his horse near the trailhead. He was looking back, apparently waiting for someone.

The horses around Charlie began to stir, restlessly. The other riders were also looking toward the trailhead. It seemed they were all waiting for someone. The mystery didn't last long. After a few more minutes Packard and Gregory rode out to the lakeshore. This seemed to be the signal for everyone to turn their attention back to the prince.

He stood with his sword in hand, watching them approach at a leisurely pace. It gave him time to reflect that the pile of broken rock he was standing on made a pretty good metaphor for his ruined political career, and that someone of a more poetic bent could probably make a pretty snappy epic out of this. But he didn't get much further with those musings. The soldiers parted to let Gagnot through. He stopped his horse to talk with some officers, pointedly ignoring Charlie. Packard and Gregory continued to the edge of the rock pile and faced it with distaste.

Gregory looked up. "I don't suppose you'd like to come down here and have a little chat."

"I'm fine right here," Charlie assured him.

Packard was already off his horse and picking his way up among the boulders. Gregory followed him, muttering imprecations under his breath. When they got to the top of the heap, Packard took off his hat and fanned himself with it. "Nice day, Charlie."

"The lake is especially lovely," Charlie agreed.

"Cut it out," snapped Gregory. "Where's the WMD? Where's Thessalonius?"

Charlie looked at Packard. "I thought I was supposed to be the short-tempered, irritable one around here."

"The original deal is still on," said Packard. "You'll get a share of the payoff and safe passage to the border. I'm sorry things didn't work out for you with Catherine, but you know, that wasn't really in the cards to begin with."

"Who do you think you're kidding? You planned to kill us both."

"Charlie, that was a mistake in judgment. But no harm has been done and we've seen the error of our ways."

"Oh really? Did Catherine go along with this?"

"We talked with her. She's still playing both sides of the fence. She slipped away to join Fortescue, but if we come back with the WMD, she'll throw her lot in with us and we'll put her on the throne of Noile."

"How convenient."

"Charlie, look around you," said Gregory. "There's half a regiment here. As soon as we get out of the way they'll be all over you. What are you going to do? Fight them all?"

"Abe won't let them attack. Not after I tell him that you two planned this insurrection. Not after he learns that you two ordered Catherine's death."

"I'm afraid he will, Charlie. Before she left, Catherine told him that you would spin a wild conspiracy story similar to what you just said and not to believe you. Just one of your paranoid fantasies, she told him, and proof that you are unfit to rule. We confirmed it, of course."

"That was nice of you." Charlie showed his annoyance by banging the point of his sword against a rock. They had figured all the angles. "Forget it. You're not getting the WMD. Thessalonius described its powers to me. You can't be trusted with it."

"Charlie, be realistic!" Gregory was on the verge of losing his temper. "*It's over*, Charlie. The grain reserves are nearly gone. The crops are wilting. There's no rain in sight. What are you going to do? Let people starve?"

"They won't starve. Fortescue has food. He'll take Damask anyway, WMD or no WMD. He's on his way already. You know that."

"But he *won't pay us, dammit*!" Gregory screeched.

"Too bad," Charlie shot right back. "I know about your plans to attack Fortescue and I won't be part of it."

Packard kept his patient tone of voice. "You're the prince regent, Charlie. You have to show some leadership now. You know Damask cannot sustain itself. Either we seize Noile, or Noile seizes Damask. Do you think Gregory and I will be worse than Fortescue? You know what kind of expansionist plans he has. Come on, Charlie. Sure, we all admired him when he pacified Noile. Sure, we all breathed easier when he brought an end to the troubles. But with the WMD, he'll give us never-ending war."

"And what are you planning to do with it? Destroy him and his army, right? Instant death for thousands, or tens of thousands of men."

"They're *soldiers*, Charlie. It's their job to die in battle. Fortescue would use it on a city. We'll do it here in the mountains. It won't go anywhere near a major population center."

"You're a true humanitarian, Uncle Packard. But it doesn't matter. The WMD is gone. Thessalonius dumped it in the lake. Like Uncle Gregory just said, be realistic. It's over."

"He dumped it in this lake?" said Packard. "Lake Organza?" He turned around to look at Gregory.

Something in the way his two uncles exchanged glances made Charlie uneasy. "Yes?"

Both men turned their backs to him now. They carefully picked their way to the bottom of the rocks. Packard called over his shoulder, "Charlie, did you know the average depth of Lake Organza is a hundred and seventy feet?"

"Um, no. It is? How do you know?"

"Your father commissioned a study some years ago. I had no idea why at the time, but there it is."

Gregory was already talking to Gagnot. "Abe, send a messenger to Damask. We'll need a shipwright up here right away. And a team of carpenters. We're going to build a raft."

"Two rafts," said Packard. "It will save time. Get two sets of chains and dredges up here. We're going to drag the lake."

"What?" said Charlie. "You can't drag Lake Organza."

They ignored him. Gregory looked around the lake. "We'll fell the timber for the barges here. Send for some axes and set your men to cutting trees."

"It won't work," said Charlie. "Dragging the lake. Thessalonius thought of that, I'm sure."

"And get some of those things for squaring off logs. What are they called, Packy?"

"Adzes, I think."

"Right. Get some adzes. Oh, and kill Charlie."

Gagnot smiled. He dismounted. "You heard the man." His glance took in a half dozen soldiers. "Behind me." The other men got off their horses and formed a wedge behind and to the side of Gagnot. They drew their swords. The mounted soldiers shifted their horses to give them room to maneuver.

Packard and Gregory reached the bottom of the heap and separated to get out of Gagnot's way. Gagnot kept his eyes fixed on Charlie. "On my command," he said, loudly enough for everyone, and especially Charlie, to hear, "we charge."

Charlie sheathed his sword, drew himself up to his full height, and favored Gagnot with what he hoped was a confident sneer. "Try it, Abe, and you're a dead man." He grabbed the chain around his neck. "I'm warning you. I have a—AAAAGH!"

His scream of pain startled the horses and echoed off the surrounding mountains. Everyone jumped. Packard and Gregory turned around. Gagnot shook his head, as if to clear it, and said, "What was that about? You have a what? A backache?"

Charlie had grabbed the chain around his neck and yanked it with all his strength, intending to snap it free in a dramatic manner. But both the chain and clasp proved unexpectedly sturdy. He had merely succeeded in driving the gold links into his skin. He rubbed his neck. A welt started to rise. More carefully, he pulled the chain over his head and held it in the air. "Ah, that was just to get your attention. I have a getting-out-of-a-tight-spot device."

It got their attention, all right. Every man on the ground took an involuntary step backward, while the men on horseback tightened their grips on the reins. Then Gagnot, not wishing to appear cowardly in front of his men, stepped to the front again. "Really," he said in a silky voice. "You know, I've never seen one before. A genuine getting-out-of-a-tight-spot device.* And what, exactly, does it do?"

"Um," said Charlie. He looked at the crystal dangling from his hand. "That I cannot tell you. . . ."

"But we'll know when the time comes," chorused Gagnot, Packard, Gregory, and, in fact, pretty much the entire army. No one smiled, but Charlie had the distinct feeling they were laughing at him. He looked around angrily.

"Fine!" he said. "Have it your way!" He grabbed the gold and crystal pendant and squeezed it. There was the tiniest click, the gold wire holding the crystal sprang open like the petals of a flower, and the crystal itself dropped into Charlie's palm. Without hesitation he flung it at Gagnot and threw up his arms to protect his face.

The crystal caught the sun as it flew through the air. The tiny, glittering object transcribed a flattened arc, struck a boulder, glanced off, hit the ground, and bounced on the rocks to stop at Gagnot's feet. Gagnot also flung up his arms in a defensive gesture, as did most of the men who stood around him. But when nothing happened, they lowered their arms and eyed it warily. Gagnot himself bent over it. He was careful not to touch it, but he studied it cautiously. The crystal gave off a brief flicker of red light, like a candle sputtering just before it dies. Then it did nothing. It did not even sparkle. It lay on ground, dull and inert. He smiled thinly and straightened up.

"My, wasn't that anticlimactic?" He ran his thumb along the edge of his sword. "Any more surprises for us,

---

*Lowe, Nick. "The Well-Tempered Plot Device," *Ansible*. July 1986. Look, a real footnote! It follows *CMS* and everything.

Prince Regent? No? Then I think it's time to put an end to this."

He made a few exploratory swipes in the air with his sword, extended it in Charlie's direction, and raised his left hand to motion his men to follow him. He paused to give them a chance to resume their formation, then threw his hand forward and down. "Attack!" And he charged up the slope.

He was about halfway to the top when he realized that no one was following him. He looked down and saw the rest of his men still gathered at the bottom of the rock pile. He looked up and saw Charlie had his sword back out and aimed at Gagnot's heart. Without a signal from his brain, Gagnot's feet quickly terminated the advance, controlled by an ancient and primordial instinct—the desire not to impale oneself on a naked blade. Then, feeling more than a little ridiculous standing by himself, waving a sword, halfway up a pile of rocks in the middle of nowhere, he tried to make surreptitious signals to his soldiers below to join him.

The problem was, they weren't looking at him.

The men on the lake side of the rock pile had turned completely around and were staring at the water. The men on the opposite side were moving around the rock pile to get a better view, quietly and politely threading their way among the men in front of them. Even the horses seemed to be jockeying for position. Gagnot looked to where they were staring, and found himself staring also.

Packard and Gregory left the group entirely and walked to the water's edge. Out in the lake, perhaps half a mile from shore, the water was roiling and bubbling. It almost looked like it was boiling, but they knew that was not the case, for they could see fish jumping and playing in the foam, and occasionally the wind brought the mist to shore, where they all could feel its coolness against their skin. Twice the height of a man, the water lifted itself from the lake surface in a great pile of foam, and bubbles that caught the sunlight and reflected iridescent gold and blue and red. At its source, the roiling and bubbling must have been quite loud, but from the shore, the soldiers could only hear a pleasant, harmonious fizzing. It was all quite hypnotic—the bubbles, constantly forming and collapsing, the flashes of color and light, the melodious fizz. Each man kept his eyes fixed on it.

Everyone except Charlie.

He looked at the crystal. From his perch on top of the stone rubble he could see it clearly. It flashed red, once, brighter this time. He looked toward the foaming lake, then back at the crystal. It flashed a third time, then a forth. He was sure the flashes were coming closer together.

It was counting down the time.

"Um, guys," he called down. "I think we better get out of here."

No one moved. The soldiers continued to look at the bubbles, pointing to them and talking to each other.

"No really," Charlie called, louder. "I don't think this is a good place to be. I think we need to back off a few miles. Starting right now." He looked over his shoulder at the crystal. It was flashing steadily now.

"Uncle Packard, Uncle Gregory! I'm pretty sure we're all in danger."

His uncles ignored him. "At least we know where it is," Packard told Gregory. "We won't have to drag the lake after all."

"One hundred seventy feet, did you say?"

"That's the average depth. It could be deeper. We should be prepared to go three hundred, if need be."

"After we get this one up we can build duplicates. Even if only Thessalonius knows the magic that underlies it, other sorcerers should still be able to copy it."

"Right. Then we can set off one or two to prove we really have them. You know, we could even sell them to other countries. We'll ask for a percentage of the spoils they take when they win their wars."

"Abe, listen to me! I surrender, okay? I put myself in your hands. I throw myself at your mercy." Charlie tossed a pebble at Gagnot to get his attention. It struck him on the shoulder. "Abe, you need to tell your men to get away from the lake."

Gagnot brushed his shoulder absently. "You know what it reminds me of?" he asked one of his officers, without taking his eyes off the foam. "It reminds me of a giant fizzy bath bomb."

"I think you're right, sir." The officer also kept his gaze directed on the lake. "I can even smell jasmine."

"No, that's lilac. It grows wild around here."

Charlie considered fleeing. Only minutes ago these men were ready to kill him, after all. He could escape alone, leave them to their fate, and if what he thought was going to happen really happened, they would be no threat to him ever again.

But he couldn't do it. These were Damask soldiers. As much as he hated to admit to an emotional tie to Damask, they were his countrymen. Most of them were fresh from their farms, forced to enlist by economic necessity. They didn't think of this fight on their own. They had been manipulated into it by Charlie's uncles, and by Charlie himself. He couldn't abandon them.

That left him with only one other choice.

He had to get their attention. He had to make a speech that would break their concentration, that would penetrate their brains, that would dissolve the glue that fixed their minds on the lake, bring them back to reality, and alert them to the danger they were in. He knew what that meant. He hated to do it. The thought revolted him, but he knew the words that he would have to say. *Desperate times demand desperate measures,* he told himself. Damask was a fairy-tale kingdom, and as much as he loathed the idea, in a situation like this, there was only one kind of speech that would do the job.

Iambic pentameter.

He quickly finger-combed his hair, dusted off his boots with a handkerchief, braced one foot on a rock, and held his sword up in what he hoped was a dramatic and dashing gesture. Then he began:

> *Abjure this evil beach, good men, fall back.*
> *Too near this water fills me up with dread.*
> *Do not be fooled by bubbles bright and gay,*
> *Or sunlight playing on the sparkling lake,*
> *Or iridescent colors in the foam.*
> *Let not your senses by these things be trapped,*
> *Nor by the gentle music of waves.*
> *For wicked magic that had slept below,*
> *Is now disturbed and like the kraken wakes,*
> *To unleash power quite beyond our ken.*
> *Doom and destruction threatens all our lives.*
> *Death waits to those who linger in its sphere,*
> *Of influence. So therefore tarry not,*
> *But emulate the crayfish on the sand.*
> *Who, sensing danger, bravely waves his claws,*
> *Yet also backs away, his hole to seek,*
> *And hides, protected by the solid rocks.*
> *Or like the hart and rabbit of the woods,*
> *Who flee the forest fires when they come.*
> *They know the conflagrations are too great,*
> *For them to combat with their puny power.*
> *And so they run away, but soon return,*
> *To graze in comfort when the ash is cold.*

It worked! Slowly at first, one man after another, but then in groups of five or six, the men turned their heads away from the spectacle of the lake and looked at Charlie with annoyed expressions. Charlie was exultant. The irritating sound of bad blank verse was breaking their concentration, cutting right through the pleasant, relaxing ambiance of the bubbling water like bagpipes at a violin concerto. He took a deep breath and continued:

> *You get my drift? Do not forsake your wives,*
> *Nor leave your mothers weeping on the hearth.*
> *Let not insurance salesmen gnash their teeth*
> *And grudging pay survivor benefits.*
> *You must not linger, 'tis no hero's death,*
> *To suffer to be blown to smithereens.*
> *Just go on home, and later you can lie.*
> *Exaggerate the bravery that you showed.*
> *Old soldiers do it all the time, you know,*
> *And glean more honor from a tale grown tall,*
> *Than simple truth carved on a graveyard stone.*
> *So grip your reins and turn your horse away.*
> *Set spur to flank and urge him to top speed,*
> *For quickly we must boogie out of here.*

Charlie stopped when he saw that all the men had turned away from the lake and were scowling at him. Even the horses looked like they wanted to kick him.

"Are you deaf or what?" he shouted. "Get going, or I'll start rhyming couplets!"

It was nearly too late. Shocked into awareness, the mounted soldiers cast a backward look at the lake. Their expressions changed with the sudden realization that the behavior of Lake Organza was far from normal. They spurred their horses into a galloping stampede and headed for the trailhead to Damask. The dozen or so men who were on foot scrambled to mount their horses, and took off only slightly behind the main group.

Charlie was left alone, standing on a pile of rock, watching them disappear. Behind him the noise of the lake changed. He turned to see the bubbling water lift up, piling on top of itself, rising above the lake's surface, until it formed a column of swirling liquid a hundred feet high. The bubbles turned green, then blue, then gold, a lovely sight by any standard. But then they turned an ominous black, as though they had been dipped in soot. Beneath his feet the crystal stopped flashing and now glowed a bright, steady red. "Time to take my own advice," said Charlie, and he scrambled down the rocky slope to flat ground, running at his best speed away from the shore, toward the surrounding ridges, not daring to look back.

Then the earth split open.

Xiaoyan, the High Priestess of Matka, who walked a path of her own footsteps, paused on a hill outside the city and beheld the ship that would take her away from Noile.

For the task of herself and her companions was finished, and no more would they need her—nor each other—and soon they would be dispersed among the world.

And she thought in her heart: *Shall I leave without sorrow? For I came here as a child and I have grown up among these people and they are all I know. But I am a child no longer and I must make my place in the world. I cannot tarry longer.*

And so she entered the city in the midst of the solemn procession, and the people of the city gathered on both sides to bid her farewell, and she looked about the city with regret, for she was certain in the knowledge that she was going to miss all the good end-of-summer sales. And she passed by the salons and thought: *I wonder if there is time to get my hair done.*

But immediately upon thinking this she grew angry with herself, and she chided herself in her heart for her vanity, and she told herself that such an action would be foolish and wasteful. *For you are going on a sea voyage, and the salt spray and the blowing wind will quickly leave your hair in disarray.* Yet even as she told herself this, the thought came unbidden to her mind: *Perhaps just a short flip cut to get it off the shoulders and make it more manageable.*

But there was no time, for as the procession wound through the city and toward the harbor, the mayor and the aldermen came out of the Great Hall of the City. And when she saw them she knew that she would have to make a speech, and glad she was that she had prepared for this day with a memorized boilerplate.

And the mayor hailed her, saying:

High Priestess of Matka, decades you have watched over us from your mountain fastness. Decades we have walked the trail to your temple and brought to you our problems and our fears. For you came to us at a time when our nation was deeply troubled, and all was in turmoil, and each man's hand was raised against his brother. The future was as a dark night to us. We could not see our way and so uncertain were we that we hesitated to move at all. But you held before us a glimmer of light so that we could see to take a first step, and thus we moved forward with our lives.

And it truly must be said that deep was your wisdom and keen was your understanding, and that your rates were not at all unreasonable, certainly a lot better than that quack the astrologer we used to have—I never understood how anyone could believe that stuff.

Now your ship rides the tide, and the wind that will carry you away from us fills its sails, and in the great play of life you seek another stage on which to perform. But there is time yet before the tide turns. Therefore we ask you speak to us and tell us of ourselves and what lies before us. For we would fain take more interest in that then hear yet another go-in-peace speech which we have all heard before, give us some credit.

Xiao bowed her head and asked: People of Noile, what can I speak of save that which is already in your hearts?

And an alderwoman stepped forward and said: Speak to us of time.

And Xiao said: Time is a gift of nature and measured by the sun and seasons. It cannot be caged nor controlled, nor counted—and to attempt to do so will only lead to unhappiness. For surely we have noted that in the summer when we need a good swimsuit, the shops are filled only with winter clothing, and yet in the winter when we seek to buy a sweater, the shelves are filled with summer clothing. We must reconcile ourselves that time is out of joint and we cannot put it right, but at least we can buy on sale after the holidays, when prices are heavily discounted.

An old woman spoke out and said: Speak to us of children.

Children are a blessing to the world and a burden to the eighth-grade teacher. They bring joy to their parents when they are born and even more joy when they are finally old enough to move out. Children fill the home with love and warmth and affection. Nonetheless, consider getting a cat instead, which will do the same thing and also keep the house free of mice.

Then a young, bearded man stepped forward and said: Tell us of Gaia, of the Earth Mother, the Goddess, the Spirit that surrounds us all and inhabits every natural thing, that quenches our thirst with her rain, and warms us with her light, and speaks to us in the wind and the rustling of the trees, yeah man, the trees, the trees *speak* to me, man, and the earth is alive, I can feel her pulse beating, I can feel *the pulse of the earth, man*, and it is like, totally cosmic.

Xiao said to him: Oh wow, like what have you been smoking? I think you need to lay off that stuff for a while, dude.

And a model slash actress raised her hand and said: Speak to us of beauty.

There is the beauty of nature and there is the beauty of art and there is the beauty of the human spirit and the beauty of the soul. There is the beauty and sorrow of the female form, for the beautiful woman inflames desire in all men, yet she is hard put to satisfy the desire of even one man. The beauty of youth is fleeting and evanescent and the joy it brings is temporary. Therefore think not to realize only your outer beauty and neglect the beauty that lies inside you. For truly it can be said that a fat woman might lose weight someday, but a skinny bitch will never develop a nice personality.

And a scholar said, speak to us of learning.

The wise man knows himself to be a fool, and the fool thinks himself wise, and both are correct. We are all wise in some small way, and all modest in knowledge of a few more things, and totally ignorant of all the rest. The philosopher seeks to know himself and believes that the unexamined life is not worth living, but never considers that the examined life might not be worth living either.

Here Xiao spread her arms to encompass the whole of the people that filled the square.

Therefore think not to understand yourself, but to understand your brothers and sisters, and your neighbors and companions, that you may be a better friend to them.

She decided it was time to wrap up this question-and-answer session, board the ship, and get into some more comfortable shoes. She lifted up her arms to the surrounding mountains.

"Seek to understand the world around you, that you may live in harmony with nature."

A light breeze sprang up, causing the front of her thin robe to shape itself to her trim body, and the rest of it to trail out behind her. She let one arm drop to her side and with the other she pointed to the distant peak where the Temple of Matka stood, where the thin blue line of the Organza River traced a path down the green slope, and a white plume marked the spot where the waterfall left Lake Organza. The crowd turned and looked to where she was pointing.

"Look to the mountains and to the sun, for change will come like a new dawn and the light of knowledge will blind those who close their eyes to it. But let your eyes be opened and you will see the truth."

As she spoke these words, a light appeared on the mountaintop, a glowing brightness like the dawn of a new sun. It wasn't exactly at the place where she was pointing, but it was close enough that she could quickly adjust her pose to make it so, before anyone noticed she was off a few degrees. The light grew into a circle, small at this distance, but so intense she had to squint to look at it. Within the white ball of light a yellow oval appeared, as though a cat's eye was staring at them. It seemed to go on forever, but in reality it lasted only a few seconds before rising into the sky and fading away.

Xiao continued to point at the mountain. She felt, before she heard, the murmur of astonishment and awe that came from the crowd. She knew, without looking down at them, that their heads were turning her way, and that shortly every eye would be upon her, for in their minds a miracle had just been performed. So she kept her face composed and relaxed, her expression inscrutable, and gave not the slightest sign that what had just occured was as unexpected and mysterious to her as it was to them. Not so much as a twitch of her lips or a flicker of her eyelids betrayed her thoughts, which were:

Wow! That was totally cool!

Then the shockwave hit.

A well-known bit of medical trivia is that people who are knocked unconcious will show a short period of amnesia. After regaining their senses, they will be unable to remember the few seconds immediately preceding the trauma. The victim of a mugging, for example, cannot recall being struck, or even the face of his assailant, if it happens quickly enough. This is so widely accepted that it is even used by investigators to determine if a purported assault victim is telling the truth or lying.

Thus Charlie, even after he was able to stand up, could not remember being thrown to the ground. He could remember running from the lake as fast as he could, trying to reach shelter behind a ridge of rock. He could remember the ground heaving beneath his feet, boulders the size of coaches bouncing around like popcorn in a hot skillet, trees with trunks as broad as a doorway shaking and swaying like freshmen at a homecoming dance, and the noise of the bubbling lake suddenly increasing to a tremendous roaring crescendo.

He could not remember diving for safety behind the ridge of rock or striking the hard ground headfirst. He could not remember the fireball that rose from the lake, the wall of water and mud that accompanied it, the blast wave, or the blistering heat. He rose disoriented, covered with dirt and mud, his head pounding and his muscles aching, and looked numbly around at the toppled trees and the scorched ground. Gradually he became aware of a pain in his left hand. Two fingers had lain outside of the shadow of the rocks. The hair was burned off the knuckles. Blisters were rising on the skin. He grimaced and wrapped the hand in a handkerchief.

Gradually coherence returned to his brain. He looked first toward the Temple of Matka, thinking to check on Thessalonius. A hard look convinced him he would be wasting his time. The ancient temple had returned to a state of ruin. The walls had fallen again, and the large dome had collapsed. Thessalonius was now buried under tons of stone. Charlie suspected the sorcerer planned it that way.

Then he looked in the other direction.

He said, "Well, I'll be damned."

He started laughing.

Eventually he heard Gregory calling to him. "It's not funny."

Charlie thought it was. He wandered to the edge of the newly formed river and sat on the bank, letting all the stress and tension of the summer release itself in a sustained burst of hysterical laughter. It was a long time before he was able to control himself. Even so, when he finally stood up and looked across the river at Gregory's angry face, he nearly started laughing again. "Hello, Uncle Gregory," he called. He had to shout to be heard over the sound of rushing water. "Where's Uncle Packard?"

Gregory pointed toward the mountain road, where soldiers were starting to filter back up, staring wide-eyed at the fallen trees and scorched earth. "Packy twisted an ankle. Tried to outrun the earthquake and got thrown from his horse. Everyone else had the sense to get down." He looked at the river. "Well, that was a waste of magic and effort. Sorcerers! Who can understand them? All that planning and research—and expense—for nothing. Your father was an idiot."

This time Charlie really did start laughing. "You still don't get it, do you, Uncle Gregory? Come on, look!" He pointed to the mountain, where a crack thirty yards wide had appeared in the granite. "It goes right through the mountain! Six miles of solid rock split right through!"

He waited until he saw the light of understanding appear on his uncle's face. Then he laughed again and did a little twirling dance step. "Sunken roads! I thought they were sunken roads. But they were *irrigation ditches*! Your brother was a genius, Uncle Gregory." Some of the soldiers had appeared behind Gregory. Charlie waited until they were at the banks. From his vantage point, safely on the other side of ninety feet of rushing water, the prince was able to smile at them cheerfully. "Dad found a way to bring the Organza River to Damask. Irrigation ditches. That's what this river flows into now. The harvest is saved. The farmers have all the water they need."

"To hell with the harvest!" snapped Gregory. "What's

wrong with you, Charlie? I thought you were on our side. We could have all retired in luxury. Now we're back where we started. We'll still just be minor nobles stuck in a provincial little country."

"Yeah, too bad," said Charlie, with no trace of sympathy. "Worse, you've got a country with a future, now. You'll have to start ruling responsibly. Whoever runs the country, that is. Jason, or Richard, or yourself, or Fortescue. No more strip-mining and clear-cutting. You'll have to start thinking about the long term."

"You're under arrest," screeched Gregory. "As far as the people of Damask are concerned, you're still a tyrant and you're still deposed. We're taking you back to stand trial."

"Come and get me." Charlie picked up a pebble and tossed it in the turbulent river.

"We'll send men around the other side of the lake. You won't get away. And when you're in jail awaiting execution, you can think that you've given them a country that's now worth fighting for. We were giving them a peaceful occupation. We wanted to avoid a war. Now there will be fighting and it's your fault."

"Look behind you."

Gregory turned around. The soldiers who had been standing behind him were now running to the trailhead.

"They're going back to their farms. They won't fight. As long as they have their land, they don't care who rules Damask."

He waited while his uncle watched the soldiers disappear. "And neither do I. I'm out of here. Give my regards to Packard and Catherine, Uncle Gregory. It's been a great summer. Ciao."

He walked away from the river without a backward glance, taking a leisurely stroll past the temple ruins, around the other side of the lake, climbing over the trunks of fallen trees, stopping once to wash his face and arms in the cool water. He was feeling rather pleased with himself.

Damask had water and a future. A terrible weapon had been kept out of the hands of men like his uncles and General Fortescue. Granted, that wasn't Charlie's doing. His father and Thessalonius had planned out the whole thing. But Charlie thought he'd helped things along, with his rationing plans and anticorruption campaign and public works projects. No one had been killed, either. Charlie figured he could take credit for that, too.

Now his role in the plan was over. He was footloose and free, with no responsibilities. The sun was setting, the evening star was out, fireflies were starting to flicker, and the air was gradually filling with the sound of crickets and night birds. A light breeze made rippling motions in the grass. All and all, it was one of the most pleasant evenings Charlie could remember and he enjoyed it thoroughly, until Fortescue's men caught and arrested him.

The night before Fortescue was due to return to Noile, Catherine slipped out of her tent, camouflaged by a dark green traveling cloak. Under it she hid pitcher of water and a muffin.

It took two days to walk from Lake Organza to Noile Harbor. Charlie spent the time in manacles and leg irons. They gave him nothing to eat and precious little to drink. At night they chained him to a tree, so that he could not even lie flat. He was groggy and nearly delirious from exhaustion and lack of sleep. Catherine took off her cloak and spread it over him. She was wearing a simple dress of plain, unbleached linen. Her long red hair was tied back with a bit of ribbon. He thought she had never looked lovelier. She held the pitcher of water to his lips while he drank.

"Bradley doesn't like you," she said.

"Who?"

"General Fortescue. He's angry with you."

Charlie looked at the manacles on his wrists. "You know, I had a wild hunch that might be the case."

"You've upset all his plans. He was really counting on getting that Weapon of Magical Destruction."

"He told me."

"I saw the fireball." Catherine tore a piece of the muffin and put it in his mouth. "It didn't look so dangerous. I mean, it was awe inspiring, but it wasn't what I'd been led to expect."

Charlie swallowed the muffin. "It was big enough. It exploded under a couple of hundred feet of water. An airburst would have been plenty enough to destroy a city. I'm not sure, but I think Thessalonius used it to trigger a fault."

"It was nobody's fault, Charlie."

"Not that kind of fault. A geologic fault."

Catherine looked blank. "Well, it wasn't your fault. That's what I told Bradley. It wasn't your plan. It was your father's plan. He manipulated you just like all the rest of us. Bradley didn't accept it. He said you did a pretty good job as prince regent and that's why it's important to put you out of the way."

"That reminds me. What happened to Oratorio?"

"He slipped across the border. He and Rosalind are on their way to Bitburgen. It turns out they'd been planning this for a long time. She said she was reluctant at first, but she talked it over with him and he persuaded her to do it."

"Elope with him?"

"Join a sorority."

"Right, right. What about Pollocks?"

"Fortescue has him."

"Damn."

"Pollocks tried to take all the blame. He told Bradley that he was in on the whole plan and you knew nothing. All you did was run the public works programs. Bradley just decided to hang you both."

"Pollocks is taking this Faithful Family Retainer business too far."

"Charlie, listen to me." Catherine lowered her voice and leaned in close to him, so close her breasts brushed his chest. Two days ago this would have had his pulse racing. Now he barely paid attention. "Charlie, I can get you out of here. You still have the best claim to the throne of Damask. I'll make the nobility realize that with viable cropland, they don't need Fortescue. We can still negotiate with them."

"Uh-huh. And if you manage to get *me* into power, how many people would I have to murder to get *you* on the throne of Noile?"*

"Only four. No more than five." She saw Charlie's expression. "Possibly only three," she amended hastily. "Dammit, Charlie, your own life is on the line. You're worth more than three of them. Besides, if we got into power, we could do things that would more than compensate for a few executions."

"Like what?"

"Oh, build schools and stuff. You know. I'm sure there's lots of things we could do."

"Can you help Pollocks to escape?"

Catherine shook her head sadly. "No. He couldn't move fast enough. And Bradley is determined to hang him as a spy."

"Then my answer is no."

Catherine sighed. "All right, Charlie. I did my best." She held the pitcher of water to his lips again. "Drink up. It will be hot tomorrow. You've got a long walk to Noile and then a short one to the scaffold. Bradley wants you hung in a public square and then your body left strung up for a few

---

*I can only think of one Donald E. Westlake novel that had a footnote. I mention this because my next novel will have a lot of Donald E. Westlake influences.

days for everyone to examine. He says that's the best way to prevent an imposter from appearing later and making a claim to the throne."

"Very practical. Despicable, but practical. I'm sure you two will get on very well together."

Catherine rose to her feet. "We probably will, Charlie. But I gave you your chance. My conscience is clear." She walked off into the gloom. "Goodbye, Charlie."

Charlie didn't say goodbye. He just watched the pale dress fade away into the darkness. He looked up, to where moonlight was filtering through the leaves of the tree, and wondered if this would be the last moonlight he'd see. Then he turned over on his side and tried to sleep.

⚜ ⚜ ⚜

Fortescue knew, as well as any general, the importance of pomp and circumstance, and putting on a good show for the masses. Thus he stopped his troops outside the city of Noile and had them change into parade uniforms, with polished buttons and sharp creases. They had waving banners, horses with curried manes and oiled harnesses, and mules with—well, there really wasn't much you could do about the mules. But it was the effort that counted. The former prince regent of Damask was left dirty and unshaven, to increase his humiliation.

Fortescue had been tempted to ride into Damask as a conquering hero, but that wasn't the story that had been created. He wasn't supposed to conquer Damask, he was merely supposed to be sending a few troops to help maintain order. Besides, it was more important to get back to Noile, his main power base, before people started asking questions. No one was going to miss the Organza River. Noile didn't need the water, and it had always been a flooding problem. But when a river like that suddenly stops flowing, someone is bound to take notice.

He sent the cavalry ahead, to blow their horns and

prance through the streets and generally let people know there was going to be a parade, so they had a chance to come outside and line up for it. He let the first of his troops enter next, then the band, blowing some splashy show tunes, to get the crowd in a festive mood. He followed the band on a spirited charger, waving his hat. An open carriage followed, holding Lady Catherine Durace (she was always popular in Noile). A few wagons followed the coach, with Bad Prince Charlie dragged along in chains behind the second wagon. And then the rest of the troops and the rest of the wagons.

He had done this plenty of times before. His army was well-rehearsed when it came to victory parades. They knew how to put on a good show. So it was quite a disappointment that no one came out to see them.

Fortescue called a halt to the procession three blocks inside the west gates. He called one of his officers over. "Where the hell is everyone?"

"Don't know, sir." The officer looked nervous.

"Where's the city garrison?"

"Don't know, sir."

Fortescue looked back. There were, of course, soldiers from the city garrison manning the gates. "Bring me one of those guards."

There was a delay while the officer turned his horse back to his troops and found a sergeant. He double-timed him over to the gate, found the ranking guard, and ordered the sergeant to order the guard to return with them to Fortescue. The general tried to hide his impatience. When the soldier arrived Fortescue smiled at him warmly and said, "Good morning, Corporal."

"Sir!" The corporal saluted.

"Where is everyone?"

"Down at the Market Square, sir!"

"Very good, Corporal. And why is that, do you know?"

"Because the High Priestess of Matka is there, sir!"

Fortescue nodded, as though he was expecting this. He was surprised though. He thought the High Priestess of Matka was to have sailed off days ago. The most likely explanation was that her ship had been delayed. He could understand why people wanted to see her. It was a bit disconcerting to have his thunder stolen, but on the other hand, he also wouldn't mind posing her a few more questions before she left. He was about to dismiss the soldier when the man added:

"She saved us from the demon, sir!"

This gave Fortescue pause. He'd been on plenty of inspections during which low-ranking soldiers, and even high-ranking officers, under the pressure of meeting their commander-in-chief, nervously blurted out something nonsensical. *Probably* that was all he just heard. Under normal circumstances he'd smile understandingly, dismiss the soldier, and send him back to his ranks feeling like a damn fool.

No. *Probably not.* Fortescue was a good judge of men. He looked down at the corporal and realized that this man was not nervously babbling, that he thought he'd contributed useful information. Fortescue wanted to know more, but he wasn't about to listen to an explanation from an enlisted man, in the middle of parade, with his officers surrounding him and his bride-to-be looking on. He'd find out about this later. He dismissed the man and told the cavalry officer, "To the Market Square."

They hardly got started again when a troop of soldiers came around the corner, and *they* were a disturbing sight. There was nothing really wrong with them. They wore the uniform of the city garrison. They were in proper dress and formation. But the uniforms looked like they'd been slept in, and the formation was a little off, as though the men were distracted, and every one of them had an expression of wild excitement. They stopped when they saw the parade. They looked over the band, the carriages, the wagons, and Fortescue himself. And then, without a word among themselves, they rushed over and surrounded Bad Prince Charlie.

"Now what the hell is this?" Fortescue demanded out loud. His own soldiers stayed in formation, but he could see them gripping their weapons more tightly at this little hint of trouble. He rode over to Charlie. The prince was taking advantage of the delay to rest, propping himself against a wagon. His eyes were closed and his chin rested on his chest. He didn't seem to notice anyone around him.

The garrison soldiers fiddled with the chains, unsure what to do. One of them looked at Fortescue. "The High Priestess, sir. She demands that we bring the Bad Prince to her."

"This is my prisoner, soldier, and you don't take orders from the Cult of Matka. Where is your commanding officer?"

He had hardly spoken the words when General Gudiron, the commander of the city garrison, galloped up on his own charger. He rode directly to Charlie, looked at the soldiers surrounding him, and snapped, "Unchain him and bring him to the square." He wheeled his horse around and was about to gallop off again when Fortescue leaned over and took him by the arm.

"Nick," he said. "Are you all right?"

Gudiron looked at him. He looked as wild as his men, the look of a man who hasn't slept in days because of inner tension. His men fell silent and watched him. "The High Priestess," he said. "She drove away the demon of Organza. Never again will the river flood. Now she demands that we deliver Bad Prince Charlie to her."

"Demon? What demon?"

"The demon of the lake. For centuries it tortured us with floods. But she called it out of the vasty deep and drove it away. It flew off into the sky. I saw it."

"That wasn't a demon! That was . . ."

"I saw it," Gudiron persisted. "It looked at me with its great glowing eye. I felt its hot breath on my cheek." His men nodded.

Fortescue was torn between the urge to snarl his disapproval and the urge to laugh out loud. He let go of Gudiron's arm. Riding over to Catherine, he bent his head to hers. "If the Cult of Matka wants to sacrifice Charlie to a demon, this ought to be worth seeing." She looked pale. "All right, Nick," he said out loud. "We're bringing over the prince regent. Let the High Priestess know we're coming."

Xiao well remembered the day when she was picked to be the new High Priestess. Thessalonius broke the news to her himself. He gave her a speech on her responsibilities, a speech he had no doubt given to many High Priestesses before her, and she recalled in particular his closing remarks. "The prophecy game and the intelligence game are not greatly different from one another," he said. "In the intelligence game you try to predict the future using sparse, erroneous, confused, and often conflicting information. In the prophecy game you do the same thing with no information at all."

"That seems like a pretty big difference," Xiao objected.

The old man smiled. "Many people would prefer to have no information than bad information. You'll find that you can do very well with just your own good sense."

Thessalonius himself was a veritable gold mine of information, in the sense that a mine is deep, dark, and mysterious. The only man she knew of that actually had some real predictive ability had been awfully closemouthed about what he thought was going to happen. Now Xiao was on her own for the first time and she had her own plan. It was risky, but the opportunity was too good to miss. Despite the title of High Priestess, she was pretty low in the organization. She got people to tell their secrets by being pretty and acting mysterious. The monks compiled it into their intelligence reports. But as long as she was in the public eye, they had to go along with her wishes. The "monks" couldn't stop her.

For two days she waited on the steps of the Great Hall of the city, neither eating, nor drinking, nor sleeping. Her kidneys ached. The people of the city remained before her, watching respectfully. Thousands brought candles to spend the night in silent vigil. The others returned each morning to fill the square. The monks had no choice but to go along with it, surrounding her, reciting chants, lighting incense, and performing brief, impromptu ceremonies with fans and scarves that they made up as they went along. Periodically Sing would move in close and hiss, "What are you up to, for God's sake? The ship is ready. Let's get out of here before you give the whole thing away." She ignored him, standing motionless with her hands clasped in front of her and her best expression of serene wisdom on her young face.

It looked like her gamble was going to pay off. Toward the end of the second afternoon Fortescue appeared at the back of the square. The people in the square clapped, cheered, and craned their heads. The monks, seeing their cue, began a complex chant. Fortescue dismounted from his horse and walked through the crowd, which parted to let him pass. Looking from beneath closed lids, Xiao saw that a couple of guards were dragging Bad Prince Charlie along in chains. Lady Catherine Durace remained in her carriage.

Fortescue reached the foot of the steps. He stared at her in a calculating way, trying to figure out if his oracle was playing him a trick. He looked like he was about to start up the steps, but the monks swarmed down, took the chains from the guards, dragged Charlie up the steps, and threw him down in front of Xiao. They took up positions on either side of the High Priestess and began chanting again.

Fortescue remained where he was. For his entire career he'd been taking advice from the Cult of Matka. He wasn't about to anger them without reason.

Charlie knelt before Xiao, his head bowed. Xiao looked over him, bowing to the east, bowing to the west, and then bowing deeply to Fortescue, who nodded back. Under her breath she said, "Took you long enough to get here."

"The leg irons slowed me down," said Charlie. He had his back to the crowd, so they couldn't see him speaking, nor could he be heard over the background of chanting.

"You always have an excuse," said Xiao. Charlie realized that by bowing, Xiao had allowed her hair to fall in front of her face, concealing the movement of her lips. He reminded himself again not to underestimate her.

"They've got Pollocks," he whispered.

"Brought him in yesterday," Xiao murmured back. "I'll take care of it." She spread her arms and motioned to the monks. They stopped chanting. A hush fell over the square. The crowd waited expectantly.

"Good citizens of Noile, honored visitors from Damask, for many decades I have walked hand in hand with you and endeavored, with my simple gifts, to find for you the true path."

Decades? thought Charlie. He did not realize that most of Xiao's supplicants couldn't tell one Eastern girl from another. They believed the same High Priestess had been operating in Matka for fifty years.

"General Fortescue," continued Xiao, looking down the steps. "Your people and your army put their trust in you and you have honored their trust. Always you have sought the true path, and always it has brought you to victory, and each victory has brought Noile closer to peace, stability, and prosperity. You have done well."

Some promotion-seeking officers started to clap. The crowd picked up on it and gave Fortescue a round of applause. Xiao waited until it died down. "But now I tell you that your path has taken a turn. The path of conquest is no longer the true path. Two days ago, summoning all of the power at our humble command, the Cult of Matka drove away the dual demon of flooding and drought."

This time the applause lasted much longer and was spontaneous. Fortescue frowned. "Freed from its cruel influence, Damask and Noile will prosper together. But it will only stay away if you follow the true path, and that is the path of negotiation and compromise. Let your army be used only for defense and the common good. General Fortescue, you can bring Damask back to Noile"—there was more applause—"through agreement and conciliation. Let their peoples join in peace, for there will be found the strength to keep the demons away."

"I can't see him," whispered Charlie, who had to maintain his kneeling position. "But he knows there was no demon. It was the WMD."

"The people are accepting it and so are his soldiers. He'll go along with it."

"Don't forget Pollocks."

"I haven't." Xiao pointed to her right, toward a knot of soldiers. "Release the Faithful Family Retainer."

The soldiers looked surprised, as did Fortescue. When they looked toward him for instruction, he nodded. They stepped apart, to reveal the bound and hooded figure in their midst. With a few quick strokes of a knife, the hood and ropes fell away. Pollocks blinked in the sunlight.

"Faithful One, you have served the royal family of Damask well. Now you shall serve the High Priestess of Matka." To Fortescue she said, "Treat this man well, for he is my eyes and ears while I am gone. Consult him as you would consult me." She held her breath, hoping that Fortescue would not go macho on her. She could see his calculating expression—he would not easily abandon his plans of conquest. But the WMD was gone. For decades he had relied on information from the Cult of Matka to further his career. To her relief, he nodded again. To Charlie she whispered, "He bought it."

"Make Catherine the queen of Noile."

"What?" Xiao cast her eyes down at him.

"Damask, also."

"Huh." Xiao's lip curled the slightest bit. "Still have the hots for her, eh?"

"No, but she'll stab and poison her way there, anyway. It will save some bloodshed if you just give it to her. And she's bound to do a better job than my uncles."

Xiao made some mystical hand-waving movements while she thought it over. "You're pushing it, Charlie."

"I know. But do it anyway."

Xiao pointed to the carriage. "Lady Catherine Durace." At the mere mention of the name there was sustained applause. Catherine really was popular. No one, at least among those present, objected when Xiao declared her heir to the thrones of Noile and Damask.

"Great," whispered Charlie as the applause died down. "Now free me and this thing is ended."

"Bad Prince Charlie." Xiao's high, clear voice rang out across the square. All who heard it fell silent. Heads turned. Every eye now focused on the prince. "There remains only to mete out justice for your crimes against the honest, innocent citizens of Damask."

The crowd responded with a murmur of assent. "You tricked your uncles into letting you usurp the throne of Damask. You laid a burden of oppressive taxation upon her nobility, besmirched the good name of her aristocracy with false accusations of corruption, and held them illegally in durance vile."

The nobles in the crowd nodded.

"You stole the food of the poor, sabotaged their crops, and forced them into slave labor for your self-glorifying public works projects."

The commoners nodded agreement.

"You treasonously attempted to betray Damask's army to General Fortescue, offering him a secret deal which he nobly refused."

Fortescue chewed the inside of his cheek for a moment, then nodded.

"You monstrously attacked your Faithful Family Retainer, and dealt him a mortal wound, one that was miraculously cured by the Cult of Matka."

"You may be going a bit too far on that one," Charlie murmured.

"And, not least of all, you kidnapped Lady Catherine and cruelly used her to satisfy your unspeakable lusts."

Everyone in the crowd turned to look sympathetically at Catherine, who sat in her carriage with her head bowed and her eyes downcast. When they turned back to Charlie their expressions were filled with anger and indignation.

"For these crimes I sentence you to permanent exile."

"Exile works for me," Charlie said.

"On pain of death is this sentence pronounced. Never are you to return to Damask or Noile. Immediately you will leave these lands. You will not set foot upon this soil, nor land on these shores, nor travel these roads again, upon immediate forfeiture of your life. All your claims to title and office are renounced."

"No problem. Strike these chains and I'll be on my way."

"Never again will you drink of its cool, refreshing waters, breathe its clean, fresh air, or gaze upon the loveliness of its mountains. Not even in death shall your body be returned."

"Enough, Xiao. Wrap it up and let me get out of here."

Xiao turned to the monks beside her. "Take him to the ship and lock him in the brig."

❧ ❧ ❧

The monks and the lower priestesses were gathered on deck, watching the sun set, and commenting on how differ-

ent a sunset at sea looked from a sunset in the mountains.
A few still wore their blue robes, but most had already
adopted clothing suitable for a sea voyage—trousers or
skirts of white cotton duck, loose shirts and blouses, and
scarves to protect their necks from the sun, salt, and wind.
Xiao was still in her high priestess outfit, standing at the
prow, with the wind whipping her long black hair and long
white robes around her. "You look great," said Sing, who
was still in his blue robes. "Very dramatic."

"How long do I have to do this? You said I could go below once we were out of sight of land."

"Too many incoming ships about. Stick with it until it
gets dark. A dramatic exit is as important as a dramatic
entrance."

"All right. How is Charlie?"

"Mad as a wet hen."

"I mean, is he okay?"

Sing smiled. "He's fine. He was hungry and a little de-
hydrated, but he's all right now."

"He's not really in the brig, is he?"

"No, we put him in a cabin next to yours. There's a connecting door. If you're not going to really use both cabins
tell us, so we can let some of the other girls spread out."

"I'll let you know."

"Why don't you come with us, Xiao? We got an offer to
set up in the far eastern kingdom of Thiam. The Thiamin
potentate is getting suspicious of Niacene, and wants to expand his intelligence system."

Xiao shook her head. The last orange sliver of sun was
sinking below the horizon. The edges of her white outfit
softened in the twilight. "Not for me, thanks. I've had
enough. I've got money and a handsome prince and that's
all I need for now."

"I think we're finished here," said Sing, looking at the
sun. "Might as well go below now."

Xiao was off like a shot. She raced down the ladder to

the deck below, skipped through the gangway to Charlie's cabin, raised her hand to knock on the door, and came to a complete stop. For a long minute she hesitated with her hand in the air. Then she lowered it and tiptoed into her cabin. Lighting a lamp, she checked her look in the mirror. *"Gaaaa!"*

Twenty minutes with a hairbrush, and a dab of lip gloss later, she was again knocking on the cabin next door. "Charlie? Are you okay?"

The roar that came back shook the mizzenmast. "GET THESE CHAINS OFF ME!"

In a moment Xiao had the door open. In another moment it was locked behind her. In a third moment she had both arms wrapped around Charlie's neck and both legs wrapped around his waist and was kissing him all over his face.

"Xiao . . . mmmph . . . can you . . . mmm . . . Xiao . . . The chains, Xiao . . . mmm. Dammit, Xiao!" Charlie tried to get a grip on the slim, squirming female body that was determined to press every inch of herself against every inch of him. But eventually she had to stop to breathe. He held out his arms and said, "Chains. Off. Now!"

"Oooo," said Xiao, stepping back to look at him. "I think they look kind of hot. Can't we leave them on for a while?"

"No!"

"Oh, come on. Just a little bit."

"No!"

"I'll let you rub almond oil on me again."

"I don't care!"

"Oh, all right."

Xiao produced a key and soon the manacles fell away. Then she launched herself at Charlie again. When she came up for air a second time he said, "How can you kiss me when I'm so grungy?"

"Good point." Xiao unlocked the connecting door to her cabin, dragged him in, and pointed to a large tin-plated bathtub, recently filled with warm water. Water splashed on the floor as she pushed him in, and even more splashed when she climbed in on top of him. "I wanted the giant double tub but they said it was too big to bring on board ship. So we'll just squeeze together."

"I can handle that."

Xiao pulled his shirt off and threw it on the deck. Charlie said, "Your robes are soaked."

"I won't be wearing them again. Would you mind tearing them off me, in a way that is savage but not brutal?"

Eventually the tearing and the splashing and the kissing died down. Charlie leaned back in the tub and said, "I'm such an idiot. I was manipulated by everyone. Dad's ghost, my uncles, Catherine, you, even Pollocks. I thought I was so smart, but everyone was playing me."

Xiao raised her head off his chest. "You're not an idiot. Thessalonius planned all this out and he could predict the future, remember? Not much, but enough to set us all up. You can't outsmart a guy with an edge like that."

"Who came up with the idea to divert the Organza River, Dad or Thessalonius?"

"Your father. He set Thessalonius to the task of triggering the earthquake. The problem then became how to keep other people from using it as a weapon and, Charlie, you did a great job. Don't be so hard on yourself. You figured out the Cult of Matka. You fed your people. You saved Pollocks from being tortured, Catherine from being executed, and you got the army away from the explosion. For one summer you ruled a kingdom, and you ruled it wisely and well. How many other boys your age can say that?"

Charlie put hands around her waist and pulled, so that her slim, wet body slid along his until her mouth was level with his own. He kissed her. "You're quite the flatterer, you know that?"

"Well, it's true."

"What do we do now?"

"Anything we want. I've got money. For years people have been paying the Cult of Matka for advice, and I've been investing my share. We're young. We've got nothing to tie us down now. The ship will drop us anywhere we want. Let's go someplace where we can have adventures. Also lots of sex."

Charlie nodded. "What's your money invested in?"

"A chain of frozen yoghurt stands. They say it's going to be the next big thing."

"Hmm. Then there's only one thing we need right now."

"What's that?"

"A fizzy bath bomb. You didn't happen to bring them, did you?"

"Your gift? Of course I did." Xiao stood up. Water and suds cascaded off her breasts and ran down her smooth thighs. Charlie watched appreciatively. She leaned over him to extract a scented, round ball from her vanity case and drop it into the tub. As the water foamed around them, she settled into his arms for another long bout of kissing.

He had, Charlie realized, no ambition to do anything else. And right then that was just fine. "But I have one remaining question."

"The answer is no," said Xiao.

"What?"

"You were about to ask me if I could really see into the future. No, it was all just part of the scam. Cold reading and conjurer's tricks. No."

"Glad we got that settled," said Charlie.

Not all men are born heroes—some have to read the instruction manual.

Heroics for Beginners
by John Moore

Prince Kevin Timberline must retrieve Ancient Artifact Model Seven from the clutches of the evil Lord Voltermeter—He Who Must Be Named—before the evil Lord unleashes his Diabolical Plan.

Luckily, Kevin wields a secret weapon that will have the Forces of Darkness running scared: *The Handbook of Practical Heroics.*

0-441-01193-4

a095

"Excellent tongue in cheek
parody fantasy."
—BookBrowser

The Unhandsome
Prince

by John Moore

Caroline kissed every frog in the swamp until
she found the one that turned into a prince—
only Prince Hal isn't the handsome specimen
she expected to find.

Unless she can learn to love the princely sum
of his parts, it'll be unhappily ever after.

0-441-01287-6

THE ULTIMATE IN
SCIENCE FICTION AND FANTASY!

From magical tales of distant worlds to stories of
technological advances beyond the grasp of man, Penguin has
everything you need to stretch your imagination to its limits.
Sign up for a monthly in-box delivery of
one of three newsletters at

penguin.com

ACE

Get the latest information on favorites like
William Gibson, T.A. Barron, Brian Jacques,
Ursula Le Guin, Sharon Shinn, and Charlaine Harris,
as well as updates on the best new authors.

ROC

Escape with Harry Turtledove, Anne Bishop,
S.M. Stirling, Simon Green, Chris Bunch, and many
others—plus news on the latest and hottest in
science fiction and fantasy.

DAW

Mercedes Lackey, Kristen Britain, Tanya Huff,
Tad Williams, C.J. Cherryh, and many more—
DAW has something to satisfy the cravings of any
science fiction and fantasy lover.
Also visit dawbooks.com.

*Sign up, and have the best of science fiction
and fantasy at your fingertips!*